Praise for This Cursed Line

"An emotional, atmospheric debut that will leave you on the edge of your seat. Hubbard weaves a beautiful tale of darkness and redemption that will linger long after you've reached the end."

- Rachel L. Schade, author of the *Cursed Empire* series

"Gritty realism, morally gray characters, and redemption arcs... real and gritty fiction I'll come back to read again and again."

- Jordan Comeaux, featured author in *The Valkyries Initiative*

"What is living when you are a pawn of the devil? *This Cursed Line* is a timely, heart-wrenching tale exploring what it means to live. Full of courage, hope, and healing, this story will live with readers long after the last words have been savored."

- Megan Gerig, editor and owner of Lamplighter Literary Creations

"With riveting clarity and a sense of storytelling that feels at once timeless and new, *This Cursed Line* will challenge you in ways you didn't see coming. Within the pages of this book is a story of the terrible burden of darkness and the sort of self-sacrificing love required to break its curse."

- Brian McBride, author of the *Mammoth* series

THIS CURSED LINE

Wistful Publishing
P.O. Box 7453
Knoxville, TN 37921-0011

Visit the author's website at morganhubbardauthor.com

Cover design by Maria Spada

ISBN 979-8-9863981-0-5

*To those who feel like they are
beyond redemption.
And to Cody, for never letting me give up.*

1

It began with the witching winds.

Outwardly, the people of Morville, Washington shrugged it away, reassuring themselves that the Devil didn't care for quiet, little towns.

Except he did care—*does* care—for quiet, little towns. Because quiet, little towns are the place to hide one's secrets.

Until those secrets ask to die.

The first of November meant payday for Alexander Pike, which found him resting in a creaky wooden chair outside of the local coffee house, feet propped up on the low table and coffee next to his open journal.

November 1, 1879

The job in Manhattan went as planned three days ago. I completed the poison job in New Jersey soon after with only a few hours to spare. That girl's laugh will prob-

ably be burned into my memory, a fitting price to pay for the treachery I committed.

Trust broken. I promised to carry her burdens and then became one myself.

The boss won't be too happy with my emotional involvement, but at least I fin-
ished the jobs this month. It's been years since I've missed one or messed one up beyond
help. For a moment, I didn't think I'd hit my deadline for October. I thought for sure
I'd have to pay the price come the first of November.

Lydia's death was also the first killing I've had to do in a while, making it a
little worse, even if poison is hands off. I almost felt out of practice, but then hundreds
of faces resurface, and I'm drowned once again in their tears.

Eyes that cannot cry . . . Lips that cannot speak . . . Yet I feel them, see them,
hear them. I can't name the countless souls I've left in my path. Which is worse:
committing the crime or paying for it myself?

Pike's hand stilled as silver flashed behind his eyelids, trying to
squeeze out the painful memories. With a shaky breath, he resumed his
journal entry.

I hope to see Mother soon. It's been a few weeks. I try to write to her when I can,
but there's not much in the vein of news that I could tell her. My life isn't something I
can share openly on a postcard. I wonder sometimes how long this debt will last. And
if I refuse to have an heir, what happens then? If something happens to me, would
my mother take over the debt?

He paused and watched the funeral procession across the street
pass, followed by a horse-pulled cart. On top of the cart, a bundle of
marigolds were held by stiff, blue hands. The breeze around Pike sounded like laughter, *her* laughter. Pike sipped his coffee to swallow down his
sorrow before he noticed an older man approaching him, red in the face.

"You bastard!" the man shouted, spit flying off his lips.

Two of the other patrons reclining outside of the coffee house
stood and apprehended the grieving man.

"You did this," the man continued in a loud voice. "We trusted you.
It's your fault that Lydia is dead." The man broke down in sobs with the
last word. He crumpled into the arms of one of the men who'd apprehended him.

Pike met the patron's eyes. The sorrow that rested behind their eyes
matched his own. The men slowly turned away and joined the funeral

procession, continuing the slow trek to the cemetery at the edge of the city. Pike took another long sip of his coffee before resuming his journal entry.

I think I'll be kicked out of New Jersey if I don't get picked up soon. Not that the boss would miss payday . . . He never misses.

Draining the last of his coffee, he sighed and brushed back his tangled blonde hair. Exhaustion had caught up with him from the long month, but his jobs never ceased.

Pike stood, stretching his arms wide, icy blue eyes constantly watching his surroundings. Leaving his empty cup on the table, he walked away from the funeral procession and into the dusk settling on the horizon. There was a chill in the air, maybe winter on the wind.

Pike began to sing in a low voice, walking the lonely road.

"'Twas a November gale, the witching winds took my lass from me. No hope, no love, no joy I have, for none of which cost is free. I-diddle-I dee die dee doe. I-diddle-I dee do. No hope, no love, no joy you have when the witching winds come for you."

"That's quite a song you're singing, Alexander Pike." The lilting voice came from the stretching shadows of the alley Pike had passed.

"Silvertongue!" Pike turned, forcing a tight smile to his lips. "I wondered when I'd see you again."

"Alexander," the man crooned, stepping partially into the light cast from the gas lamps on the cobbled streets. His sharp smirk glinted in the flickering, pale-yellow light. "It's the first of the month. Did you not expect to see me? Or are you too emotional to even comprehend what day it is?"

Pike stiffened. "Of course I know what day it is, Silvertongue."

"You should take heed calling me by that name here in the open," the shadowy man cocked his head.

"Would you prefer your given name from centuries ago? Or shall I call you fiendish devil like everyone else does? If I can't call you by your name, you shouldn't call me by my father's name."

"But it is your given name. You come from a long line of—"

"Of Alexander Pikes. Yes, I know my own family history." Pike shifted, averting his eyes. "I don't need a reminder."

Silence hung between them. Silvertongue wrinkled his pale nose at Pike. But his expression changed to one of contemplation. It was unsettling, the way his skin almost rippled. To an untrained eye, it would've looked like a trick of the light. To Pike, however, it seemed ominous.

"Pike, I like you. Out of all the men in your family lineage, you have been my favorite to work with." He lifted a hand, stopping Pike from speaking. "No, I don't just say that to anyone. Your ancestors have an unfortunate need to chitchat. You, on the other hand, like to get straight to business."

Pike shifted his weight again, and the man stared him dead in the eye, dark pupils seemingly void of emotion.

"I like that about you, Pike. I like you." He cracked his neck methodically. "So don't do anything to make me regret that. You wouldn't want your mother taking over for you, would you now? Not when we're so close to the end."

"The end?" Pike asked warily.

Rolling his eyes, the man nodded. "Yes, Pike. That's how debts work. Eventually they get paid off."

Pike held the man's gaze, trying to hide any emotion that he'd struck a nerve. Silvertongue practically fed off the fear in Pike's heart. The lamplight flickered over them, sensing the evil presence lurking in the street.

"So, your job sites for November." The dark man examined his perfectly kept *human* fingernails. "Greenwich, Lankin, Jethro, and Jovy. Which is your first pick?"

"I have a choice this time?" Pike ran his hands through his unruly hair, furrowing his eyebrows. "Am I supposed to know which one I should pick?"

"Pike, what did I just say?" the man snapped. "Pick one so we can get going."

"I guess. . . Jethro."

The man's smirk turned into a sickeningly happy snarl. "Excellent."

In two strides, the man was at Pike's side, strong hand digging into Pike's shoulder. Pike braced himself for what would happen, squeezing his eyes shut to avoid the nausea.

The world spun, and shadows curled around them in an unearthly grasp. Smells turned from the dusty scent of a town nestled in the woods to the briny salt of sea air. Waves crashed nearby as they came to an abrupt halt, feet sinking slightly in wet sand.

After his eyes adjusted to the pale moonlight, Pike noticed the underside of a dock above their heads, the waning light of the rising moon shining through the cracks, the sky a lilac purple. The crash of the waves beside them rolled like the warning hidden deep in Pike's heart.

"Name?" he asked, glancing around surreptitiously, looking for anything that might give him an edge on his assignment. Culture, class ranking, religions. . . anything that might be of use to him.

The sharp-angled man brushed off his perfectly tailored suit, black vest and coat matching his coal black hair. "Oliver Eames. You'll find him tomorrow at the trading post. His boat will dock in the early morning."

"First, you tell me you like me. Then, you give me a choice. Now, you're helping me. In the seven years that I've worked for you, you've never done this. What part of this game am I missing?"

"Nothing you need to know. . . yet." The man shifted his weight, clenching and unclenching his human-skinned hands, a motion that caused a cold chill to run down Pike's spine. "I'll come back to check on your progress, *Alexander.*"

"Thanks, *Silvertongue.* I'll be waiting at the crossroads."

With a hiss and a snarl, the shadowy man vanished into the humid air.

Pike sighed heavily. Six generations. *Six* generations of Alexander Pikes and still more debt to be paid. Surely he was close to being debt free. Maybe that could be why Silvertongue had been so odd. But was one ever free when indebted to the Devil?

Pike's shoulders shivered despite the warm breeze coming in from the gulf. He rolled his shoulders back and made his way down the beach and up a rocky stretch of the shore.

Overall, it seemed to be a peaceful evening. The low tide shrunk from the shores, leaving plenty of beach to stroll across. Pike envisioned a different time in a different life where he strolled along the beach between his mother and a beautiful woman.

His wife would have been beautiful but not in a traditional sense.

Beautiful and *wild*.

She would have had long, dark hair matching the colors of his hometown in Morville, Washington. Her eyes would have been piercing and seeing. She would have been cunning and yet kind, knowing when to be sharp and when to soothe with her words. She would have laughed with reckless abandonment and danced like the breeze. Most of all, she would have been real.

But that was the thing about dream girls, they were always that.

A dream.

Two men—he assumed collectors waiting to take payment from those docking overnight—stood throwing pebbles off the side of the dock, trying to hit the hull of an overturned fishing boat on the sand.

"Excuse me!" Pike called. "Can either of you direct me to the local public house?"

"Where'd you come from then?" one stiffened immediately. The other promptly elbowed the first in the side, shaking his head.

The second cleared his throat. "Up the street, take a right and then an immediate left."

Pike nodded. "Thank you very much." He turned and smoothed down his sleeves to cover his forearms before being seen up close. He couldn't afford to have anyone recognize the shadow man.

The tense man called after him. "Are you looking for anyone? Maybe we can help."

Pike hesitated. He didn't like to let people in on his jobs, even if it meant help. People typically banded together against him, harboring the damned. Their time had come anyway, there was no use in prolonging it. But normal people—people not in Pike's situation—didn't understand it.

Something in the man's voice sounded like he'd help with the promise of money. Most street rats would sell their own family if it meant a meal to eat. And even if Pike didn't plan on giving any money, the man didn't need to know that.

He halfway turned, looking back at the man and his friend, the tense one clearly trying to look important despite having the night shift.

"I assume you'd want something in return?" Pike asked.

"I'd be stupid not to ask when making a deal with the Devil."

Pike laughed. Actually laughed.

However young and innocent this man seemed, his eyes were observant enough to catch the markings on Pike's forearms before Pike could get his sleeves down. "No, I'm not him. He's not quite as *polite* as I am." He stepped in their direction, the second man taking a step back. "I'm looking for Oliver Eames."

"Sorry?" the tense man asked, eyebrows raised.

"I'm looking for Mr. Oliver Eames."

"Hank, you don't think he means Ollie?" the timid man gasped. He grabbed Hank's arm, eyes wide and reflecting in the moonlight.

"You know him?" Pike raised an eyebrow.

Hank's jaw tensed. "Are you sure you're not mistaken?"

"I need Oliver Eames. He arrives on a ship tomorrow. Someone told me I'd find him at the trading post."

The timid man looked at Hank and shook his head. Hank leaned closer and whispered something to his friend then turned to close the gap between him and Pike. He dropped off the dock to where Pike stood on the sand. Hank was young, maybe younger than twenty, but Pike couldn't be sure. Either way, he was cunning and bold enough to attempt an alliance.

"I can make sure you find him if you promise payment in return."

Pike smiled warmly. "If you deliver, you'll get what you're owed." Pike stuck his hand out, and after a moment of hesitation, Hank took it.

The timid friend threw a handful of rocks in their direction.

"You're a coward!" he shouted and stormed to the end of the dock where he disappeared behind one of the few ships harbored overnight.

Pike regarded the man who still stood grasping his hand. "Hank, is it?"

"Henry. My friends call me Hank."

The boy seemed deflated, shoulders slumped forward. He'd clearly crossed a line with his friend, but Pike didn't need messy ties causing problems. Pike pulled his hand back and patted him on the shoulder.

"Hank, you did the right thing. Death comes for us all. In the end, we are not cowards for facing it. We are brave. Death is nothing to fear."

Silver flames flashed in Pike's memories.

His father's screams echoed in his ears.

Hands, claws, blood. So much blood.

But he blinked and only the young man standing in front of him by the blue-tinted light of the moon remained.

Hank nodded.

"I presume I will see you tomorrow morning?"

"I'll be waiting by the door of the post."

Pike awkwardly patted Hank's shoulder again. "Have a good night then."

Stepping onto sandy streets under the Spanish moss, Pike began to sing again to himself. His melodic voice drifted in the humid sea air, almost drowned out by the drone of the waves crashing against the shore.

"I-diddle-I dee die dee doe. I-diddle-I dee do. No hope, no love, no joy you have when the witching winds come for you."

Dawn found Pike leaning against the side of the trading post building, shadows shrinking from the sunlight angled into the alley. The town still slept, but these were the moments Pike craved. The moments when no one recognized the monster that he had become over the years.

He desperately longed for the day that he could be free again. Truly free. Not scarred by memories and the marks on his skin that set him apart from everyone else.

He still dreamt of the burning that had flooded his body when he received his tattoos—one for each arm, like shackles binding him to the Devil's service until his debt was satisfied.

The Devil had brought his father, Alexander Pike V, back from a job in such a fury that it had woken fifteen-year-old Pike from his dreams of running through the piney woods of Washington State. By the time he'd stumbled outside where his mother watched and his father lay taking a beating from the Devil, Pike could only stare. He didn't even cry.

And after the silver flames consumed Pike's father, Silvertongue had put on his human skin, like a robe over his tar black beastly figure. He slid his hands into the human fingers, like putting on leather riding gloves. And he cracked his neck like always, settling back into his disguise like second nature.

He'd strolled over to Pike, rubbing his hands together, malicious machinations coming together in his devious mind. After bending down to be at Pike's eye level, Silvertongue had taken Pike's arm and pushed his shirtsleeve past his elbow, sending a burning sensation through Pike's body. Taking a long fingernail, the Devil traced curvy lines three times down each forearm. Pike felt the ache in his jaw from clenching his teeth shut even now. It had taken everything in him not to pull against the grasp on his arms. An unearthly fire had sprung up at the base of Pike's elbows, causing the skin beneath to turn dark and ashy. The flames leapt and licked the tender flesh of his arms but cut off in a sharp line several inches away from his wrist.

Pike often wondered what might happen to his marks if the time ever came when the debt was fulfilled. Would the flames on his arms disappear? Or would he be scarred for life?

Two years after the tattoos were burned into his flesh, his mother found him in the bathroom in the middle of the night, bent over the sink crying. He had rubbed his arms raw trying to scrub the flames off, to be free of such a fate, but no amount of effort or soap or remedy would get rid of the unholy signs. Anger bubbled up, directed at himself and the Devil. But more importantly, anger boiled for his father.

When he had died, his father had not only left Pike with the blood curse, but he had left his son as sole protector of Pike's mother, a mere fifteen-year-old boy. At that age, what did he know about protection and provision?

Worse yet, what did he know about murder? About arson? About treason? About kidnapping and deception?

But the choice had been made. So Pike, seven years after inheriting this awful curse, still lived in service to that monster. But who was he to judge? Pike's nature had shifted to mirror the beast he served.

At some point, Pike had grown a bit numb to it all. He'd ended so many lives, each one stacked up like empty glasses in a cabinet, hidden in the dark.

No.

They were shattered glasses, *dead and useless.*

The sound of gulls pulled Pike out of his memory, a coastal breeze ruffling his hair, running through the branches of the palms. As the red sun rose over the waters cresting the horizon, Hank shuffled towards him.

"Morning, Hank," Pike said.

Hank shook his head. "Let's get this over with."

"Where's that brave spirit from last night?"

"I don't know about other towns, but in Jethro, people don't enjoy having a traitor in their midst."

"Oh," Pike sighed, squinting his eyes into the early morning sunlight. "So that's what they're calling it these days."

Hank looked up at him, with brows deeply furrowed. "What do you mean?"

Pike needed trust and confidence from Hank, not despair. And lies slipped from Pike's lips so often that it felt like second nature. Lying got the job done.

"I would've called it strong. Heroic even. I mean, to willingly offer to help me find someone whose time has come. You are quite brave, Henry. Quite brave, indeed."

Hank took a deep breath and let it shudder away into the morning breeze. He squinted into the rising sun. "These gales are something else. It's been a while since we've had this much wind." He lifted his head. "The winds . . . It's you, isn't it? Like the shadow man legends say?"

Pike shrugged but said nothing.

"You know, I wouldn't have recognized what you were if I hadn't seen your arms. You pulled your sleeves down, and I . . ." Hank grew silent, neck reddening.

Maybe Hank had realized what he'd said, but Pike made no reaction or response. No expression to show that saying *what* instead of *who* had any impact on his feelings. Feelings weren't allowed in this business.

"I'm no legend," Pike muttered. "Those are stories. And besides, legends get too much publicity."

Hank chuckled half-heartedly, and they settled into a semi-peaceful quiet.

Jethro began to bustle in the early morning light, the temperature rising slightly. The town yawned and stretched, its houses basking in the shining sun, unaware that one of its visitors would never again step foot on its cobbled streets.

"Oliver is here, by the way," Hank looked down. "Saw him at the market. You sure he'll be at the post?"

"Positive."

"How are you so sure?"

Pike closed his eyes in the sunlight, taking in its warmth. "I can feel it . . . in the movement of the tide, in the warmth of the sun, in the weight of my bones." He opened his eyes and turned to Hank, evidently awestruck. Pike's lips quirked slightly, hiding the smirk that tried to escape. "It's fate."

Hank blinked a few times, pulling himself out of a stupor, and sized Pike up. "You're joking with me, aren't you?"

"Absolutely," Pike grinning internally, though he kept his face blank. "I have very good intelligence. Perfect, actually. It never misses a single step."

Hank grew quiet and Pike thanked him silently. Less talk meant less room for error. They waited as scores of crew members from several ships, locals, traveling merchants, and every person in between shuffled through the trading post doorway to make a living.

"Have you seen him enter?" Pike whispered.

Hank shifted his weight. "Not yet. Are you—"

"He'll be here."

Counting to five, Pike exhaled and released the tension in his midsection. He was getting antsy, and antsy was an easy way to screw up a job. He didn't need that. He felt the tides changing with Silvertongue. His demeanor and word choice, it all felt so . . . formal.

It can't be a good sign, can it?

"There he is," Hank muttered. "The smaller one."

He'd spoken so quietly that Pike had to look at him to make sure he had spoken at all. Hank's eyes were fixated to the side where a young man walked along the path with a group of other shipmates all decked out in a rough uniform. The boy, no older than fifteen, laughed gleefully with his crew, sweeping his shaggy brown hair out of his eyes and back under his hat, as he and his friends entered the trading post.

Pike swallowed. No wonder the man from the night before had been so upset. Oliver was merely a kid.

Pike hesitated, foot half raised to walk after Oliver, but he stopped, frozen on the street. He reminded Pike of himself when he'd taken over from his father. The Devil hadn't said what he should do with the boy, so what did that mean for the kid's future?

Pike wondered what Oliver had done to attract the Devil's attention.

Pike, being unlucky enough to be the last Alexander Pike's son, had no choice but to take over. But Oliver? Maybe he'd heard about God on his travels. Maybe an idea had been forming to start a church in Jethro. Maybe he loved his family a little too much. Or maybe he was meant to do something *greater*, and Silvertongue wanted to hinder him as much as possible.

Regardless of the boy's destiny, Pike couldn't let it eat him up with guilt, even if the kid reminded him of himself.

Don't get soft now, Pike.

He had a debt to pay. One that wouldn't pay itself. In fact, if he didn't do the job, *he* would pay. Afterall, payday came once a month, and if he hadn't performed well enough. . .

Flashes of shadows and silver overwhelmed him. Pain radiated beneath his shirt, reminders scratched in pale, puffy skin.

You deserved it.

Pike struggled to swallow.

"Hank, if you want to testify freely without a guilty conscience, you can leave," Pike pulled his favorite knife from his belt.

Hank sucked in a heavy breath. "You're going to do it here? Now?"

"It's none of your business what happens. If you get tangled in this,

I may be visiting Jethro again very soon." He met Hank's gaze with the darkest look he could muster, eyebrows drawn together.

Hank's eyes were full of fear, but Pike wondered what Hank saw in him. Did the man see a monster? Were Pike's icy blue eyes empty and soulless? Maybe Pike *was* soulless. Perhaps that was part of his debt, losing his soul.

"Hank. Leave."

The young man stumbled backward and skirted up the alley. Licking the back of his teeth, Pike straightened his shoulders and merged into the flow of bodies entering the trading post.

Inside the dim room, Pike's eyes adjusted. Trading tables, men, and women trying to sell food and clothes clustered together in the center. Pike joined the line closest to the door and began searching again for Oliver. When Pike caught a glimpse of him outside, he noted that the boy grew closer to average height and wore the same thing everyone else wore. But his smile Pike would remember, beaming and exuding joy.

Joy that wouldn't last for very much longer.

Oliver stood in a group around the spice table. Pike slowly zig-zagged his way over to him, stepping through lines of people here and there. Finally, he stood several feet away, acting interested in silks for a few moments before stepping right behind the kid.

"Oliver Eames. Don't move and don't speak," Pike muttered in Oliver's ear.

Oliver visibly tensed and nearly backed into the knife Pike held low to avoid being observed in the packed room.

"I said, don't move," Pike warned.

The boy barely nodded.

"Come with me, and no one else has to get hurt."

Oliver nodded once more, almost imperceptibly. The boy's head tilted, trying to get a view of his threat, but Pike grabbed his arm and forced him out of the packed room, back into the sunlight.

Pike dragged Oliver down a sidestreet and away from the port. His heart pounded in his ears like it always did when completing a job, bright eyes scanning the street behind them as he pulled the boy along.

"You're going to kill me, aren't you?" Oliver asked.

"No."

"So I'm not going to die?"

"No."

"But you said—"

Pike turned swiftly and pinned Oliver against the wall with his forearm braced against the boy's neck, dark flame tattoos mocking them both. For a moment, they both took in quick, shuddering breaths. The gulls called in the distance, and despite standing in the shadows of the alley, Pike could feel the warmth of the sun speaking of the tepid day to come. A gale kicked up trash, and it swirled past Pike's feet, almost whispering as it went.

"Death comes for us all, kid," Pike finally growled. "We have to face it eventually."

Oliver swallowed hard, and Pike released him.

"Will it hurt?"

"I'm not dead, am I?" Pike rolled his eyes.

"Why me?"

"Why not you?"

Oliver stood in defeated silence, his final question standing in front of them like a temptress in the lamplit streets of a busy town.

"Where am I going?" Oliver whispered, face blanching as the words escaped his lips.

Pike wasn't allowed to answer that question. Truth be told, he didn't know. He wasn't so sure that all of his jobs ended up in the same place. Not all of them died either. Some went on to live long and relatively decent lives.

He resumed his hold on Oliver's shirt collar and continued the trek through winding streets. Many people visibly turned to watch them as they went, but Pike moved relentlessly. No one asked questions which made things easier, yet at the same time, it perturbed him how unconcerned these people were.

Maybe they think I'm his father or an angry boss.

They reached the edge of the Alabama port town where palm trees still decorated the area. Pike slowed his steps, but continued pulling Oliver behind until they reached a crossroads.

The trees were now a mix of tropical and pine, and Pike promptly forced Oliver to sit at the base of one, tucked in the dappled shade. Then, Pike dropped on the grass a few feet away, ready and alert.

They sat watching each other for a while. Pike observed the boy seated in front of him who nibbled at the skin around his fingernails. Oliver had no idea what he would face, no clue how things could change so swiftly like the wind. Despite his best efforts, Pike pitied the boy. He wondered if people had pitied him when his father had passed.

What I wouldn't give to be young and innocent once more.

The sun beat down directly overhead, and Pike made no move to leave the spot he'd chosen earlier, a few paces from the crossroads.

"You know," Oliver mumbled, shifting where he sat. "We have stories about you. The shadow man, coming in the night to steal us away, glaring down at his victims with unearthly, ice blue eyes, flames consuming him. I never imagined you to be like this."

"How do you mean?" Pike asked.

Oliver shrugged, pulling grass up by his feet. "You're always cruel and murderous in the folktales."

"Who's to say I'm not cruel and murderous?" Pike asked, mildly offended.

"You haven't impaled me, beheaded me, or sawed me in half yet, so I'd say you're pretty normal comparatively."

He laughed, the sound vibrating deep in his chest. "Are those the stories spreading about me?"

It was humorous that this child believed what he saw before ever hearing or seeing the truth. Pike briefly wondered if he had ever been so innocent. His chuckle faded to mild irritation.

"I have done everything you've listed. I have impaled traitors, be-headed queens, and sawed one person in half. I've also strangled and drowned people, tortured some, humiliated others. I've cut many throats. I've burned people alive."

Pike hesitated, watching Oliver carefully. All of the color had drained from his face, but he wasn't shaking and he wasn't running, meaning he had taken this better than most of the people that asked too many questions.

"I am a monster, but only when necessary," Pike shrugged. "It's rude to be a monster unnecessarily." With a stretch and a yawn, he recalled his fitful night spent in a lumpy bed at an inn. Exhaustion drained him, body sore from tossing and turning in such a creaky bed.

"Listen, kid, I don't care to talk about myself. I'm doing my job. So please—"

"What about your markings? Were you born with them? Or did you earn them somehow by proving yourself?"

Pike froze momentarily, mind flashing to the lines of fire on his forearms, like brands on his pale skin. To avoid someone seeing them, he always wore long sleeves and never anything shorter. It had been necessary for survival.

A mark of the beast.

"They were a gift. . . from my boss. . ."

"How did you get this job?" Oliver ran his hands down his pant legs, tilting his head in curiosity.

"Why? Are you interested?" When tense silence from the boy greeted him, he shook his head. "You want to become *greater* and strike fear in peoples' hearts when they set eyes on you? You want every possibility of a happy future to be dashed into the sea? You want to surrender every ounce of control for a life that isn't even yours? You want to burn someone else's life to the ground, letting their dreams crumble like ash while your image in their mind becomes twisted and wretched?" He wasn't sure what made him ask. Maybe the boy's age or his innocence, but cruel memories of a ruined childhood flashed behind Pike's eyes, the guilty feeling from before washing back over him like the tide. When silence lingered, Pike continued. "It passed to me. End of story. Now keep quiet."

Pike leaned back on his hands, reclining in the grass. Oliver fidgeted with his hat, but for once he wasn't talking. Pike's thoughts drifted away with the light coastal breeze that ruffled his sandy colored hair. He wondered if the Devil's purpose for Oliver was more evil than he first expected. Tension seized his stomach at the idea, though he knew even if he wanted to help that his hands were bound. Reality grabbed Pike's attention when a dark figure materialized at the crossroads.

"Get up," Pike huffed, pushing himself to his feet.

Oliver stood and kept behind Pike as they made their way towards the shadowy man. The Devil smiled at Oliver with lifeless eyes.

"Hello, Oliver Eames," the Devil crooned.

Oliver nodded his head in greeting, but didn't look Silvertongue in the eye.

"Mmm," the man turned to Pike. "Very polite. How nice." He brushed off his suit. "Well, easy job first. What town next?"

"Another choice?" Pike asked.

The man rolled his eyes. "I need an answer. It's not like I have all of eternity to waste standing here with you." He raised his eyebrows. "Oh wait, I do. But I'd rather get back to business. It's a simple question, so what will it be?"

Greenwich, Lankin, or Jovy.

"I'll take Greenwich."

"Delicious," the man grinned and licked his white, sharp teeth with appalling happiness. "I think you'll enjoy Greenwich immensely." With a terrible screeching laugh, the man grabbed Pike and Oliver's shoulders. The world spun once again, salty air meshing with the piney scent of a conifer forest and rain.

Great, I had to pick the one with rain.

They stood on top of a bald hill overlooking a mountain town flickering in the distance, a bright spot in the gloomy weather. Things were tinted orange and the autumn air invaded Pike's lungs.

Oliver stumbled, attempting to gain his footing after the jump. The sound of retching accompanied his stumbling and Pike averted his eyes.

"I'll be back." The man again reached for Oliver's shoulder but hesitated. He slowly turned his gaze to Pike. "I suggest you get acquainted with the town. This one is a little more. . . difficult."

"What about the name?"

The Devil grinned at Pike. "I'll see you soon. Don't wait up."

And with that, the man and the sick looking boy disappeared.

"Great." Pike brushed his hair and the rain out of his face. "This is Manhattan all over again."

He turned, taking in his surroundings, albeit wet and grim.

Better watch out, Greenwich. Hell is coming for you.

3

The hike into town was atrocious.

By the time Pike reached the edge of cobblestoned Main Street around lunchtime, his feet and shoes were soaked, squishing as he walked. Mud covered everything up to his knee. His loose, white shirt stuck to his chest beneath his coat, restricting his movement, and everything else he owned was damp.

He felt for the journal tucked in his pocket, lamenting wet pages and smeared ink. Muttering curses under his breath, he jogged under the cover of a shop awning, thinking the whole time of his job at hand.

What job? I don't even have a name yet.

After combing his hair out of his face, he took his first real look at the mountain town around him.

Across the street, a red brick building with high steeples jutted out of a grove of auburn-colored trees. It reminded him of a Sunday back home in Morville, running with the other children in the park. Down the street, grand houses in a variety of colors glowed from the warm light of fires and gas lights within, looking like nostalgia in physical form. A wagon rumbled past, splashing rainwater in its wake dousing Pike's feet with another wave of water. A bathhouse bustled with customers, but all the other establishments looked mostly empty. He wondered if any of the faces inside felt their time coming to an end.

Pike gazed upward towards the hills he'd come from, but the mountains past it were shrouded in clouds much like his purpose in Greenwich. Squinting through the slowing rain, Pike observed that each building had large letters painted on the side declaring what it offered, from ammunition to hardware to studio photographs and bustle gowns.

Behind him stood a postal service building where the postmaster sat sheltered from the rain. Pike knocked on the door, not wanting to be impolite nor wanting to get the things inside the office covered in muck.

The postmaster shuffled to the door.

"Dear heavens, come in!" he cried. The man ushered Pike in without a question and closed the door after him. While surprised by the genuine act of kindness, Pike expressed his immense gratitude to be let in from the rain.

On closer inspection, Pike noticed the man had thin gray hair and seemed a bit frazzled, though that could have been from a stranger turning up on his doorstep in the middle of a rainstorm. Even the rainstorm alone could have ruined a person's day. The man pulled a wooden chair up close to his small wood-burning stove and beckoned Pike to sit.

With a grateful sigh, Pike sat and shivered involuntarily. "Thank you for your kindness, sir."

The man nodded. "The blasted rain. . . comes in when it wants and leaves when it wants. Ruining plans. . ."

The man went away muttering and left Pike to himself for a moment, giving him ample time to take in as much information as he could.

While small, the office felt lived in, and paper, wrapping supplies, and postage littered the desk. Pike leaned to the side and rifled through a few of the letters.

Emilina Jackson.
Madeline Stooksbury.

Anne Thomas.

Evan Collins.

Letting the letters fall back to their original place, he turned his attention to the wall. Certificates and newspaper clippings were posted with respect alongside a framed CDV photo of a family standing in front of the postal service building.

"Here you are." The man returned with a glass of amber-colored liquid. "It's not the best Greenwich has to offer, but I hope it'll warm you up."

Pike accepted it, turning the corner of his lips in a smile. He took a sip and exhaled heavily.

"So, you're not from here," the postmaster stated more than asked.

"No, sir." Pike chuckled. "I'm from Washington."

The postmaster settled into a seat across from him. "The great Washington Territory. What's brought you so far from home? Are you visiting for the debutante ball later this week?"

"That is my primary purpose," Pike lied, thinking that whoever his job ended up being would most likely be at such an important social event. If not, it meant dinner and a dance which wouldn't be completely terrible. "I also came for business. I do contract work, and I'm hoping to strike a deal."

"I'm assuming you have a place to stay?"

"Not yet," Pike scratched his forehead while attempting to craft a story for his arrival. "Arrive on the last train, and there weren't any carriage drivers. Hiked the last mile or so and showed up at your door a few minutes ago."

The postmaster chuckled. "I'll take you down to the Greenwich Hotel. They have excellent service. And despite our influx of visitors in preparation for the ball, I'm sure they'll have a room for you."

After Pike finished his drink, the postmaster walked him down the cobbled street, turning up a muddy lane labeled 2nd Street. The Greenwich Hotel, shining brightly through the rain, stood down the road. The sight of it alone, opulent and glamorous, made Pike's heart leap in his ribcage. They walked past a tea house and more residential houses before standing in front of the extravagant building, gaslights glowing in the gray atmosphere of drizzly, afternoon weather.

Stepping inside, Pike thanked the postmaster, clothes and shoes still damp and squishy. Marble pillars framed the doorways to side rooms filled with sounds of laughter, billiards, and music. In the billiard room, a group of men chuckled, puffing on cigars. They all wore Hessian boots with similar short trimmed hairstyles and wax-styled facial hair.

This job won't be easy with all of the men dressing alike these days. Everyone looks almost exactly the same, like perfect clones of the other.

Pulling off his coat, he snapped it in the air to knock out some of the water onto the marble flooring before draping his coat over his arm and stepping to the lobby counter.

"Excuse me, who can I talk to about my room?" he asked the porter.

"I can do that for you, sir," the man nodded, unkempt hair falling in his grubby face. "How many nights?"

Pike bit his bottom lip. He could pay for a room, or instead he could buy time until he disappeared without a trace when Silvertongue picked him up. "I do apologize." He cleared his throat then continued, "My employer sent a telegram last week to have a room prepared for Mr. James Pike for one week."

The porter sifted through some papers behind the desk before saying, "My apologies, sir. I have misplaced the telegram, but I can have a room prepared immediately."

"Thank you very much."

"So you're here for the deb ball?" The man scratched a few words onto a sheet of ledgers.

"I am, yes. I wondered where I might find a shop where I can replace my clothes."

No sense packing for a trip when you never know what you'll need to wear.

Pike gestured to his clothes. "I've had an unfortunate incident with my luggage. This weather has been the death of me."

The man laughed. "You and I both. I'd recommend the shop down Main Street, Irene's. She'll have everything you need."

The porter turned and unlocked a glass box with dozens of keys on hooks. He pulled a set off, relocked the door, then picked up a few pieces of paper.

"If you will follow me, Mr. Pike, I can take you to your room."

Pike smiled and fell in step behind the porter.

The hotel wasn't the fanciest place Pike had ever seen, but most places he'd visited paled in comparison. Its gas lamps burned bright to fend off the dull weather, and somewhere, music played.

They went up one set of stairs and around a balcony where they stopped in front of a plain white wooden door.

"Welcome to Greenwich, Mr. Pike." The porter unlocked the door for him. "If you have any questions, please don't hesitate to ask! And we'll continue to search for that missing telegram. I apologize again for any inconvenience."

"Thank you very much." Pike shook the man's hand and left him a small tip. "I'll try to contact my boss tomorrow and see what I can find out."

With that, the porter left Pike with the keys to his room and a small map of Greenwich.

Pike relieved himself before heading down the halls, testing doorknobs here and there. His days with the Devil had taught him that money wasn't always guaranteed. Any chance to make a few more dollars—whether honestly or dishonestly obtained—was well received on all accounts.

A few of the other guest rooms were unlocked. Pike slipped into a room that looked similar to his own, only fancy clothes filled the closet. Stuffing his hands into the coat pockets, Pike found a bunch of folded bills. On the side table, he slid a gold coated watch around his wrist, tightening it to fit snugly beneath his shirtsleeve.

He slipped quietly out of that room, down the hall, and through another unlocked door. Pike tiptoed his way around the messy room, only taking a pair of gloves that had been discarded on the floor.

Heading back downstairs, his keys and coins jingled lightly in his pocket alongside the bills of different amounts. After slipping on his coat, he stepped outside into the rain and headed down back to Main at a brisk pace. It only drizzled now, but mud coated Pike despite his best efforts.

At the end of Main Street close to the other side of the town, a clothing store stood, looking like the kind of place that overcharged based solely on a name or title. A bell jingled as Pike opened the door.

"Good afternoon," a voice called from the back. "Come inside!"

An older woman, maybe in her late fifties, came around the front to Pike. Draped in a garish purple dress and lined in black lace and ruffles, she walked with a bustle bouncing behind that seemed almost as big as her.

She led him to a lush lounge area decorated with lavish sofas and an oriental rug, giving him a black coffee with a spoonful of sugar before pulling several options of suits that he might like. By the end of it, Pike left with a business suit, promising to pick up his dinner attire the next day.

He headed back to the hotel with a new suit and new shoes both wrapped and boxed carefully to avoid the rain. Up in his room, he changed fast, not wanting to miss the evening dinner chatter. Downstairs once again, he followed the sound of music.

Rounding the corner, he reached the dining hall which sat across from the cigar lounge and billiards room. Pike strolled over to the bar, stuffing his hands in his pockets, hiding his stolen watch.

"Americano, please," he waved at the bartender.

He leaned his back against the bar and surveyed the room. The dining area consisted of dozens of white cloth-covered tables outfitted with flowers and general cutlery. The other guests were mostly of a higher class, women dressed in the new colors and striped styles that had recently become popular. The men were mostly in their evening dress suits. A few groups had already sat down to eat an early dinner, and among them, Pike heard the chatter about a garden party.

"Of course, it'll be the prelude to the ball on Saturday," one woman said, an extravagant, yet teeny, hat bobbing in her hair. "We'll get coffee and tea while being delightfully entertained by the season. I wonder about those Collins boys. Or poor Miss Thomas. This is her third season, you know."

Another lady launched into gossip about the poor Miss Thomas, and Pike promptly checked out.

The bartender slid a tall glass across the counter to Pike. Red in color and garnished with a lemon peel, the drink enticed him, looking as fancy as he felt.

"Might I ask you a question?" Pike asked, then took a sip.

The man nodded.

"I'm supposed to be here for an event. Tomorrow, I believe. But I've misplaced the address on my way to town. I'm sure several other people here are attending. It's the garden party. You don't happen to know the place?"

Pike pulled out the map that the porter had provided him with and slid it to the bartender, who examined the streets with precision.

"Here," he pointed. "The Stooksbury House. They host all the fancy house events in Greenwich."

Pike slid a tip to the bartender. "Thank you very much, sir."

After eavesdropping some more and savoring the last of his drink, Pike stood and retired to his room. He needed to prepare to look and act his best at this garden party. Either he'd find out valuable information or get kicked out of Greenwich before he could even begin.

4

Pike woke up in a bed draped in sheets softer than he'd ever slept under. The sunlight barely gleamed around the edges of the curtains, and for once in a very long time, Pike felt somewhat calm.

The urge to go back to bed nearly overwhelmed him, and he almost gave in.

Almost.

More was at stake than his rest.

Pulling himself from the comfort and relative safety of the bed, Pike stood to face the day. He pulled on his new dress shirt and pants then buckled his belt.

The question of the previous night still loomed in the shadows of the hotel room.

How am I going to charm my way into this garden party?

It's not like he hadn't done similar things before, but he'd always had names of people he "knew" as leverage. This time, he would walk in blind. It unsettled him, causing his hands to sweat. It was difficult *not* to connect with people, making the act of harming someone that much more intense. He found it hard to keep to himself. Normal people, humans not bound to the Devil, had a freedom Pike only dreamed about.

Irresistible, and off limits.

After brushing his hair out with his fingers and rubbing the sleep from his eyes, he headed down the main stairs where he found breakfast already started in the dining hall.

"Morning." He nodded to those he made eye contact with, silently wondering if one of these people would soon have to face the Devil.

A waiter seated him with a few other men and promptly handed Pike a mug of coffee.

Pike smiled his thanks before the waiter sped off to the next table to give coffee to other guests. While Pike waited for breakfast to be served, he savored the deliciously sweet coffee he'd been given. It warmed him to the center, and he wished he could climb back in bed instead of working.

The hotel's clientele were speaking in hushed tones. Pike picked up conversations of war and politics, more talk about the garden party, and gossip about the young ladies of the season.

Breakfast was served, and Pike immediately dug in.

The Greenwich Hotel certainly knows how to do breakfast.

They served platters with sausage, bacon, cold ham, eggs, toast, apples, and all varieties of jams, jellies, and marmalades.

By the end of the meal, Pike's stomach had been stuffed with anything he wanted. He drank the rest of his coffee, enjoying every drop, before heading out to find the house that belonged to the Stooksbury family.

His walk around town was much less horrendous than the previous day in the rain. The clouds hung low, but they had been emptied of the rain they carried. The bright gray morning lit up the hillsides, yellows and oranges along with reds and browns peeking through the mist which clung to the mountains. Rolling hills stretched as far as the eye could see, twisting and curving into the wilderness of the Appalachian mountain range.

Water pooled on the streets, but the ground had drunk enough of it to leave dry patches where people walked. The cobblestone was slick and the damp dirt streets stuck to Pike's shoes, but he thoroughly enjoyed his morning walk.

As it turned out, it wasn't all that difficult to find, especially with the bartender's help from the night before. Half the town bustled about in preparation for the party which began right at midday.

Pike had no trouble getting onto the premises. In fact, he'd hardly gotten any words out when someone handed him several boxes and ushered him to the backyard where chaos awaited. Tents were being erected and banners hung. Tables and chairs needed moving and food needed preparing.

Never once did the woman giving orders make eye contact with Pike. No one doubted his identity. They assumed he had been hired to work like everyone else that arrived early, which fell in his favor.

Given the liberties that he had as a server and greeter with guest belongings, Pike found himself several hundred dollars richer. He even nicked a forgotten ring from the Stooksbury's house in addition to a pair of gloves for serving. Slipping them on, he mused to himself.

Never waste a good opportunity.

It's exactly what his father would have said.

Clenching his jaw and pushing back the memory of his father, Pike opened the French doors that lead to the yard where all the festivities were taking place. At the service tent, a cook passed him a tray of hors d'oeuvres to begin serving the guests. Unsurprised and frankly grateful not to make too much small talk with society's rich and powerful, Pike straightened and headed for the nearest table.

The band began to play a relaxing tune and women were starting their gossip when Pike asked a table of gentlemen if they would be interested in a cucumber sandwich.

"My God," a young man sat up quickly. "You were at the Greenwich this morning. Why on earth are you in servant's gloves?"

Pike had seen him at breakfast, assuming he was visiting Greenwich as well.

Pike bent his head apologetically. "Late this morning, I arrived early to the party to ask for Mr. Stooksbury. I wanted to show my thanks to our wonderful host, but instead a few boxes were handed to me. My mother taught me to always lend a hand when one needed help, so I decided not to say anything in hopes I wouldn't embarrass the host for the mistake."

The man shook his head. "My apologies on their behalf. Please sit." He lifted the tray from Pike's hand and slid a few sandwiches onto his own plate before setting the tray down in the center of the table. Several other men took a sandwich, chuckling amongst friends.

Pike sat in the chair next to the man, relishing a chance to rest after being on his feet for a few hours.

"I'm Liam," the kind man held his hand out.

"James," Pike shook Liam's hand.

"So James," one of the other men leaned forward, "we were just discussing the current politics in South America. The Saltpeter War has caused quite the stir in the southern hemisphere."

Pike smiled politely. "I confess to not know much about South America's political climate. I've been more concerned with current advancements on our own soil."

"What advancements interest you?" Liam sipped on his drink, leaning back with a sort of leisure Pike only wished he conveyed or even felt.

Pike cleared his throat before he began. "I've been impressed thus far with the Transcontinental Railroad. Some weren't even sure that would stick. But with Edison working on better ways of harnessing electricity and the invention of telephones . . . The world is full of intelligent people, and I believe that a good deal of them ended up here in our country."

Liam chuckled. "I couldn't agree more. The scientific community is making leaps and strides. New elements are being discovered, and they're finding certain chemicals to be better painkillers than what we've been using."

"So you're a doctor then?" Pike asked, picking up a cucumber sandwich.

"Medical lawyer."

"Next time I run into any medical issues, you'll be the first person I call."

Liam laughed. "By all means! You would help pay my bills. Someone find this man a stunt to pull." Liam stood and waved jokingly, chuckling the whole time. Sitting back down, he tilted his head sideways. "Do you have any plans this weekend?"

"I do, actually." Pike nodded. "I'm in town for the debutante ball on Saturday. Why do you ask?"

Liam beamed. "Excellent! I wanted to invite you. I don't believe in love at first sight, but I do believe in friendship at first introduction. I'd love for you to meet a woman."

Pike raised an eyebrow. "You want me limiting the amount of women whom you'll get to talk to?"

Despite his remark, his insides turned.

I barely know this man and he's trying to get me married…

But part of Pike ached for a friendship close enough to bind two families together, to forge a bond that lasted a lifetime. Yet, his fate lingered elsewhere. Was there any point in hoping for such a friend?

Liam's face broke into a smirk. "Not just any woman. I want to introduce you to someone specific. Someone I know. In fact, she should be here somewhere."

With that, Liam stood, craning his neck to find one face among dozens of flowery, frocked women in wild new colors and silly hats.

Pike sat alone with the other men momentarily, but the older gentlemen spoke only of wars while the younger men spoke only of what existed under the women's skirts. Finding both very dull, Pike stood to seek company elsewhere.

He meandered around the leaf-covered garden, inspecting the trees and the last flowers of autumn. The hue of oranges and browns draped the landscape. He'd been to his fair share of parties, but never a debutante. Being in the trade he was, Pike had no choice but to adapt and learn to fit in wherever placed. He'd learned early on how not to embarrass himself at nice dinners and among the higher society.

"Champagne?"

He turned to face a waiter who held a tray of champagne flutes, the liquid fizzy and enticing.

"Thank you very much." He took one and turned back to the flowers he had been inspecting previously.

As he tipped the glass to sip his champagne, his gaze gravitated to a woman strolling past a section of chrysanthemums. But not just any woman.

Delicately wrapped in a deep orange and lined with black lace, she practically glided on the breeze. Her hair had been twisted up in curls and topped with a small hat to match her dress, every detail intentional. She carried herself like a queen, confident and bold. And she was observant of her surroundings though her eyes never met his own.

She seemed simultaneously beautiful and wild.

His dream girl.

Of course, he had no idea if she shared the personality of the woman he'd dreamed up for himself, but she looked almost exactly like he'd imagined her to be had she truly existed. And *here*, a vision before his very eyes.

He made his way back towards where she had stood, dodging partygoers and waiters alike all dressed in bright garments, sashes, and hats. He nearly toppled over a young servant boy and mumbled his apologies, turning around. When he made it to the line of chrysanthemums where he'd last seen her, the woman had long since disappeared.

Heart racing, Pike turned in circles looking for her, but he couldn't find the delicate orange in a sea of color.

Maybe she was a dream, he thought to himself.

"James!" Liam grabbed his shoulder.

Pike flinched, mind flashing immediately to the Devil who always grabbed his shoulder right before traveling to a new place.

"Oh, are you all right?" Liam asked, concern evident in his voice.

"Fine, sorry." Pike shook his head lightly. "You scared me out of my thoughts, that's all."

Liam nodded. "Listen, I had every intention of introducing you to my sister. However, she and my mother and youngest sister are heading back to my house to retire for the afternoon. They're unfortunately only visiting me here in Greenwich."

Many parts of Liam's words had intrigued Pike, but one stuck out the most.

"You live in Greenwich? Were you not staying at the hotel?"

"I see how that could be confusing." Liam smirked. "Apologies, but I was visiting a friend who's staying in town for the deb. Our schedules never quite meet up well, so I went to him instead."

"This ball must be very important for the town," Pike glanced around. "People have come from all over to attend."

"It's certainly one of the bigger events Greenwich sees throughout the year," Liam sipped at his own glass. "But it's necessary. A town full of beautiful and *eligible* women. . . Why not?"

Pike smiled. "And your sister is supposed to be there?"

Liam fiddled with his glass but wouldn't meet Pike's gaze. "You must think I'm rather strange, pushing my sister at you when you and I have barely even met." He glanced up and laughed quietly. "I always did have a knack for making connections. It helps in the practice of law to have them."

"So why introduce me to your sister?" Pike scratched at the facial hair on his chin. He internally cursed his ulterior motives. It did not bode well for him that the Devil had said Greenwich would be difficult. Had he known already that it would be difficult for Pike to keep his emotions at bay?

Liam half shrugged. "You will know when you meet her. She's graceful and honest. Not that all women are liars, but she doesn't avoid hard things." Liam shook his head. "She's tenacious and yet overwhelmingly kind."

"Does she have any faults?" Pike grinned at the man next to him.

"She's completely stubborn," Liam chuckled. "She disappears for long solitary walks in the city, and she's not afraid to get into trouble when she's curious."

"She sounds like a handful."

Liam nodded. "She may be, but I think you two would fit well together. I saw how comfortable you were this morning, listening to the conversations of others. And serving this afternoon... Most men I know would throw a fit if someone assumed they were a servant. Instead, you lent a hand. And clearly you're educated, what with all the conversation about railroads, inventions, and whatnot."

Pike smiled but shook his head. "I'm a handful myself. I'm not so sure you'd want the two of us together."

Shrugging, Liam drank the last of his drink. "You never know. Maybe it would be the perfect match."

"You'll have to introduce us then."

Before Liam could say anymore, a few men approached.

"Dr. Jackson! We need to talk about the Orson case."

With an apologetic shrug, Liam allowed himself to be led away. "Until Saturday, James!"

With a sorrow filled sigh, Pike stood and headed to the service tent, thoughts swirling with dancing and colorful dresses. . . Or maybe the champagne had flooded his senses. He cleared his throat, poking his head inside.

"Do give my compliments to the host. I had the most pleasurable afternoon."

And with that, he showed himself out and back to the hotel. He did stop on his way by Irene's clothing store to pick up his debutante attire. Pike noticed that there were several people buying their own outfits while waiting for his suit to be brought out to him. Many of them wanted to look their best, if not *the* best. Pike didn't blame them.

Despite knowing he could never truly settle down unless he received freedom from his enslavement under Silvertongue, Pike wanted to look his best for Liam's sister. He found himself wondering what she was like or how pretty she looked. He hoped she might help him get his mind off that woman at the garden party even if for a moment. Because seeing his dream in reality made him pine even more for a future of freedom rather than slavery.

He climbed into his bed that night and stared at the ceiling.

"What are you thinking, Pike?" he muttered to himself aloud.

He couldn't get the woman out of his mind. Gentle curves, a round face, and those eyes. . . He wondered what type of life she lived in Greenwich. He wondered who she knew and what she did for fun. If he possessed freedom, he wondered if she would agree to move to Morville with him to be close to his mother. He wondered if this mystery woman knew how to cook or if she had a cook. He wondered if she would sing songs in the drawing room, working on embroidery. He wondered if she would draw close to him at night when it grew cold and snowy in Washington.

Worst of all, he wondered if she could even love him if the chance arose.

Am I capable of being loved?

Pike shook his head, trying to shake away the thoughts.

Will I ever be free?

He ran through several different scenarios, of him asking the Devil nicely for freedom. Of him offering to pay with his firstborn like the old legends. Of him offering his soul in the end if he could only spend what years he had left on the earth with a loving wife and a family. Would that mean his children would be enslaved still?

With a sigh of resignation, Pike pushed all thoughts of marriage aside. He assumed that the Devil would merely use the information for some new form of mental and emotional torture, rubbing salt in the generations-old wounds.

5

Six days.

Pike had been in the town six days, yet he still didn't have a name. It was Friday. He was getting antsy. Ansty didn't bode well for him.

Friday evening while wandering the town's dirt side streets asking himself existential questions, he ran into his employer again. The Devil walked towards Pike with a sleek cane and a set look of determination on his human mask, black eyes glinting in the light.

"Silvertongue, finally."

"Alexander, please. I've had a hell of a week."

Pike coughed, trying to hide his laughter.

The Devil sneered. "Please keep it together for a moment and stop acting like a child. Do you want this job or the alternative? Or shall I ask your mother to help me instead?"

Pike stiffened. "You know I want the job."

The Devil shrugged. "You haven't shown much initiative with this one. I figured since—"

"I want the job. I've been doing my best to meet people around town, but you haven't given me a name. We both know I want the job more than the alternative."

A greedy look flashed in the Devil's eyes, but it quickly faded away with a nonchalant shrug.

"Predictable," the man scoffed, knocking his cane into the ground. "Though I do love testing your self-control by making you wait. Patience is not your strong suit, Alexander." The Devil licked his teeth, then bent his head to examine his cane before he continued. "Harper Benson. She's the wife of a coal man. Not just any coal man, the white collar who runs the whole operation. There's a debutante ball tomorrow night. I suggest you find a nicer suit."

Silvertongue looked down at Pike's new business attire.

"I've already handled it," Pike brushed his hair back out of his face. "I've had that covered since Monday, no thanks to you."

The man hissed and his face warped slightly. "I suggest you try not to get under my skin. You don't want to see me angry. . . again."

Pike swallowed.

"I must say, I am disappointed," the Devil sighed. "It's been a while since you've refused a job."

"I learned quickly." Pike clenched his jaw shut, willing memories not to overflow like tears.

"To each his own, I suppose." The man turned to leave, but Pike stopped him by the arm, the Devil stiffening beneath his grasp.

The Devil's body pulled taut, tension rippling beneath the thin layer of human skin.

What have I done?

It was inescapable now. His gut reaction had been to stop Silvertongue, to ask him the question that had resurfaced over and over. The question had been scribbled all over his most recent journal entry.

Pike had to ask, had to know.

"What happened to Oliver Eames?"

"Pardon?" The Devil cocked his head to the side, every feature tense, wound tight like a clock. His humanoid fingers were turning white around the head of the cane.

"Oliver. What did you do to him? You never said what you wanted with him."

Silvertongue furrowed his brows and stepped back holding his cane in one hand. "Seven years of working for me, and you have never once asked about the fate of one of your jobs."

Pike blinked a few times. "I– I guess I never thought I could ask."

Silvertongue barked out a laugh. "That's because you can't."

Pike's heart sank. He'd feel the guilt of that assignment for a while, remembering how young the boy had been. He hoped Oliver had gotten out of having too much heartache, but he would never be certain. "What about Harper Benson? What did she do?"

The Devil twitched like a broken windup toy. "Harper? Harper has done absolutely nothing. But Mr. Benson will pay for his sins through his sweet wife. He will be tormented for the rest of his rather short life. He will doubt, and he will question, he will make this whole city doubt its beliefs, and then he will end his own life."

Pike's whole body shuddered as the Devil continued.

"Mrs. Benson will not die tonight or even this week. But once you bring her to me, she'll start the process of a long, slow, and agonizing death from poor health. It's quite depressing, which makes me rather cheerful." Silvertongue regarded Pike coolly. "She will rot from the inside out while his soul festers like an open wound. He will renounce what he thinks he believes and kill himself in the middle of the town on a busy night. A story to tell for *centuries*."

Pike tried not to show his emotions though he knew his face probably paled, telling the world and his boss exactly how sick his stomach felt. His vision wavered momentarily, focus drifting to the dirt under his feet.

"Is that too much information for you, Alexander?" Something a little dangerous flickered in the Devil's voice while he crept closer.

Pike hesitated before shaking his head, hands resting on the knife always strapped to his belt. He wasn't quite sure how this conversation would turn out.

"Do you regret asking your silly questions?" The Devil hissed in

Pike's face, breath reeking of rust and smoke.

"No, sir," Pike whispered, closing his eyes.

The Devil's face twitched in a snarl. In one quick motion, Silvertongue swung the head of his cane around and smashed Pike in the nose. Stumbling back, Pike's eyes immediately flooded with tears, searing pain overwhelming his senses. Bringing his hands up to his face, Pike's body surged with regret. The next blow came to the backs of his legs, bringing him to his knees. He let out a muffled shout, trying to blink away the tears that were mingling with blood.

So much blood.

His face stung. But his pride stung more.

"Don't ask questions," the Devil hissed, face disfigured into a ghoulish apparition, though Pike couldn't tell if he saw reality or if the disfiguration came from his blurry vision. "Get up. Do your job. I'll see you tomorrow at midnight. Do not fail me."

And with that, he left Pike alone, assaulted in the street.

He pushed up to one knee and spit on the dirt, blood mixing with tears. A terrible metallic taste coated his tongue and blood dripped from his nose. A few people passed him by in a wide arc on the other side of the street. Pike gingerly wiped his tears away and winced at the contact with his nose, his hands covered in a deep crimson. A wave of nausea nearly overcame him, but he swallowed it back. Other people's blood didn't bother him too much anymore, but seeing his own was another story.

The last time he'd seen so much of his blood, it'd taken him weeks to recover. He'd nearly died in Nashville, blood coating his lips and torso. He thought he might've been hit in the head, but he honestly couldn't remember. After transporting him back to his mother's house, the Devil left him and didn't return for a fortnight. Pike had crumpled in the dirt and stared at the trees until his mother had come home and cleaned him up.

A shiver ran down Pike's spine while he tried to beat away the memory. Pain filled all his senses.

Movement and the shuffle of shoes on the dirt pulled him out of his thoughts. He wasn't alone anymore.

Sliding his knife out his belt, Pike turned around.

From what little he could see through his tears, a woman laced her hands in front of her. Her face twisted in concern.

"Can I help you, sir?"

Her sweet southern voice hung in the night like a sunset on a summer evening, cicadas singing in the humid air.

Pike tilted his head to the side and furrowed his brow, causing pain to radiate through his facial bones again. "Why do you care?"

He choked on blood and the words, spitting blood on the ground.

"You've been injured. The least I can do is help you up." She took a small step forward and bent down. "Looks like you were hit fairly hard. Nothing a little care won't fix. My father is a doctor. He can help you. If you want help, that is." She smiled with the last words, and it made Pike's heart flip. He sincerely hoped this wasn't Harper Benson.

With her closer to him, he could smell the faint lingering scent of roses. And he could focus on her face better. His heart squeezed with ache.

The woman scrutinizing his injuries was the same woman he had been thinking of daily, the one from the garden party. The whole week, he'd been looking for her, and here she stumbled into his path the moment his face had been horribly bloodied and disfigured.

Damn my luck, Pike thought.

He wondered why she walked at night all alone or if some other man had already caught her attention. But most of all, he wondered what this young lady thought she was doing, associating herself with a brute bleeding on the street.

"Who are you?" he asked, spitting again and sliding his knife back into his belt, dreading her answer. He hoped if she wasn't Mrs. Benson that she wasn't a "Mrs." at all.

She blushed with a light smile, and amusement lit up her features. "Goodness, I thought this town was small enough. I have to admit, I'm surprised we haven't already been introduced. Do you really not know who I am?"

Pike shook his head once dizzy from the pain, and looked up at her. "I'm from out of town. I don't believe I've had the pleasure of being properly acquainted with you."

She blinked a few times deep brown eyes full of wonder, tilting her head to the side. "I am also visiting Greenwich." She frowned and her forehead wrinkled, making Pike's stomach jump to his heart. She met his gaze, amusement still dancing in her eyes. "My name is Cassidy Jackson. But you can call me Cass. . . if you'd like."

Jackson...

Pike leaned forward on his knee in a half bow, inclining his head, spitting more blood as he did so. "Pleased to make your acquaintance, Miss Cass. My name is James Pike. I would properly bow and greet you, but under current circumstances, I'd hate to stain your gloves red."

They both stood, Cass with a light blush and Pike with eyes squeezed shut. He stifled a groan, and he regained his balance as they started walking down Main Street.

"What did I do to deserve such kindness from a stranger?" he asked.

Cass mused to herself for a moment. "I suppose because everyone deserves kindness."

"I am sincerely glad that you believe in such goodness. If your father manages to clean me up, it means I might look my best for tomorrow's debutante."

"You're attending the debutante?" Cass beamed. "That's wonderful! I'm not sure how much we can help, but my father and I will do our best to keep you from looking all beaten and bruised."

"I like a woman who's ambitious." Pike smirked at her from the side.

He succeeded in obtaining the reaction he desired. She blushed madly and turned her face slightly down and away. "Mr. Pike, you are quite forward. I hesitate in assuming so, but you aren't from the south are you?"

Pike shook his head. "No, ma'am. I am originally from Manhattan; however, my father relocated our family out west, railroads and all."

"You know, I've always wanted to go out west," Cass looped her

41

arm through Pike's so comfortably it startled him.

Pike shifted his body and hands away from Cass while still keeping her arm around his own. Her touch alone intoxicated him. He didn't want to lose that feeling, but he was hyper aware of his blood still drying on his hands and his face.

If Cass noticed, she didn't acknowledge it. "Ever since I was a little girl, I've loved the idea of horses and an endless horizon as far as you can see. And I finally get to go, though I doubt it'll be like my childish fantasies."

"What's taking you so far?" Pike looked sideways at her, desperate to know her more. Her presence, though by any means not magical, seemed to dull his pain if only slightly. He wondered what it would be like to kiss her.

"My father's profession. He's starting his own practice out in Washington State. My mother, sister, and I will go with him, leaving my brother behind here in Greenwich working as a medical lawyer. He's slightly famous in this region, criminal cases and all."

"Well, I hope my home state is welcoming. It's a beautiful place. I guess I might be biased since it's where I live, but it really is beautiful." After a moment or two, Pike cleared his throat. "Your brother isn't by chance named Liam, is he?"

Please say yes. Please say yes.

Pike's heart beat quickly in his chest. Could this woman be the sister that Liam wanted to introduce him to at the party? And all along, his dream woman had been around the corner. . .

"It is," Cass watched him carefully. "Have you two met?"

Pike chuckled, sending new pain radiating against the pressure built up in his face. Pinching his nose, he grunted. "I believe he wanted us to meet. He and I met earlier this week at the garden party."

"You looked familiar, but I couldn't place how! No wonder. I must have seen you at the Stooksbury's House then. Liam did mention to our father that he wanted to introduce me to a friend. Now the mystery has been solved."

"Then, at long last, it's a pleasure to finally make your acquaintance,

Miss Cassidy Jackson."

"So. . . Mr. James Pike, what's brought you so far? It can't be solely for the debutante," Cass asked, watching people walk past them.

"Well, partly the ball. But I'm also here to do business."

"Business?" Cass turned to him now. "What kind?"

"Contract work." Pike shrugged, careful to keep his bloodied hand away from Cass while he held his nose with the other. "So Liam is who brought you to Greenwich?"

"Well he lives and works here, and it's a nice stopping point to see him before making our trek out west."

"It sounds like you're going to miss him very much," Pike smiled sadly at her. He knew how much it hurt to leave behind someone you loved.

She returned his smile with her own and gazed up at the flashy house in front of which they stopped. A grand two-story home towered over them, an elegant front porch framing the front. Lights were on in almost every window, lighting up the yellow-painted boards of the house.

"Here we are." Cass pulled her skirts up slightly and stepped up the stairs to the porch.

"I'm afraid I am severely underdressed for this time of day."

"Nonsense." Cass waved her hand, dropping the knocker. "I'm sure you've been working today, and besides, my father has seen a lot worse. And I'm sure Liam won't mind."

Pike felt slightly woozy now that they had stopped walking.

The door opened, and a well-dressed butler opened the door. "Miss Jackson, welcome back. Done exploring so soon?" He raised an eyebrow, eyeing Pike carefully.

Pike gave him credit that he hadn't been shocked to see such a bloody mess. Nevertheless, Pike's jaw tightened, aware of being scrutinized. Butlers of doctors must be used to blood and gore. And apparently the daughters of doctors were, too.

"Henderson, this is Mr. James Pike. I admit to having stumbled upon him on my walk, and I couldn't help but offer my assistance. That is, my father's assistance. Is he free?"

Henderson grinned ruefully. "You always do find someone or something to help, Miss. He's in the cigar room."

Cass grinned and nodded her thanks. They made their way down the hall, through an unoccupied yet opulent sitting room with paintings of people and places on every wall, and found themselves surrounded by sweet cigar smoke in a back room.

"Father?" Cass questioned, stepping confidently into the room. "Do you have your medical equipment handy?"

"Good Lord." Dr. Jackson quickly rose to his feet. "What in the devil did you get into on your walk?" He turned, addressing Cass. "You didn't do this, did you?"

Pike gave Cass a wry smile, causing her cheeks to adopt that light pink color yet again. It sent Pike's heart tumbling in his chest so much that he almost forgot to breathe.

She shook her head. "Not this time, father. Can you help him? He was attacked in the street tonight, but he's supposed to be going to the debutante ball tomorrow night. Coincidentally, he's the friend that Liam wanted to introduce to me. Mr. Pike simply cannot go to the ball like this."

Dr. Jackson stepped over to them with a grunt. "My, my. . . you took a hard hit, young man. Come into the sitting room. Cass, get me a bowl with warm water."

Cass set off, looking thrilled to be invited to help. Dr. Jackson sat Pike down on the couch and sat next to him.

"I don't believe I've had the pleasure of your acquaintance," the doctor removed his glasses and cleaned them with a handkerchief.

Pike cleared his throat, choking on blood again. "James A. Pike, sir. I do contract work, and I'm supposed to be meeting someone at the ball tomorrow night. I apologize for my appearance, I feel very unprofessional right now." He met the doctor's eyes which were full of genuine kindness. "I am extremely grateful for your generosity towards me. I even told Miss Jackson on our way to the house. A complete stranger doesn't often show this much kindness. It's unheard of and honestly very disarming."

Dr. Jackson laughed heartily as Cass came back in with a bowl of water and a cloth. She set it on the low table in front of the couch and left once more without a word. But she smiled warmly at Pike right before she walked away.

"Now, let's see here," Dr. Jackson stood, walking over to a cabinet. "Are you a brandy man or more of a scotch fellow?"

"Dealer's choice," Pike replied, craning his neck around, making his head rather dizzy. He cursed quietly and went to squeeze the top of his nose again, a horrible idea. He hissed in pain and removed his hand, now covered in fresh blood bright against the dried blood from earlier.

"Oh, I wouldn't recommend touching it quite yet." Dr. Jackson chuckled to himself. "The skin and bone will both be sensitive. But I do recommend a drink. To your health, son."

He passed the glass to Pike who downed it quickly, tongue still tasting like iron. "Thank you."

"All right, now the heavy work." Dr. Jackson set the bowl on his lap and dabbed the cloth in the water. "This will not feel any better until we are completely through for the night. I want to make you aware of the amount of pain you might feel."

"Pain isn't a new acquaintance for me, doctor." Pike clenched his jaw. "In fact, we're old friends, pain and I."

The doctor regarded him curiously, but began dabbing away blood without asking questions. Pike pinched his eyes closed. He didn't want to tear up again, especially not in front of this doctor, but it hurt worse than many of his previous injuries. Injuries that had left scars littered across his body. The alcohol helped the pain in his face subside, but the pressure right underneath his eyes was almost unbearable. Crying with an injury like this seemed normal and involuntary, but Pike didn't want to be weak in front of this man. Or in front of Cass.

"So," Dr. Jackson began, working on cleaning away the blood that quickly soiled the damp cloth and bowl of water, "you do contract work?"

"Yes, sir," Pike managed to grunt through the pain.

"Might I ask with whom you are working? I might be able to introduce you tomorrow. I'm assuming this is your first time to Greenwich."

"Yes, sir, it is. I'm supposed to meet a Mr. Benson? He works as—"

"I know William," Dr. Jackson interrupted. He muttered a few words under his breath while he continued his dabbing. "There a reason you decided to do business with him?"

Pike shifted his weight. "Well, he offered me a job. Well, my employer offered me the job with Mr. Benson. I've never met the man before, so why would I judge him before he's gotten the chance to introduce himself?"

Dr. Jackson huffed, shaking his head. "You're right, of course. But he's not the best man to be doing business with if you know what I mean. He—"

Cass walked back into the sitting room with a briefcase in tow and a fresh towel. Dr. Jackson grew quickly quiet. Clearly whatever things Mr. Benson did were not proper for a young lady's ears which could mean several things all too dark to discuss in polite company. She set the case down next to her father's feet and took the cloth from him. Replacing the old towel, she continued the cleaning work, starting with Pike's hands. She gently washed the blood away from each finger and each palm. Breath escaped him as this woman completely captivated him. An intelligent and fascinating young lady sat before him, the woman who had consumed his thoughts since he'd seen her earlier that week.

"It's broken, yes?" she asked her father, going back to work on cleaning Pike's face, almost seeing past him.

"Quite," the doctor replied, rummaging through his case.

Pike watched Cass carefully who did not look him in the eyes, rather she focused on his injury. She almost didn't see him at all.

"You were lucky, Mr. Pike, to have fallen in the path of my daughter," the doctor spoke, opening a bottle of a clear liquid with a smile. "She can't refuse the need to help those in trouble."

"I do consider myself quite lucky," Pike said, still looking at Cass.

And he did. She, of all people, had happened on him and offered to help. Cass, a dream and an entirely fascinating woman. And since she would be attending the ball as a debutante, he knew she wasn't married or being courted. In fact, that meant she was very available, his chances being much higher than he previously expected.

"All right," Dr. Jackson doused a small cloth in the clear liquid. "This will hurt."

Pike chuckled. He'd handled pain before, but words didn't want to come out at that moment.

Cass raised her eyebrows and shared a look with her father that worried Pike. They doubted his pain tolerance, causing him to be highly concerned with the level of pain he would feel.

Dr. Jackson stepped forward right in front of Pike. At that proximity, Pike could smell the cologne he'd worn intermixed with the sweet smell of a cigar. Feeling slightly uncomfortable, Pike pulled his hands into his lap.

Dr. Jackson carefully felt the bone all the way up the nose, Pike's pain going from small to immense in a few seconds. Pike squirmed in his seat, trying desperately not to move away. The doctor gave him a look with eyebrows raised while placing the wet cloth gently over Pike's nose. The liquid quickly sank into the busted skin and stung like alcohol on a cut. With a horrible thought, Pike realized that's exactly what happened and felt rather than heard the alcohol sizzling away, sterilizing his wound. He immediately tensed, desperately wanting to scratch his face. Without hesitation, the doctor lined both hands up with the edges of Pike's nose putting excruciating pressure on both sides of Pike's face. He folded all of his fingers down except for the pinky fingers, which lay against Pike's cheek bones, and squeezed with both hands.

"One," Dr. Jackson adjusted his hands.

Pike groaned in pain but clenched his mouth shut, jaw tensing.

"Two."

It hurt quite a bit, but he could tolerate the pain at least for a moment. And then, without saying three, the doctor snapped his hands to the right and a sickening crack accompanied it.

"Oh my—" Pike started. "Ow!"

Dr. Jackson stepped back and tossed the blood-covered cloth into the bowl of soiled water. He stepped around the table where his daughter stood, thoroughly unimpressed. Forgetting the pain from before,

Pike reached up and pressed on the bridge of his nose. The pain still bothered him from where his skin had split, but the pressure and intense shooting pains from the break were nearly gone. His pain had gone from excruciatingly high to almost nothing in seconds. Pike met the doctor's eyes in surprise.

"The bleeding should stop momentarily. You should be completely fine if you keep it clean," Dr. Jackson grinned and chuckled. "I did try to warn you."

Pike rubbed his nose gently. "You did. And while I am familiar with pain, that was something entirely different."

"Broken noses are relatively simple fixes," Cass packed up the briefcase. "It's broken eye sockets that cause the most trouble. They're trickier to heal."

"Luckily, you had none of that," Dr. Jackson said. "Best to wash your hands." He nodded to Pike's hands. "The washroom is down the hall."

Pike stepped down the hall and opened a door that led to a small washroom. The golden framed mirror stood against the wall, glimmering in the gas lamplight. The face that looked back at Pike didn't look the same. His nose had swollen along with the upper parts of his cheeks under his eyes, now framed with slightly dark circles. A small gash ran over the bridge of his nose where it ached the most, but Dr. Jackson did his job very well. Pike examined it up close, noticing that the blood had already stopped flowing from his nose and the gash.

Pike bent over the basin and washed his hands, ensuring that he had cleaned off the rest of the blood. He thought back to the countless times he'd done a similar thing, washing his hands of someone else's blood. It had become almost a ritual, a messy and sickening ritual that he'd grown numb to over the years. He rinsed off his face before heading back to the cigar lounge.

"James!" Liam stepped down the last few stairs. "I heard you had a little boxing match on the street."

"News travels fast." Pike laughed. "I'm lucky that your sister found me."

Liam patted Pike's shoulder. "Lucky indeed! Welcome to my home." He threw out his hand, gesturing to the house, and accompanied Pike to the lounge. "My family is staying until they head west in a week."

Pike stepped to the doctor, sticking out his hand. "I am indebted to you, Dr. Jackson." They shook hands, and Dr. Jackson patted him on the back.

"There might still be some bruising for a few days, but as long as you keep it clean, it should heal fine. Maybe not in time for the debutante, but certainly in time before you head back home, wherever that may be." He turned his head to the side. "Can I interest you in a cigar?"

"Or tea?" Cass interjected.

"Or both," Liam added.

Pike looked at each of them, knowing he needed to get out, to prepare for the next evening. With a heavy sigh, he shook his head. "I really wish I could, but I have to get some business things in order for tomorrow night. My sincerest apologies."

"You'll have to come again soon." Liam offered. "I can give you a proper tour of the place."

"I'll show you out." Cass headed for the door.

"I'll check on you tomorrow evening at the debutante, young man. I can introduce you to William," the doctor called after him, a suspicious look in his eyes.

Despite the anxiety bubbling within him, Pike managed to nod.

Who is William Benson to elicit such tension?

"Thank you again, Dr. Jackson. It was a pleasure finally meeting you. And thank you, Liam."

Both men waved as Pike followed Cass to the door.

Outside, Pike turned to her. "Please make sure your father knows how grateful I am that he would welcome me in and take care of me tonight. It means the world."

Cass smiled lightly. "I think he already knows. Hopefully you won't swell or bruise too badly by tomorrow." She lifted her gloveless hand up and ran her thumb down the edge of his nose, forefinger grazing his chin. Pike froze, holding his breath. Her touch felt like the electric lights that were starting to become more common. Cass blinked and quickly muttered an apology, removing her hand instantly.

As she lowered her hand, Pike caught it and placed a gentle kiss on her bare knuckles, the feeling of her skin on his lips sending shivers throughout his entire body like a small electrical shock. The things he wanted to say to her. . . "I hope to see you tomorrow."

Her cheeks flushed with color. "As do I."

"Goodnight, Miss Jackson."

"Goodnight," she practically whispered as he stepped out into the street.

6

The next morning, Alexander Pike—that is Mr. James A. Pike, the contractor—sat sipping on a cup of tea at the local tea house on 2nd Street. He scanned the newspaper, brushing up on current events, when a familiar figure glided through the doors.

He straightened in his chair as Cass, dressed in a blue striped day dress, whispered to an older woman by her side, never losing eye contact. They made their way around tables to stand with him next to the bar.

"Good morning, Miss Cassidy Jackson." He beamed, standing to greet them properly. "And you must be the other Miss Jackson?" Pike reached for her hand and kissed her gloved knuckles.

The woman laughed. "You flatter me, sir. I'm Mrs. Jackson, Cassidy's mother."

"Mr. James Pike." He nodded to her.

"I'm sorry to hear about the incident last night," Mrs. Jackson began. "It must've been one of those leeches who hang around here." She turned to Cass. "You know they always show up unannounced at Liam's door begging for help. Unwarranted business."

"My brother." Cass rolled her eyes. "But did you recognize the man who attacked you at all? Perhaps Liam knows of the man."

"I confess that I didn't get a good look at him," Pike lied, looking at his new shoes. His eyes dragged to his gloves laying on the counter as he sipped his steaming cup of white tea, minty and fresh in flavor.

It reminded him of Cass, light and charming.

"You're not too bruised today!" Cass started. "Just over the bridge of your nose and right under your eyes. You look quite good. I mean—" She fidgeted where she stood. "I only meant that your injuries have taken to healing quite nicely in a manner which doesn't distract or take away from your. . . face."

Mrs. Jackson, with an amused smile, raised an eyebrow at Cass who looked at her own shoes.

"Pardon my tardiness, Mother, I got caught up in the street." Another young woman rushed forward. She seemed to be a year or so younger than Cass, maybe seventeen or eighteen. Her face was rounder and complexion more freckled. Her hair was wound in a bun like the tight hairstyle that young women preferred. The color of her hair reminded him of his own rather than her sister's dark hair color. She met Pike's observing gaze and her face reddened.

"Hallie," Cass began. "This is Mr. James Pike, the man from last night. Mr. Pike, this is my younger sister, Miss Harriet Jackson."

Hallie blushed as Pike lifted her hand and kissed it the same way he'd kissed Cassidy's the night before, only Hallie wore her gloves and the motion was more a formality anyway. "It's a pleasure to meet you. Miss Cassidy Jackson has told me you all are traveling west soon for Dr. Jackson's work."

Mrs. Jackson beamed. "We are! As a matter of fact, we leave tomorrow after breakfast. We'll of course stop several times along the way, but we hope to be there in a few weeks to settle in before December."

"That is a rather ambitious goal."

"It may be," Cass said. "But with trains these days, a journey that once took six months now only takes a few weeks."

"I do not doubt it. The trains are an ever-evolving convenience," Pike replied, looking at his tea, feeling his time with Cass slipping away even as they spoke. "I don't want to keep you wonderful ladies from your morning fun, boring you with current events and politics."

"You're never a bore," Cass mumbled, avoiding his gaze.

"It was lovely to meet you, Mr. Pike," Mrs. Jackson gave Hallie a look.

She gave a quick dip of her head. "Yes, lovely to meet you, Mr. Pike."

Hallie scurried off behind her sister, blushing the color of Alba roses on a sunny midsummer day. Pike wondered if he unnerved her with roguish good looks or if his face looked wretched after his injury.

With a sigh he returned to reading the paper, though his mind constantly drifted to the events of the night before. Cassidy's hand on his nose, the look in her eyes, the intense longing he had to be with her.

"Sir?" the shop owner asked.

"Sorry?" Pike shook himself out of his thoughts.

"Telegram for you." The woman, dressed in a yellow and purple striped frock, slid a slip of paper to Pike.

The note read: *Business built on friendship can be murder. Rockefeller. - ST*

Pike gazed over at the table the Jackson women occupied. They giggled together, but Cass looked up at him and smiled. He nodded his head politely, but the motion was tense and measured.

Someone kept an eye on him. And that *person* wasn't happy.

Friday morning seemed to pass with aching slowness at the teahouse, but the afternoon finally arrived. Pike hated when things were slow before a job. Silvertongue knew this. And there Pike sat, waiting. And waiting some more. He had made his way to a gentleman's cigar club, where he sat smoking and calculating how much time he had left in the month.

He'd completed the job in Alabama. He would soon complete the

Greenwich job. Then what? Either Lankin, Montana or Jovy, Oklahoma. Both of those must be longer assignments like Pike's current one to take up the other twenty-two days in the month, twenty-one if Silvertongue took his sweet time to get back to North Carolina after Pike obtained Mrs. Benson. Or unless he had more jobs after those two, but he at least hoped that the Devil would make him aware of his quota like he usually did.

He wasn't sure which brought more fear: Silvertongue being early or late to pick him. He shuddered at the thought and puffed again at his cigar, musing over his plan for that evening.

He intended first to eat, collect information from the other guests, have a dance with Cass if she would allow him one, and then track down Mr. Benson. He knew he would be able to find Mrs. Benson if he could only find her husband.

Pike sighed, regretting that he couldn't do what he wanted. Every moment had to be for the job. What he wouldn't have given to have his own life again, his own house, a place to sit on the porch watching the sunset, sipping on a drink. Maybe a wife and kids someday. Maybe Cass.

But his whole life would instead be spent in services for the Devil.

He sighed, shaking his head.

"Can I get you any more whiskey, sir?" a young man dressed in a nice suit stood by the couch where Pike reclined.

Pike smiled at him. "I am perfectly comfortable, thank you. I'm actually on my way out."

The man nodded. "Of course. Let me get your coat."

The young man briskly walked away, presumably to the back to fetch Pike's coat that he'd bought only a few days previous.

Pike brushed off his hands and was slipping his gloves back on when a group of three men waltzed into the club like they owned the place.

Pike stepped to the side behind a room divider when the men approached. He glanced around the room, and from what he could tell, no one had noticed him moving to eavesdrop on them.

"We have the quarterly review coming up. Surely he has a solution," one old voice said.

"Benson doesn't have a solution. He is far too busy with his little *friends*," another younger voice piped up.

This received a hearty laugh from the third man who had a deep voice.

"Oh please," the deep voice said. "You can't be jealous of his girls. You have one of the most esteemed women as a wife and your mistress is a close second."

"Men, back to business," the first man nearly shouted.

"Mr. Benson said to supply the numbers," the third voice offered. "So do that."

"You want to lie on official government documents?" the old voice trembled slightly, whether from fear or old age, Pike couldn't tell.

"Everyone does it. Sign his name instead if you're scared."

Pike stepped around the divider and passed the group on his way to the door. No one even glanced at him. The young man who worked at the lounge handed Pike his coat on the way outside into the chilly afternoon air.

"It's going to be a very cold evening," Pike sighed, strolling back to the hotel where his evening clothes waited.

The night would be eventful, though not necessarily the kind of events Pike wished would occur. He hoped he could squeeze a dance in with Cass, even if they were pretending for one night. Even if it had to be a lie, he would take his chances.

7

Gaslit lamps and new arc lamps from Europe decorated the town hall in such elaborate displays that it looked more like a firework frozen in time than lighting fixtures. There were countless white cloth-covered tables littered with flowers and greenery and hundreds of candles flickering gently. The whole of it felt like magic, like the air teemed with possibility.

Pike had slicked his blonde hair back for the occasion, icy eyes wandering over heads in the crowd looking for two specific individuals. One he wanted for a job, but the other he wanted to. . . well, he wasn't exactly sure what yet, but he couldn't help looking for her. He decided he would allow himself a dance with her and mild flirtation at the most.

Harmless.

The band tuned up to begin the setlist, drawing Pike's attention away from the incoming crowd. When he turned around, Cassidy Jackson headed his way, Hallie Jackson in tow, both draped in white. Cass was wrapped in a gorgeous evening gown that accentuated her shoulders and collarbone, drawing his attention up to her pink lips, shimmery brown eyes, and chestnut brown hair tied up tightly, dotted with pearl adornments. Her dress was short-sleeved, paired with gloves that came past her elbows. The top of her dress was beaded, but at the waist it erupted into folds of sheer lacy fabric that fell to the floor in waves. She looked every bit a debutante, as well as a bride, making Pike's stomach churn with nervousness he hadn't felt in a long time.

"Well, if it isn't Mr. James Pike," Cass mused with a dazzling smile.

"How do you do, Miss Cassidy Jackson? You look ravishing this evening." He bowed his head towards her. "And please, call me James." Pike turned to Cass's younger sister, equally stunning. "Miss Hallie Jackson, I hope you are well. You look every bit as wonderful as your sister." He gave Cass a quick wink after obtaining a blush from Hallie. "I believe I am sitting at table six."

"Oh, wonderful!" Cass exclaimed. "We're at table six!"

"I'm at table seven with our mother and father," Hallie interjected.

"That's odd." Cass frowned. "Usually they put us all together."

Pike silently hoped that no one would go asking why an older gentleman sat at table seven with the Jackson family instead of their oldest daughter, who now sat conveniently next to Pike. Dr. and Mrs. Jackson, both dressed in exquisite attire, walked up behind their daughters.

"James," Dr. Jackson held a gloved hand out.. "Good to see you again, son."

Pike firmly shook his hand. "Glad to be here, sir. I have to thank you again for helping me out last night. Without you, today would've been a true disaster."

With a hearty laugh, Dr. Jackson patted him gently on the shoulder. "I am glad you're healing so nicely. Your bruising seems to be minimal, and the break should heal back relatively straight. Are you in any pain?"

Pike shook his head. "Nearly none at all. There's a slight twinge occasionally. But besides that and sometimes getting the urge to itch my nose, I am quite without pain."

"Good to hear." Dr. Jackson smiled. His eyes slid past Pike and lit up. "Well, they let anyone in here, don't they?"

Pike turned to see Liam dressed in a sleek suit striding towards them, positively beaming.

"Father," Liam shook Dr. Jackson's hand.

Liam turned to Pike with a grin and outstretched hand. "And I see you've met my other beautiful sister."

Pike shook his hand. "I have. Your family has welcomed me in, for which I am indebted to you all."

Pike moved his gaze around at the Jackson family, practically wrapped in money yet exuding none of the arrogance that typically accompanied people of that class. It was surprising and completely refreshing. Somewhere a bright chime rang, and all the debutante guests began taking their seats.

"Oh, they're starting the first course." Mrs. Jackson pulled her husband towards table seven. Hallie and Liam followed, the latter giving Pike a wink as he moved to his seat.

"Selfishly," Pike whispered, slipping his arm around Cass's. "I am quite happy that the seating didn't work out like it normally would. I'll have you all to myself and won't have to share."

"Mr. Pike—" Cass began, her face reddening.

"Please, call me James."

Cass hesitated, mouth still open to finish her previous sentence. She cleared her throat awkwardly. "Mr. Ja—"

"Just James, if you don't mind."

She squinted her eyes up at him, but a smile edged her lips. "You do not have to fight hard for my attention. . . James."

"There," Pike crooned. "Was that so difficult?"

Cass rolled her eyes. "You flatter yourself, *Mr. Pike*. That was a fluke and nothing more." A wry grin twisted her lips and mischievousness danced in her eyes.

I should be ruthless, Pike's mind screamed. *I should make her hate me. I can't do this.*

Pike knew it felt easier to leave when someone wasn't attached. But at that moment, none of his thoughts moved past the idea of kissing her pink lips. Every other thought escaped him.

Pike pulled out a chair for Cass. He took his seat and couldn't help but stare at her.

"Isn't it beautiful?" Cass asked. Pike watched her gaze around at the gleaming lights and elegant ladies dressed in only the finest attire accompanied by men dressed in only the finest suits. Of course, the purpose for the evening was to parade the socially available ladies so the eligible bachelors were able to get an idea of which lucky lady might catch their affections.

Pike hadn't been able to attend such an event as a child, being that he wasn't old enough to look for a wife when he had gotten *promoted*. He never knew what the first Alexander did to infuriate the Devil, but it meant their family line couldn't really participate in normal society, for better or for worse.

"James?"

Pike blinked a few times and found himself meeting Cass's gaze, shimmering brown eyes reflecting all of the beauty around them, except her eyes were only on him.

"I do apologize." He cleared his throat. "I confess to be a little nervous in your presence."

Cass smirked, tucking loose strands of her dark hair behind her ears. "As if that could ever happen. I doubt you have ever been nervous in your life."

Brief flashes of canes and silver flames and weapons of all kinds came and went in the blink of an eye, but the phantom pain still lingered in the raised skin beneath Pike's shirt. And the image of his father being flung into those flames would never leave his mind. He laughed awkwardly and sipped his water, running his free hand on his slacks.

Cass put a hand to her chest. "I am so sorry. You actually are nervous, aren't you?"

Pike swallowed. "I'm only trying to find the words to. . ." He looked over at Cass again, whose eyes were full of pity and regret, no doubt about making him more nervous. Though, Pike knew it wasn't due to childish nervousness in front of a lady. "I am trying to find the words to ask you for a dance."

Cass beamed, tilting her head slightly to the side. "I would absolutely love to dance with you, James. Would the first dance be all right?"

Pike laughed. "And here you talk about me being forward while you ask me for the first dance! Truly, Cass, I am surprised you are not already engaged."

Cass's eyes widened as she placed a hand over her collarbone. "James, I—"

Pike rushed to correct his mistake, face burning from his words. "In dance! Engaged in a first dance, not—"

"Right." Cass cleared her throat. "Of course. I apologize for misunderstanding."

"No, I should've—"

"I didn't mean—"

"—explained more precisely."

"—to suggest anything untoward."

Pike and Cass both averted their eyes elsewhere. Cass fidgeted with the beading on the front of her dress. Pike straightened his tie and brushed off his sleeves, but stopped in the motion after a moment.

"You said my name," he stated.

"Pardon?" The space between Cass's eyebrows wrinkled.

"You used my name, my first name."

"And you used mine."

Pike observed this girl sitting next to him, so elegant yet so oblivious to her dazzling effect on the world around her. Everyone noticed her when she walked by. It was difficult not to. Her face radiated pure joy regardless of where she stood, what she did, or who she conversed with. And here she was, talking with him, a man so undeserving of such grace.

"Good evening, ladies and gentlemen," a servant approached their table and interrupted Pike's intrusive thoughts. "Tonight, we begin our first course with a lettuce-based salad garnished with dandelion, and a classic vinaigrette, served alongside roasted turkey."

As he spoke, the waiters placed salad bowls in front of each guest at the table. Though Pike didn't prefer fancy, he could admit to himself that the turkey tasted better than any meat he'd cooked himself—though he would've preferred more turkey than salad.

Throughout the salad course, Cass politely conversed with the other attendees at their table. One of the bigger topics they discussed was the President's declaration of an annual national day of thanksgiving and prayer set on the twenty-seventh of November. All of the excitement centered mainly around the parties that would have to be arranged, rather than the gratitude and prayer. Pike would have loved to spend time with his mother baking and being together, which made him feel more sour about everyone else's celebrations. Everything discussed after circled around local gossip, but Cass seemed to be in her element so Pike didn't mind paying attention.

The servant came back out and announced the palate cleanser, a champagne sorbet. Cass gave Pike a dubious look as Pike raised his eyebrows at her. If he couldn't celebrate thanksgiving with his mother, he could at least enjoy his moments with Cass. He sipped his champagne then ate bite after bite of the mouthwatering sorbet. The flavors melted in his mouth and danced on his tongue.

"I could get used to champagne sorbet," he whispered in Cassidy's ear, breath dancing with the hairs that had escaped her tightly coiled updo.

Cass hid laughter behind a gloved hand. Pike desperately wished to remove the glove and kiss each and every finger. He'd replayed the night before in his head until his brain went dizzy with the thought of it. The feeling of her hands holding his while she cleaned off the blood, her finger running down his nose, the warmth of her hand in his, pressing his lips to her knuckles. He wondered how she kept her skin so soft.

Knowing he could never have her as his wife made it all the worse. And his subconscious ate him alive. She had been captivated by a lie, a façade of a man that she barely knew. Or maybe she wasn't captivated at all. Maybe he was the one caught in a trance, caught in her own delicately woven web of beauty. A true black widow.

I'd gladly die at her hands, Pike thought.

Pike laughed shortly and finished off his flute of champagne before waving a waiter over to their table. "May I get another glass of champagne for myself and one for Miss Jackson here?"

The waiter nodded and left immediately.

Cass shook her head with a grin. "Are you trying to get me intoxicated?"

"I'm trying to get you to loosen up. Have a little fun, debutante." He leaned back in his chair, sighing and letting his eyes flutter closed.

He would have plenty of time to find Mrs. Benson when the dancing began. Well, after his dance with Cass. He wasn't missing that for the world.

"How do you have fun, Mr. Pike?" she asked, mischievousness evident in her voice.

"Back to formalities, are we?" He opened his eyes and peered down at her.

"You are avoiding my question. Now answer!"

When Pike did not answer, Cass placed her hand over his. The sensation of her bare skin touching him stupefied his senses momentarily.

"Please?" she asked politely.

"Do you—do you really care to know what I do for fun?"

"I would like to know, yes."

If Pike were honest, he couldn't think of a single thing he did for fun besides maybe having a drink or a woman to help him forget his problems for a moment. But he felt that he couldn't count on those, and nothing else that came to mind seemed even remotely fun.

Pike sighed. "Well, if it says anything, this is the most fun I have had in about seven or eight years."

"That cannot possibly be true." Cass laughed incredulously. "I mean, I really do love the debutante balls, though this is my first time being a debutante myself." At this comment, she blushed and removed her hand from Pike's, leaving him feeling absent and cold. But his heart warmed at the thought of Cass not having any previous suitors.

"But surely you do other things for fun." She tucked her flyaway hair behind her ears again.

"I travel quite a bit, though I don't get to do much of what I enjoy," Pike thought of how many things he must have missed out on while following commands instead of his desires. He shifted in his seat and tore his gaze away from Cassidy's. "I've been working tirelessly for seven years."

"That's quite a long time for someone your age."

Shrugging, Pike fidgeted with the greenery on the table. "I had to earn an income somehow."

"What do you hope to gain besides money from working so hard?" Cass asked.

Freedom.

But the word stuck in his throat right under his chin.

"Do you hope to be able to provide for a family?" Cass suggested. "Or there's a special lady you hope to marry one day?"

Pike smiled sadly. "I would love to have a wife and a family. . . someday. But I don't know that it's in the cards for me."

Cass sighed. "Don't say that."

"My *profession*. It doesn't allow me to make any roots. I go where my boss tells me to go. I stay where he tells me to stay. Wherever I am needed, I am there. I couldn't possibly ask a lady to be dragged along with me, and I couldn't possibly ask her to stay home alone, wherever our home would be."

Pike's words were choked out by the one wanting to escape most.

Freedom.

But he dared not say it in fear that the Devil would hear, because of course he would hear. And Pike would get punished again.

Cass's hand rested once again over Pike's, but this time it felt more earnest. "But what if a woman didn't mind? What if she wanted to see the world? Surely then you could entertain the thought."

Pike's jaw tightened as he looked into the pure, young woman's eyes. He wanted so much. He wanted Cass.

But he couldn't have what he wanted. His heart squeezed from emotion as he cleared his throat. "Unfortunately, I don't believe she exists. No, I'm not sure I'll ever marry. I might die alone, whispering of the things that could have been."

"That's awfully sad," Cass whispered, still holding his hand.

The servant returned, and Pike quickly removed his hand from Cassidy's.

"For our third course," the waiter held his hands behind his back, "we have our seared beef filet with red wine sauce served alongside roasted and buttered petite potatoes."

"Your champagne." A man set down a flute while another man set down the beef filet which smelled divine. But Pike's appetite had since dwindled.

He took another sip of the bubbly beverage before he began to cut into his steak, hoping that he could drown his sorrows in red wine sauce and champagne. But he knew the dread that pooled in his stomach would not be easily removed, nor the memories easily replaced.

8

After several painfully dull conversations and the fourth course—coffee mousse dusted with cinnamon and grated chocolate—they were finally able to move about freely and converse with whom they wished.

"Miss Cassidy Jackson," Pike hummed, pulling her gently from her chair, "I do believe that I owe you a dance."

Cass blushed madly, but followed Pike to the ballroom across the hall with such gracefulness that it made his heart ache.

"Look how many couples," she whispered. "They all look so lovely."

Pike glanced around the ballroom, noting all fifteen dancing couples and plenty more debutante ladies and bachelors milling about. Pike's eyes drifted from man to man, looking for the men he'd seen at the cigar lounge.

Maybe Mr. Benson will be with them.

His eyes landed on a familiar face, wiggling his eyebrows at Pike. Liam smirked before turning to his father, resuming their conversation.

Pike felt his face grow hot.

How is it so easy to get embarrassed once feelings are involved?

He wished in that moment to be of more noble birth, or at least twice the man he was. Had he been born to a family without such a heritage, maybe he might have had a life, had a woman like Cass, had a life of privilege and opulence. A life of freedom.

The band began to play a jaunty waltz with strings and flutes. Pike slid his gloved hand into Cass's.

"What do you believe your father thinks of you dancing with the strange working-class man who got pummeled in the face and broke his nose?" Pike lightly spun Cass around the room.

"Oh, please. My father is not very orthodox with his views of debutantes. This is mostly for show anyway with us visiting Liam. It's what's expected. Father knows that I want to help him in his field, which of course leaves no room for romance. And most men are rather offended by a woman wanting to work outside of the restaurant industry. But Father loves it when I help him."

"You enjoy it."

Cass frowned. "That wasn't a question, was it?"

"No, it was clear from how focused you were last night that you want to help and heal. You didn't even squirm when he reset my nose."

Cass laughed. "Well, I've seen much worse."

"Worse how?" Pike raised an eyebrow.

Cass laughed again, eyes crinkling from amusement. "Mr. Pike, I believe we're supposed to be talking about things other than broken noses and medical injuries."

"Is that so? How unfortunate." He sighed dramatically. "I guess I could talk about how lovely your eyes look with your hair pinned back. Or how light almost emanates from your skin. Or how much I've wanted to steal you away in the past twenty-four hours."

"I don't understand," Cass shook her head. "You seemed so resolute about never being married. About not wanting romance."

"I never said that I didn't want romance. . . that I didn't want you." Pike moved them around another couple. "I only said I wasn't sure if I'd ever marry. You're moving across the country, and I'm bound to never settle. I don't see it working well, but I can't deny how much you affect me, Cass."

"James," Cass breathed as Pike spun her once more.

"You don't have to answer," Pike whispered into her ear now. "I know that we were doomed from the start. I'm always addicted to the wrong things. I happened to befriend your brother, who instantly wanted to introduce us. I met you completely by chance after getting my face smashed by my own boss, and I feel as if I could die in peace merely knowing you existed."

"Your own boss broke your nose?" Cass asked. "But last night you said—"

"I thought we weren't allowed to talk of broken noses and medical injuries."

Cass sighed, eyebrows pinched together. "I can't figure you out, James. It's like when you open your eyes, all you see is darkness. You're so sad for someone so young. Young people, people *our* age, are supposed to experience the world and learn and enjoy. We're supposed to live, James. And yet death hangs over you like a shadow isolated from the sun."

"Death and I have been scandalously close for some time," Pike muttered lowly.

"How do you mean?"

"It's more than I can explain in one dance." His words were almost drowned out in the band's big finish. "I wish I could tell you more."

"Tell me your secrets," Cass gripped his hands, stepping closer.

"And they'll die with me."

Pike leaned down in a bow and slowly kissed her gloved hand as the song ended. She held his gaze until he stood upright again.

"It was lovely to dance with you, Miss Jackson, even once." Pike squeezed her hand gently for what he dreaded would be the last time.

"Please don't leave," Cass whispered.

Pike smiled, looking over her shoulder, and bowed his head, stepping back. Another man took his place, but Cass held Pike's gaze, even while her new dance partner spun her away across the ballroom floor, leaving Pike hopelessly alone.

He stalked over to the bar where a waiter stood.

"How can I help you, sir?"

Pike put his fingers above his right eyeball. "I'll take a shot of whiskey, straight."

The waiter nodded, stepping away momentarily, and passed Pike the glass. He downed it in one gulp, the liquid burning his throat and warming his insides. Coupled with all the champagne he'd had, he wondered how much his head would hurt in the morning. Pike passed the glass to the bartender and murmured a thank you as he backed into one of the corners.

"You look good together."

Pike jumped at the sound of Hallie Jackson's voice next to him. "Hallie! I mean, Miss Jackson," Pike cleared his throat, straightening his suit. "My apologies. You frightened me."

Hallie blushed. "Oh, it's all right. And you can call me Hallie. You're practically family now."

"What do you mean?" Pike gingerly felt the bridge of his nose.

"Well, father loves your honest nature, and with the way you and Cass interact, it's not surprising if—"

"No!" Pike nearly shouted, eyes wide. "Hallie, you have the wrong idea. I can't—"

"Mr. Pike!" The most sickeningly smooth voice called, the worst possible sound that he could hear at this present moment.

Pike's heart pounded wildly in his chest.

No, please not now.

"Mr. Jack Smith!" Pike forced himself to turn and face the Devil, who had a look of malice shining in his eyes despite the smile on his lips. Silvertongue had dressed in a suit and tie like usual; however, he'd replaced his black bow tie for a white one and his coat for tails. Every detail, from his fob watch chain to his handkerchief, exuded wealth and luxury.

Show off.

Pike shifted on his feet. "What a surprise to see you here! I didn't think that you could make it."

"I moved some things around. I wouldn't want to miss out on all the *festivities*. Who is your little debutante friend here?"

"Mr. Smith," Pike began, words short and spine stiff, "this is Miss Harriet Jackson."

"How do you do, sir?" Hallie curtsied lightly.

"It's such a pleasure to make your acquaintance, Miss Jackson." Silvertongue smiled fully, and it turned Pike's stomach. None of his facial expressions ever seemed quite human once you looked at him for too long.

"Mr. Smith," Pike interrupted, "if we're going to conduct business, we'd better get going. We wouldn't want to lose our golden opportunity."

The Devil pulled out his fob watch, a beautifully polished silver with flames wrapping around the edges. He popped it open and watched the hands for a moment, eyebrows knitted together. Pike heard the *tick-tick* of the watch and waited with bated breath for his boss's response.

"My thoughts exactly," Silvertongue mused.

"Miss Jackson," Pike turned to Hallie, "tell your sister goodnight for me, in case I don't get the chance to myself."

Hallie nodded, opening her mouth to reply, but before she could voice any concern or offer any polite invitation, Pike pushed through the crowd. They parted easier than he'd expected. He always had the sinking feeling that people somehow knew why he was there and maybe even knew his true identity.

Absurd.

Impossible.

Silvertongue had even risked showing up at the ball, meaning that either something extra devious might occur or he wanted to watch the *fun* unravel.

"Benson's in the ladies' lavatory," the Devil whispered. "I suggest you get in there and make a scene. That way, we can get Mrs. Benson alone after all the commotion. You know how I detest crowds. . . My own personal hell."

"Which is why I was surprised you showed up early tonight," Pike hissed under his breath. "Pickup isn't until midnight." Pike stopped walking. "Wait, the *ladies'* lavatory?"

"Yes," Silvertongue sang with a dangerous annoyance that rippled below the surface of his skin. "It appears that Mr. *James* is getting too distracted playing a romantic. I need you to focus, Alexander."

Pike nodded, afraid that if he spoke his voice would give away his heart.

"Go," his boss said once they were in the hall. "I'll keep watch."

"You make it sound like you aren't lord of Hell. What are you watching out for?"

Silvertongue rolled his eyes. "Well, for all intents and purposes, you cannot disappear and I can. Do you want to get blamed for whatever is about to occur?"

"Actually, I don't think I'd mind, considering I'll be in Jovy tomorrow."

The Devil smiled another one of those shiver-causing smiles. "Good. You're getting decent at this semi-freewill game we're playing, given our time together is almost up."

Pike inhaled deeply, letting his eyes close for a moment.

This is how it has been for the past seven years. This is the way it has to be until the debt is paid. It's a small price for a life of freedom.

If he could cause enough of a distraction with Mr. Benson, it might give him time to find Mrs. Benson. He stretched his shoulders briefly before pushing open the ladies' lavatory door, stepping into the unknown.

He heard Mr. Benson muttering before he could see him. Then the sound of a girl crying, whimpering more like. Pike's blood began to boil, piecing together what he thought of the situation around the corner.

Around the divider, Mr. Benson cornered one of the debutantes, hands on her waist and pressing her back against the wall. Her lip trembled as she arched her head away from the plump middle aged man.

"Hey!" Pike shouted, making his voice as deep and as loud as he could.

Mr. Benson snapped around. "Get out. This is none of your

business."

Pike clenched his jaw and began pulling off his gloves one finger at a time. "You know, I think you misunderstood the purpose of having a debutante ball."

"I said get out!" Mr. Benson shouted, causing the poor girl behind him to flinch and whimper, tears still streaming down her face.

"Debutantes are a showcase of beautiful young women, like this lovely lady you have trapped here. And the *eligible bachelors* can find the most charming of them all to dance with and maybe one day ask to be their wife." Pike slipped his gloves into the inside pocket of his coat then pulled his coat off entirely, never losing eye contact with Mr. Benson. "The trouble is, you don't seem to be eligible. . . or a bachelor."

"Who do you think you are?"

"Let this young woman go." Pike growled. "What's about to happen isn't for a lady to witness."

The girl made a move to leave, but Mr. Benson grabbed her arm. "Don't listen to him."

"Miss, I do apologize for this poor example of the male side of humanity." Pike smiled sadly. "I promise there is a wonderful young man out there somewhere who will make you very, very happy. Now, please, William, let her go on her way."

Mr. Benson, clenching his teeth shut, released the young girl who ran from the lavatory crying as she went. After the girl had safely exited the room, Pike looked back at Mr. Benson. He didn't have much time until others came to find Mr. Benson to punish him for his sins.

They'll be too late.

Pike tilted his head with a smirk. "Was that so bad, Benson?" He began rolling up his sleeves, tattooed flames revealing themselves a little at a time. "Now, here's what's about to happen. When a child does something bad, there are consequences for his actions. And I think you've gone too long without discipline."

"You think you can waltz in here like a hero?" Mr. Benson started. "You don't know the kind of sway I have in this town."

"You clearly don't know who I am then." Pike shrugged and turned his forearms so that his opponent could see very clearly *what* he was. He slid his knife out from his belt raising an eyebrow at his latest victim as he spun the knife twice in his palm.

Instead of fury, fear filled Mr. Benson's eyes. "Have mercy on me."

"Do you have any dignity? How *dare* you beg for mercy after what you were doing to that young woman!" The fire of hell glistened in his ice-cold eyes. White knuckles gripped the knife. His jaw pulsed under gritted teeth. "Do it! Beg again."

Mr. Benson's hands were shaking now, but Pike was already moving towards him. He slammed his free hand into Benson's shoulders and propelled him into the wall with a thud. A grunt escaped Benson's lips from the impact.

"Beg!" Pike screamed in his face.

"Please!" Mr. Benson whined.

Pike swung his elbow up to hit the weak man in the face. Before Mr. Benson could so much as cry out, Pike slid the knife light and quick across the round man's cheek. Mr. Benson went to grab his now bleeding face, leaving his torso and below unguarded, and Pike took advantage of this, debilitating his prey easily.

With a pull, Pike threw the overweight man to the floor then growled, "I said, beg!"

He slid his knife back into its place, and Pike held the man down with his bodyweight.

"Please!" Mr. Benson cried, making the grown man look like a child in comparison. He sniveled, face turning red, blood dripping down staining the marble floor.

As Pike held Mr. Benson down with his knees, his blonde hair slipped out of place, falling in his eyes. "You don't get mercy," he snarled. "Do unto others as you want done to you, William Benson."

Hit after hit, Pike channeled his rage into this fight that he had clearly already won. He wanted William Benson to feel his wrath, his sorrow for all of the women Benson had taken advantage of. He vented his grief over the loss of innocence and the fear of the unknown in that girl's position. And at some point, Pike found he grieved his *own* lost childhood.

After only a half a minute or so, the Devil pulled Pike off of Mr. Benson. Then, Pike realized how hard he'd been hitting the man and how much blood stained his hands and his white dress shirt. Hands shaking, his eyes glazed over the bathroom tile.

"Mrs. Benson is the job, Alexander, not her husband." The Devil had two arms under Pike's, pulling him back towards the door. He looked back at the bloodied figure groaning on the stained bathroom tile. "Though, I must admit, you do some great work when you let your demons out."

Pike could hear the grin in the Devil's voice.

He felt heavy and weighted to the floor while his boss let go of his arms, leaving Pike swaying where he stood, still in a stupor. Silvertongue picked up the suit coat from the sink, and they slipped out of the lavatory, leaving Mr. Benson behind. The only thing Pike could hear was the echo of the word *demons* from the Devil's previous statement.

I am a monster.

9

In the hall, the band played and people chatted and laughed. With an ache in his heart, Pike wondered what Cass would think if she saw him now without his fabricated reality to guard him. Suddenly, a group of angry men came rushing out of the banquet hall, dressed in fine suits and leather shoes. They all stopped in their tracks when they saw Pike, bloodstained and dazed.

Pike straightened. "He's received retribution for what he's done."

The man in the front of the group—presumably the poor girl's father—rushed towards the lavatory with rage still in his eyes. Some of the men followed, but some watched Pike and his companion with cautionary looks.

"Mrs. Benson," the Devil hissed, grabbing Pike's attention.

He quickly glanced around. Some people were beginning to come into the hall and notice him, covered in the blood of a sinner. His brain was too foggy to think straight, the alcohol mixing with the adrenaline.

"Where is she?" Pike whispered frantically. The sand in the hour-glass slipped by quickly.

Silvertongue rolled his eyes, pulling Pike down the hall. "Honestly, do I have to do everything myself?"

Ducking into a side room, he grabbed Pike's shoulder, and the world disappeared and reappeared outside what appeared to be the back door of the ballroom that led to the garden. No one stood out in the chilly night, leaving the two men alone. Gaslit lampposts flickered while the two slipped past the big windows. Around the corner of the building, they heard a muffled groan.

"Mrs. Benson?" Pike called out, turning back to look at Silvertongue with furrowed eyebrows. Behind the Devil's dark emotionless eyes, nothing moved or hinted to any feeling, leaving only a hollow space where a soul should be. But around the corner, something moved.

The Devil disappeared in a spark of silver flames as Mrs. Benson rounded the corner, stumbling. Her elegant ball gown contrasted her sunken eyes and a bruise poorly covered in powder. Her hair had escaped its tight clips and stuck to her tear stained face. She looked like a wreck.

"God in Heaven," she gasped, most likely noticing the blood.

"Mrs. Benson, your husband—" Pike started.

"Is he dead?" She kept her gaze on Pike's hands and chest.

Pike hesitated. The hazy look in her eyes and her eagerness for her husband's death made him uneasy. Still, he persisted. "He was caught with a debutante. He'd trapped her in the bathroom. I—" He tried to swallow the uncomfortable feeling that had lodged itself in his throat. "I did what I had to. I'm sorry."

Brief images of the bloodied marble tile filled his head. A flash of his reflection in the mirror haunted him. He'd looked more like the Devil than himself. He let in a shaky breath and let it out slowly.

Mrs. Benson sighed and staggered around the corner of the building. Pike followed warily and found her slouching against the wall with a bottle in hand and pouring more amber colored liquid into a glass.

"Why are you apologizing to me? You know what he is," she slurred. "He is worthless. Less of a man than I am."

Pike kept silent, but accepted when she held out the bottle to him.

After taking it from her, she lifted her half-full glass to him.

"Here's to another day in Hell. God come quick," and she swiftly downed the liquid, making a pained face in the process. She sniffled, letting a few more tears fall.

Pike took a swig from the bottle. "Would you like some company?"

Mrs. Benson shrugged. "Any company is better than my husband's."

Pike wished that it had been the other way around. That Mr. Benson would die a slow and painful death and not this poor woman. He hoped that God would receive her when her time arrived.

If God really existed.

How could a God who claimed to be good allow such atrocities to happen to good people?

She began to weep, laying her glass to the side. Mrs. Benson cursed her husband's name, curling her body forwards, rocking in place.

Slowly, her sobs subsided and her rocking slowed as she slumped back against the wall. In only a few minutes, no more sound came from her save the deep breaths of intoxicated sleep. Pike cradled her in his arms like a child and began his hunt for the closest crossroads, ready to be done with Greenwich. When he rounded the corner, he stopped in his tracks. Cass stood by the garden entrance, looking pale and frightened in the waning moonlight. Whether he or the sight of Mrs. Benson frightened her, Pike couldn't tell.

"Cass, I can explain," Pike gently laid Mrs. Benson down against the wall, careful not to let her hit her head on the stone in her state of stupor.

"Is it true?" Cass looked up and down at his ruined dress shirt. "Is it true what you did? There were rumors, and—"

Pike stepped towards her. "Yes, it is. It's part of what I do. I—"

Cass closed the space between them, gently planting a kiss on his cheek, gloved hand on his chin. His whole body froze like it had the night before, though some level of guilt accompanied him that Cass wouldn't understand even if he tried to explain. As soon as she'd done it, she had stepped away again leaving Pike feeling cold in her absence. His body burned for her to be close to him.

"I am so sorry, James, I didn't—"

Pike closed the gap between them and ran his hand gently over her cheek. He slipped his other hand around her waist and tugged her close. She gazed up at him, eyes betraying the mix of fear and passion she had kept so guarded. Seeing that look on her face made the yearning more intense. "Don't apologize to me, Cass. I've been wanting to kiss you since we met."

She inhaled sharply as he ran his lips across her jawline. Her perfume smelled like a spring morning, and it overwhelmed his senses. And then he kissed her fully, surrendering his heart and every other part of him to this kind-hearted woman.

Cass pulled back again. "James."

Pike chuckled. "Am I so incredibly handsome that you can only say my name?"

Cass turned her blushing face away. With gentle pressure, Pike tilted her chin back up so that she would look at him.

He lowered his voice to a whisper. "You are extraordinary, Cassidy Jackson. But I have a job to do." He smiled sadly. "Unfortunately, that means I have to leave."

"Please. Let me come with you. I'll follow you like we talked about earlier. I don't mind moving from place to place."

"Cass," Pike's heart sank, "you can't. That's ridiculous."

"Why not? We could help people and—"

"It's not proper."

"Who cares about proper?"

"Everyone cares about proper, Cassidy."

"But I—"

"No, Cassidy." Pike clenched his teeth together. He inhaled deeply, looking at the ground before daring to speak again. "You don't know me. You shouldn't trust me."

"But things can change." Cass's eyes darted back and forth between his own, wide and frantic. "I want to get to know you, James!"

"I've already done too much. I should never have kissed you."

"You regret kissing me?"

"No!" He squeezed his eyes shut, frustrated that his words weren't making sense. He needed her to see him as he was: broken. He shook his head. "Cass, look at me."

He waited. Her eyes turned down. He hated every second of this.

"Cassidy Jackson, look at me. Tell me what you see."

She looked at him, eyes brimming with tears. "I see a brave man who stopped a very bad thing from happening."

"No, Cassidy. You see a broken man. Someone who isn't free to do what he wants." He swallowed, hating that he admitted to his sins. "I've killed people, Cass. I am a monster. I'm worthless."

"James—"

"My name isn't James. . . Not my first name anyway. I am Alexander Pike VI. Look at my arms." Pike stepped back, holding out his forearms so she could see what he truly was.

Underneath the splatters of blood, the markings contrasted with his pale skin. The flames practically moved in the moonlight.

An unearthly magic.

"Don't you see?" Pike growled, face contorting in anger for his lack of freedom. "I am only shadows. I was raised to be a weapon. I am the Devil's puppet, and he is my puppeteer."

No hope.

No love.

No joy.

No freedom.

"James—"

"Pike!" He shouted, hating how much he sounded like his father. "My name is Pike. Please, Cassidy. Please. . . don't try to save me like you do with everything else."

Cass stood still for a moment, eyebrows pinched together, seemingly wrestling with new information. She took one step forward reaching out, and he took one step back like some twisted sort of dance. For a moment, Pike wondered what it would be like if he led Cass right back onto the ballroom floor and danced the rest of the night away, forgetting everything that had happened.

"Pike," she began, swallowing the word. "You are not worthless.

You are so much more than that. What you did tonight—"

"I'm not free to be more. I'm not even free to be having this conversation with you right now." Pike put his head in his hands, sighing heavily. "He's going to get me good this time. I'll be severely punished. Jovy and Lankin will get pushed back. And November will end before I can get out of bed again."

"What are you talking about?" Cass shook her head.

"It doesn't matter. *This* doesn't matter." Pike swallowed and met her gaze. "I can't see you again. I don't want this."

"Pike, I don't understand. I don't care about what's happened in the past." She sniffled, holding back her tears. "You kissed me. I thought. . ." Pike moved to step back. "Please don't leave. Help me understand."

"Cass," Pike looked down at his shoes, "you are nothing to me. You can't be anything. We both have to be okay with that."

Cass shook her head. Her tears caught the glint of moonlight, and each one that fell threatened to break Pike's carefully crafted reputation.

"Cass, listen to me. You have such a grand life ahead of you. You're going to go to another debutante soon, one that's less exciting, but you're going to meet a dashing young man with matching brown hair and the same depth in those chocolate brown eyes of yours. And you'll chat about helping people and what the latest medical discoveries are. And you'll get married in the summer when the weather is nice in the Washington Territory."

"No," Cass whispered. "I don't want it."

"You'll have musicians play some tunes, a feast will follow," Pike said with more force now, nodding like he agreed with himself. "And then you'll go abroad for a month to see the sights. And one day, you'll have kids running around with the same bright smiles and eyes full of wonder at every little thing. And they'll laugh like you and sing like him, and they'll be the world's most curious children there ever were."

Cass cried, arms crossed over her stomach. She looked as miserable as Pike felt. It was his fault anyway. He hadn't stopped it when he should have. He'd been living like he acted in a romantic play for far too long.

He cleared his throat to rid it of the emotion that had bubbled up from his twisted stomach. "And Cassidy Jackson will have a long and beautiful life with her family, watching the sun set over the western horizon."

Cass shook her head. "No. I don't want it. You can't leave. I haven't gotten to know you like I want to know you."

"Cass, I'm not leaving. . . Not until you smile." Pike smiled sadly at her.

She laughed, shaking her head, tears still racing down her cheeks. It shattered what little was left of the dam that held back his tears.

"There's that beautiful face." He sighed, lips beginning to tremble. "I swear, Miss Jackson, you could end a war by smiling."

He stepped forward, lifting her gloved hand, placing a kiss on her knuckles. Then, he stepped back and let her fingers slip through his.

"Pike." She shuddered, taking in staggered breaths.

"I have to go," he whispered. He took a few more steps back toward Mrs. Benson who still slept on the ground.

As Pike knelt to pick Mrs. Benson up, Cass pulled his arm back with force. "Pike."

"What do you think you're doing?" He pulled his arm out of her hand.

"Where are you taking her?" Cass straightened her shoulders.

The breath stuck to his lungs, his heart sinking. "I have a job to do. I can't fail. I can't—"

Cass moved to step between Pike and Mrs. Benson. Anger taking over, Pike growled. Tucking one hand under Cassidy's knees and the other behind her shoulders, Pike scooped her up, then carried her towards the back door of the ballroom.

"Alexander, let me go!" She kicked, trying to get out of his grasp.

Dropping her roughly, he pinned Cass against the wall, hands on either side of her face. Her eyes, once filled with fiery passion, had been doused with fear.

"You don't know what I am capable of, Miss Jackson." He lowered his eyes so that he met hers. "My hands are tied. I am bound to do this job. If I could fight it, I would. But I can't."

A tear slipped over Cass's trembling lips. Pike gently wiped it away, heart aching at how she flinched at his touch.

"Please don't get in my way," he whispered. "I don't want to break a perfect thing. . . Maybe one day you can forgive me."

He quickly returned to Mrs. Benson. After lifting her up, he glanced back at the debutante behind him. She stood by the door now, hand grasping her other arm.

"Pike," she whispered.

"Forget me, Cass." When she didn't respond, Pike's breath caught in his throat. "Miss Jackson, it was an absolute pleasure to know that you exist."

Cass said nothing as he walked away. And he hiked through the garden, leaving a possible future behind, carrying Mrs. Benson to a midnight meeting with the Devil.

10

He cried all the way to the crossroads where he'd arrived on his first day in Greenwich, stopping only a few times to catch his breath. Mrs. Benson didn't speak a word the entire journey.

And what would Silvertongue say when Pike arrived red faced and crumbling in confusion? Would he gloat? Would he rebuke? Would he not mention any of it? Pike doubted the latter.

When they arrived, he gently sat Mrs. Benson in the middle of their path and crumpled to his knees in exhaustion. Mrs. Benson groaned, rolling over, stirring slightly. Pike shuddered, remembering his fury and the figure of Mr. Benson lying bloody on the ladies' lavatory floor. Silvertongue's words echoed in his mind:

You do some great work when you let your demons out.

Looking down at the dried blood on his hands, Pike wondered if he was beyond redemption. Was he truly becoming a monster? How could he face his reflection if he lost all of his humanity?

More than anything, Pike thought of Cass's face when he left her, probably forever. He wondered if she saw the monster in him. He wondered if she would forgive him. She hadn't seen Mr. Benson's deformed face, but Pike knew if she had seen what he'd done, she would never be able to look at Pike the same way again.

With the balls of his hands pressed tight against his eyes, he went over the events of his life, wondering how he had come to such a conclusion. He wondered if he really did have inner demons haunting him. Maybe that's why his ancestor had gotten their family mixed up in all of this in the first place.

He wasn't sure how much time had passed when the Devil cleared his throat only an arm's length away. Pike stood with aching bones and helped Mrs. Benson, now semi-conscious, to her feet.

"This man is capable of many things. On your feet," Pike whispered to her.

She stood with slight stumbling limbs, leaning on Pike's arm.

"Did you decide having her intoxicated was the best option?" The Devil scoffed.

"You know I didn't do this. Get it over with, demon," Pike muttered.

"Demon?" Silvertongue let the word hang in the air.

Pike measured his breaths, counting and he stared back at his boss. It took about six seconds before he lowered his eyes. Demon hadn't been the right word to use. He'd pay for it eventually.

Beside Pike, Mrs. Benson shook. Whether from fear or exhaustion, he wasn't sure. After all, she'd had as bad of a night as Pike had. And she could expect much worse.

Pike sighed, looking back up at the Devil. "I don't want to play this game tonight. Get on with it, and let's get on to Jovy."

Silvertongue's skin rippled, his face distorting as he scowled at his slave. As he placed his hand on Mrs. Benson's forehead, she shouted for a brief moment. Then she had no voice, though her mouth hung wide open.

Pike had only seen this process a few times. He wasn't sure how it exactly worked. Was it painful? Did the victim remember it after, through déjà vu or restless nightmares? He wasn't sure, but he didn't want to find out.

The Devil was crafty when it came to his mischievous plans. Long term illness, mental disorders, and stone cold hearts were all things he could precisely time out. They were like explosives, set to go off at specific moments. Except you couldn't stop these from exploding.

Silver seeped from between the Devil's fingertips, oozing like tar. The heat from his hands felt like a fire radiating from Mrs. Benson. He wondered how her body could withstand such a brutal force. Then again, he wondered how he had kept himself together having the Devil as a constant companion.

Pike squinted, the Devil's human mask and skin stripping away in pieces while Silvertongue did the supernatural. His dark, leathery figure could be glimpsed beneath the slices of human skin desperately trying to cling to his bones. Holes burned through his mask like fire through paper. Pike looked away, not being able to look the Devil in the face now that his true nature peeked through. Real evil like that could never be seen without causing irreparable damage, and Pike didn't want that. Though, he wasn't so sure he'd truly escaped that fate.

Mrs. Benson's skin felt like burning coals in Pike's hands before the Devil backed away. The woman collapsed in Pike's arms. And though his heart ached for her fate, at least the air felt breathable again.

"What should I do with her?" Pike asked, still purposefully not looking his boss in the face.

The Devil scoffed. "You can look at me now, Alexander." He slicked back his refreshed jet black hair and brushed off his suit like he wanted to look nice and approachable after the sins that he had committed. "I suppose you can hand her to me. I'll put her back in her own bed. But you and I need to have a little chat in a moment. Stay put."

Pike nodded, only half listening now while he passed Mrs. Benson over to the Devil. Her twisted and horrible fate had been decided without her consent. In a moment, Silvertongue disappeared.

The woods around them seemed too quiet for the autumn. In the mountains, leaves were starting to fade from their blazing oranges and yellows to deep reds and browns, on their path of death for winter like

Pike's own soul, rotting from within. The pines still stood, green against the rest of the woods. But despite the amount of leaves lying helpless on the ground, nothing rustled or crunched from wild animals, no twittering of birds before the darkest of night. Almost like they knew what tragedy had taken place.

Looking up at the moon, Pike wondered if Cass had gone back to Liam's house yet, getting ready to sleep. He wondered if she looked at the crescent-shaped moon too. Perhaps she thought about him, wondering about his true identity.

With a resounding crackle like wood in a fire, the Devil appeared in another spark of silver flame, disrupting both Pike's thoughts and the tranquility of the night around them.

"Well, where were we?" the Devil asked cheerfully, clasping his hands together.

"Our little chat." Pike sighed.

"Right." Silvertongue smiled eerily. "Jovy is canceled. Instead, you and I get to have some *bonding* moments. We won't have many more of them."

Pike stumbled backwards out of direct reach of the Devil. His heart sank deep within him. "Please! I want to do the job in Jovy. Please. Tell me what to do, and I'll do it."

The Devil actually seemed to consider it, weighing it back and forth for a moment before disappearing without a word.

Pike turned around with vigilant awareness. The Devil was playing games now. Pike was paying for getting involved, paying for calling the Devil a demon. . . paying for that kiss, though he thought it was almost worth it.

Almost.

The twisted mind games were one of the worst parts about the job. It was strange how numb one could get to stabbing or killing people, so long as he didn't get too attached. But as soon as the Devil's eyes were fixed on a person, something feral woke inside of them. Pike's body tensed, ready to bolt from the fight or flight reaction, a human instinct. But nothing seemed human about fighting the Devil, nor could he ex-

 85

pect to outrun him.

Pike's gaze flicked over tree limbs, bushes, scattered leaves, stumps, fallen branches, and all of their shadows. He knew shadows could move, though most people wouldn't believe him.

"Hello there!" Silvertongue sang, leaning against a tree nearby where he hadn't been a moment before.

Pike turned to face him, but the fiend had disappeared again. Pike cursed and stood in the center of the crossroads, hoping that being able to see most of the area would give him somewhat of an advantage.

"Really, Alexander," Silvertongue walked out of the woods on the opposite side of the road, "you need to start being more careful. I can only protect you from so much."

"What are you talking about?" Pike decided to play dumb, heart pounding as he hoped the beast in front of him would believe he was ignorant and innocent. Instead, dread settled in his stomach.

The Devil's laugh rumbled, first deep and low then growing into a cackle, fading like an echo in the night when he vanished. As soon as Pike thought he was alone, pairs of red eyes illuminated around him.

Pike's throat went dry.

A shadow at the edge of the road began expanding, and before Pike could think, his feet began running in the other direction, into the dark woods. Stumbling in the dark, Pike fell over a log. Rolling with his fall, he hopped back on his feet, sprinting through the woods as fast as his feet would take him.

He burst through the other side of the patch of woods, faint light visible ahead. In the field, he passed a house and a barn, running through freshly harvested wheat that snagged at his pant legs, and a herd of cows, already fast asleep. Behind him, the sound of howling cut through the pounding in his ears.

The demon dogs had his scent.

His legs ached while he ran, diving back into more trees on the other side of the field, leaves crunching beneath his pounding footfalls.

Don't stop now. You're dead if you stop running.

The shelter of the woods ended again, quicker than Pike would've liked. In the next field, Pike skidded to a stop, nearly falling into a pond hidden behind shrubs. The bark of the dogs behind him pushed his feet to action once again. Skirting around the edge, Pike sprinted. Feet pounding, heart thundering, he ran and ran.

The hounds of Hell were almost on him when he ducked into another patch of woods. The hair on his neck stood as a chill ran down his spine. He wanted to stop running. He couldn't breathe. His heart felt like it could burst any moment.

Never stop running.

Pike risked a glance back and, despite the thickness of the trees, was met with dozens of red eyes in hot pursuit.

And then he rolled in the dirt. Pain shot up his right leg when he pushed himself to stand.

But the forest had grown quiet again. Too quiet.

Against every instinct in him, Pike stopped running.

Looking around, Pike found himself in a clearing, a dark, black circle of earth around him void of any grass or plants of any kind. He glanced up at the crescent moon, hiding from the Devil's terror behind the clouds.

Looking around him again, Pike noticed the Hell hounds had stopped around the edges of the circle. Their breath puffed in the chilly air, their beady eyes watching him from the shadows.

"Alexander," the Devil crooned.

Pike wheeled around. Silvertongue leaned against a tree at the edge of the clearing, blowing smoke from a cigar.

"Mad as the sea and wind when both contend which is the mightier." The Devil closed his eyes, lifting his face to the moonlight.

Dark veins crept up from the Devil's neck where human skin should have been.

And the Devil disappeared again.

"Come out. Face me!" Pike growled in desperation. He inhaled heavy breaths as he wheeled about looking for his assailant. "I want the job. Please!"

He paused. The quiet in the unnatural clearing felt suffocating. The darkness filled up the very space around him.

Shadows from the waning moonlight creeped around his feet despite originating from too far away to be natural. The shadows crafted hands and claws from their abyss, reaching for Pike's feet, hoping that today would be the day they could claim his soul.

"Not yet," the Devil hissed down Pike's neck, and the shadows retreated.

Pike jumped to the side and stumbled back a few steps.

Silvertongue chuckled. "Alexander Pike, you know the rules."

"There are no rules!" Pike shouted, head disoriented from the chase, seeing the red eyes leering at him from the shadows of the trees.

The Devil was so close.

Why had the dogs not ripped his body apart yet?

The Devil huffed. "There are rules now. No asking questions. And no getting involved. It causes too many problems." Silvertongue paused, mouth open to continue. Instead, his conversational face melted into a despicable grin. "And besides. . . Cassidy doesn't have the same bravado that your mother has, dear friend."

Pike held his gaze, wondering why the Devil's emotions had shifted so quickly. He felt the slight tremor of his hands. He didn't like the idea that the Devil thought about his mother, or Cass for that matter.

They stood observing each other. He wondered what the Devil really thought of him. He noticed how his boss absorbed every detail, every shift in footing. He noticed the cigar half smoked and tails still in pristine condition. He wondered how the Devil obtained his costumes, both skin and clothing. Mostly, Pike wondered if he was being tricked.

Neither of them moved, though the shadows grew restless and fully returned to their natural boundaries.

Silvertongue stretched his neck and puffed again at his cigar, blowing smoke into Pike's face. Finally, he groaned. "All right, I'm growing tired of this human skin. It's been itching all night. Let's get to the Oklahoma Territory so you can do this damned job."

In a flash, his hand snagged Pike's shoulder and they twisted and warped until they stood on a dusty road under a sky full of stars. A small orange light danced on the horizon, and Silvertongue pushed Pike roughly towards it.

"No questions. No emotions." His whole body twitched and convulsed. "This damn skin!" His fury bellowed into the night while the skin melted off slowly.

Pike shielded his face as a silver fire appeared behind Silvertongue's contorted frame, though it seemed to shine through him rather than around him.

"Watson Moore," a grating voice screeched in the night, different from the typical crooning of the Devil's human voice. "Kill him. Dispose of the body however you wish. You have seventy-two hours."

And with a burst of silver flame, the Devil vanished into the night.

11

Pike stood still for several minutes, taking air in slowly and breathing it back out at an equal pace. He had escaped another beating, a near miss.

Usually when the Devil erupted like that, Pike received the short end of the metaphorical stick, or physical depending on the Devil's mood. He had only been beaten a few times, but enough to make him terrified of seeing those silver flames. It meant danger and pain, but it also meant death.

Those silver flames were how Pike had inherited the job in the first place.

Those flames had devoured his father.

Pike shuddered and began walking toward the orange glow of normal fire, rolling his sleeves down as he walked, though it wouldn't do much to hide the blood on his shirt. He sighed, remembering the nice business suit that lay across the bed he'd slept in at the Greenwich Hotel. But he still had his knife, and he could do a lot with that in a pinch.

The dust he kicked up blew to his right, walking one step after the other down the long straight road. The wind rustled the brambles on either side of the dirt road, but he was alone.

Jovy is a wasteland.

The orange glow grew closer and closer, even though the road felt never-ending. After a while, he began to hear the faint squeal of a harmonica chugging a tune into the endless night sky.

Endless, endless, endless.

All of it was endless.

For a moment, he let his thoughts linger on the woman's life he'd ruined.

That the Devil had ruined.

He wondered when Mr. Benson would take his own life. Would it be soon? Or would the Devil bide his time? Would Liam be a representative in court for the case?

Pike's pace slowed as he began to make out the camp ahead of him. Three small canvas tents were pitched in a haphazard circle around the fire. The orange flames outlined at least two figures, but with three horses standing nearby, Pike assumed there might be at least one more person hiding out somewhere.

I can take on three men, Pike thought to himself.

The horses noticed his presence first, then the cowboys that reclined by the fire. The harmonica music stopped abruptly, and the men jumped to their feet, dirt crunching under their boots. Silhouetted by the firelight, a broad-shouldered man stepped into the firelight and cocked his gun.

"Stay where you are, stranger."

Pike stopped moving forward, hands raised in the air. He stood only a few steps away now, within the circle of the light cutting through the darkness. They had to see the blood. He heard two other guns click.

"Who are you?" the broad-shouldered man asked.

"My name is Alexander James. Friends call me Jay. I'm honestly not sure where I am right now. I don't remember how I arrived here. I woke up in a patch of bushes a few miles back." He motioned back to where

 91

he'd come from. "I saw your firelight and figured I'd risk it if it meant warmth from the wind and company."

"You look like hell," the man with the gun said, the silhouette of his scarf blowing in the breeze. "You don't belong out here."

The man shifted his weight, no doubt trying to gauge how much of Pike's story rang true. It was like he knew the secret, which was bad news for Pike. His hands started to sweat.

The man motioned with his head, and his two companions sidled up to Pike, feeling his belt and pockets. Pike held his hands up over his head while they searched, and he observed them as best as he could out of the corners of his eyes. They both seemed young, like children compared to the first man. One of them had a clean shaven face while the other had a mustache curled at both ends. They were both tense, and he didn't blame them.

"Knife," the mustached man pulled Pike's knife from its hiding place on his belt and tossed it to the ground.

The clean-shaven man jabbed his gun against Pike's side. The mustached man held onto Pike's shoulder.

Damn, Pike thought. *So much for being subtle.*

"I'm going to ask you again. Who are you?" The man with the gun stepped forward, Winchester rifle brandished in hand.

"I'm a contract worker." Pike swallowed, fear settling in his gut.

"What brought you out here?" The man looked him up and down. "And why are you covered in blood?"

Pike took a deep breath, glancing at the clean-shaven man who cocked his gun. Pike hoped his lie would be convincing enough. "I was thrown into a fight with a man who was trying to double cross me and my partner. Things got ugly, and I can't remember what happened after that. I can't. . ."

Pike shook his head, furrowing his eyebrows. He needed to sell it, but the only way he'd have a real enough reaction is if he delved into his memories. He forced himself to think about his father's death, reliving the emotional pain.

The crack of his body hitting the ground. The way his skin had been shredded and dangled off his arms in parts. The sound of his pleading before shadowy hands threw him into those silver flames.

Pike forced himself to remember his *bonding moments* with the Devil, reliving the physical pain.

The heavy force of the blows. The sharp teeth of the dogs biting through his flesh. The shadow men always reaching for him, holding him down. The bruises and the scars.

He couldn't keep his hands from trembling.

"Boss," the clean-shaven man sounded scared.

The one they called boss shook his head. "Jay, I'm going to ask you to sit down. But be aware that I'm not afraid to defend myself."

"Of course," Pike murmured, looking at the ground. After a moment, he added, "I can help. I can prove myself. I'll do anything."

"Anything?" The man slightly lowered his rifle. The other two cowboys snapped their heads towards the older man. They didn't want Pike there, and it showed. Their bodies were both tense, the gun pressed painfully in Pike's ribs and the other with his hand still gripping Pike's shoulder.

"Anything." Pike nodded. "I swear on my very soul."

The man sniffed, shifting his weight again, flames still crackling behind him. His shoulders relaxed. Pike exhaled slowly, hoping that meant good things.

"That's a big promise. One I'll keep you to. Sit. Eat." The man tilted his head to the side again, and the two others returned to their places among the small tents and packs.

The horses huffed at the edge of the circle of firelight as Pike took a seat near the man with the rifle. At the moment, he was grateful to not have a bullet in his side.

Now that he could see him fully, the man was broad shouldered and dark skinned. He seemed older but clean shaven with wrinkles around his eyes and between his eyebrows. He had worn clothes and beat up leather boots coated in a layer of dust. But his brown eyes were searching, like they could see Pike's soul.

"Well, Jay," the man started. "My name is Watson Moore. I manage this land. I wrangle for a nearby ranch among some other things. Whose blood are you covered in?"

The other two cowboys tensed at the question. Neither of them had said a word, and it didn't seem like they were keen on speaking to Pike, neither did it seem like they wanted to become friends. Inwardly, Pike didn't blame them for keeping their guards up since he would've done the same thing in their position. But the roles weren't switched, and Pike found himself sitting next to the very man he'd been sent to kill. He wasn't sure if he was elated that he didn't have to wait a week like he had in Greenwich or anxious about trying not to get caught before he could complete his assignment.

I am at his mercy.

Pike cleared his throat before answering the question. "A man who tried to harm an innocent person."

Watson sighed, shaking his head. "Can't say I'm comfortable with someone of your kind. I'm against any unnecessary violence."

"But you're a cowboy aren't you? Aren't you known for being a bit. . ." Pike floundered for the right word.

"Lawless?" the mustached young man snapped. His green eyes were sharp and hawklike.

Pike raised an eyebrow, turning to the younger wranglers. "Well, yes. I didn't expect a cowboy to be a pacifist. With famous people like Wyatt Earp and Doc Holiday keeping the peace. . ."

Watson chuckled, the laugh a rumble in his chest. "I'm no pacifist. I did my time in the war. That's what brought me out here actually. I found my way to Fort Blunt, away from the south."

"You fought for the Union?" Pike asked, turning back to Watson.

A cloud of memory passed in front of his eyes. But when he leaned back, it blew away as quick as it came. The wrangler with a mustache pulled his harmonica out again with a heavy sigh and began to play an old song Pike knew from his mother. The other man hadn't stopped staring at Pike since they all sat down.

Watson settled in his seat with a grunt. "Ethan, get Jay some extra clothes so we can burn those he's got on. No point in walking around in another sinner's blood. It's unsightly."

The clean-shaven man hesitated, watching Pike carefully. After a few seconds of tense silence, Ethan moved to rummage through one of the bags. He shoved a clean shirt, new pants, and a square piece of silk fabric into Pike's arms.

"Wild rag is for the dust," Ethan told Pike.

"Thank you." He nodded as he stood.

Pike walked away until he knew he'd slipped out of sight of the men. The younger two definitely wanted to dispose of him. But at least he'd found his assignment rather quickly.

After changing and buckling his new denim pants, he walked back towards the fire carrying his old clothes. Voices made him stop in his tracks. It sounded like a discussion turned into an argument.

"Watson, you can't actually trust this guy," the mustached man hissed.

"It's not your concern, Benji. You and Ethan have business elsewhere tomorrow. I think I can handle myself alone with him."

"I don't like it," Ethan said, flatly. "You saw what he looked like. There's still blood on his hands. What do you think he did to that guy?"

"And who's to say he's not lying to you?" Benji asked.

Pike could see Watson's face in the light of the flames. He appeared exhausted, but whether it was from his job or from their conversation, Pike couldn't say.

"That's enough," Watson commanded. "He'll be back soon. I expect you to be kind to him. No one shall be deprived of life, liberty, or property without due process of law. Innocent until proven guilty."

"But he is guilty, Watson!" the one called Benji barked, standing up from where he sat before. "You can't be that blind!"

"Benji, please."

Benji sank back down, holding his head in his hands.

"I won't sleep easy tonight," Ethan grumbled.

"I'll keep the first watch," Watson said. "That way you two can get some sleep. You can't be dragging tomorrow afternoon. You both have a lot of land to cover after our midday meal."

And with those words, the two younger wranglers grew tensely quiet. Benji resumed his song, and Ethan poked at the low fire with his boot.

Pike wondered what he could say or do to convince the other two cowboys that he wasn't a threat. What made it more difficult is that he *was* a threat and waltzed in looking like one, too.

Pike cursed quietly. He knew he wouldn't impress them with his nonexistent riding skills, nor did he know anything that would count as a conversation starter.

After a few more minutes of silence from the cowboys, Pike made his way back to the group. "I think I look a bit ridiculous wearing dress shoes with this. And I cannot for the life of me figure out how to tie this scarf thing."

Watson chuckled, and the younger men scoffed at Pike's ignorance. Pike had decided that would be the best plan. People liked to be around someone that's dumber than them. It would give them a chance to show off.

Watson shook his head with an amused look. "We can see about getting you some boots and maybe a hat when we're back at the ranch to-morrow morning. About two hours north. There we can get you cleaned up and on your way. Tomorrow morning, you'll ride with Benji until we reach the ranch."

Watson pointed at Benji who still played his harmonica. Benji paused and gave Pike a tight, unfriendly smile before diving back into his song.

Watson raised his eyebrows at Ethan, and the man stood with a sigh.

"Let me help you with that." Ethan stepped over to stand next to Pike. "It's not easy, but it's part of the dress code."

Ethan took the wild rag from Pike, folding it against his thigh until the fabric was the width of his hand and had a little tail. Turning the strip of fabric around, he stepped uncomfortably close to Pike.

"You have dress codes?" Pike raised his eyebrows, leaning his head back.

Ethan looked smug as he lined the tail of the fabric up with Pike's shirt, wrapping the fabric lightly around Pike's neck. "We do indeed. What do they teach you about us in the city?"

Pike smirked. "I'm no city boy. And though I've not had much experience riding horses, I appreciate your way of life. Out in the open, free from rules."

Ethan raised his eyebrows with a jesting look on his face as he tied a square knot in the front, securing the fabric around Pike's neck. It felt cozy and warm and surprisingly not suffocating.

"My apologies. You aren't lawless. But you can't tell me that the freedom of it isn't exhilarating."

"It absolutely is," Ethan agreed. "One of the best jobs in the world. But we still have to sacrifice quite a bit to be out here."

"Do you all need any help tomorrow?" Pike asked, sitting back down next to Watson, who passed him a bowl of some sort of steaming stew and took the old clothes. Though Pike had eaten dinner nearly five hours previous, his stomach rumbled at the smell. The dance felt like another age completely.

"Help meaning what exactly?" Watson asked, tossing the shirt into the fire first.

Pike felt his stomach turn as he lamented wasted money. He shrugged, swallowing down any feeling. "Wrangling, managing, whatever else you might need? Maybe until I get picked up or situate my traveling back to the Washington Territory."

"Ah, so you're from Washington?" Ethan asked.

"What's in Washington?" Benji asked.

"Home," Pike thought of his childhood home in Morville, Washington. He loved the pine trees and the sunsets blazing through their boughs. "But there's not much else. Railroads and loggers."

Thinking of Washington had him thinking of the Jackson family's trek out west. He wondered where they would end up. Maybe someday he'd find Cass again, somewhere hidden in the pine forests and mountains, or somewhere by the coast watching the whales and waves.

"Well, Jay," Watson stood and stretched, "I'll tell you what. You can help me tomorrow and the next day if that's not too much for you."

"That sounds wonderful." Pike nodded.

"It was quite fortuitous running into you out here." Watson smiled to himself. "I'm on the first watch. Boys, don't stay up too long. One story, then turn in. It's going to be a long day tomorrow."

With that, Watson left the circle of light, Winchester rifle in hand, and dissolved into the night.

12

Pike turned to Ethan and Benji. "You all tell stories?"

Benji shrugged.

Ethan nodded. "Personal stories, folk tales, sometimes legends."

"You have a favorite?" Pike asked, taking another bite of the stew Watson had given him, tasting of some sort of hot spice and vegetables. It tasted like Thanksgiving dinner.

Benji cleared his throat. "Do you want the short version or the long version?"

Pike looked at Ethan who had a sideways grin plastered on his face. Pike turned back to Benji with an eyebrow raised. "Long, please."

Ethan cleared his throat. "All right, Jay. Get comfortable. You're about to hear the story of how ole Watson Moore met the Devil."

Ice had replaced all the blood in his veins. Chills ran down Pike's spine, and his breath evaporated from his lungs.

Definitely a folk tale. It has to be.

Benji began to play a chugging song that sounded like a train rolling on its tracks, and Pike could almost hear its whistle in the distance. Ethan cleared his throat then started, "The year was 1872, the war between the states, despite ending a few years previous, had all sorts of repercussions on the country. The leaves were beginning to fall from the trees as they are today. And old Watson was on his way west for a new future after fighting in the war. He arrived in Fort Blunt back east a ways. The plan was to settle down, maybe build a family, but Watson never got far before he ran into some trouble."

Benji's song turned eerie and too well mimicked the sound of the Devil's grating voice. Pike clenched his jaw in an effort to stop himself from interrupting. He didn't want to look scared in front of these men, despite the terror building in his gut. He'd rather face mental anguish than humiliation.

Ethan continued on with his story. "Later that first night after securing land outside of town, Watson paid a visit to the local saloon. He met the owner and some other townsfolk, played a few rounds of cards, and observed a curious man in the corner having a hushed debate with one of the locals. Well, soon enough the conversation grew sour, and quicker than you can say '*Wake Snakes*', the curious man whipped out his pistol and killed the other man."

Pike's stomach turned, the stew no longer appealing to him.

"Gunfights aren't uncommon, but Watson didn't like that. He'd had enough death in the war, so he whipped his gun out, pointing it at the curious man who had wild ice blue eyes. . ." Ethan paused and stared directly at Pike. "I've always imagined something similar to yours, Jay."

Pike swallowed hard, trying to dislodge the uncomfortable lump in his throat. He tried to fake a smile, but he thought it probably looked more like a grimace.

He knew this story.

Too well.

"So, there ole Watson Moore stood with his gun pointed at this murderer and the murderer had his pointed at ole Watson. And the rest of the men had guns drawn at one of the two men so that each of them had at least four or five guns pointed at him. The barkeep, being the

good man that he was, snuck out the back to get the constable who was.
. . preoccupied."

Ethan cleared his throat. Benji began to play an intense sounding tune when Ethan continued.

"Not much had changed in the past few years as there were still *lawless* cowboys around causing a ruckus with local law enforcement. Watson figured it had to be one of those unhinged men who always sought after blood."

Benji's song grew softer like he knew what to expect. And it felt as if all of Oklahoma paused for what would happen.

"Watson was the first one to speak up, asking the murderer who he was and why he would do such a thing when peace existed between the states once again. The murderer retaliated with a slew of insulting names for people like Watson and then claimed that he was the Devil's infamous right-hand man, Alexander Pike. Apparently the man he'd killed had finally been called to judgment, so he'd been sent to finish the job. Now, we all know that the Devil gets impatient, so Watson told the man to take him to his boss. He wanted a word.

"So out they went, everyone else still on edge when the two men left, Alexander Pike carrying the body of the deceased. Some men followed to watch the story unfold, but after walking a mile or so, they stopped as if held back by some invisible barrier. The two living men and the dead man continued their journey west out of town. After walking for some time, they arrived at a crossroads. At first, Watson thought it was a mirage, but when they came closer, a dark-suited man stood tall, his hands in his pockets, relaxed and perfectly comfortable, alone in the dark. The stranger had dressed to the nines, and everyone knows the Devil wears a suit and tie. The midnight moon cast an eerie shadow to cut the Devil's face in half. The shadows of the brambles and stones stretched far into their path as if vying for their skin. Watson Moore said himself that it was difficult to look him in the eyes, that Devil. Something supernatural about it."

Benji had stopped playing at some point in the story, and Pike had just noticed. The crackling of the fire seemed almost too loud. The last of the crickets chittered in the dark abyss, alive under the light of the crescent moon. And worst of all, the wind rustled brambles in the dark, causing a chill to bristle across Pike's skin despite the cracking of the dwindling fire. In the distance, a coyote howled, lonesome in the night.

Pike wondered if Watson could hear Ethan's story way out there in the dark where he kept watch. He wondered if his dark brown eyes were watching him even now. He wondered if Watson knew.

After a minute or so of silence, Ethan shifted, clearing his throat again. "Watson could go more into detail. He tells it better than I do, first-hand experience and all. But in the end, the Devil promised he'd come for Watson one day. He'd never know when. So every night, Watson takes the midnight shift, knowing his fate could be waiting."

Pike took intentional breaths. He felt sick.

The night from the story was the same night his father died.

Silvertongue had brought his father back to the house, throwing him to the ground outside and spewing curses left and right. Pike hadn't gotten a good look at the Devil from the window of their small cabin, but he could see unnaturally long bent legs. And instead of human skin that adopted a blue tint at night, the Devil's shone like leather, black like charcoal. A black so dark that it stood out against the shadows of the night. Pike had run outside, but his mother pulled him back by the door. She cried, but made no sound, restraining him. At fifteen he could've easily overpowered her, but it would've been a losing battle in the end.

That grating voice had cut through the night almost like it screeched in Pike's own head. He'd watched his father get beaten unrecognizable and those dreaded silver flames that burned behind Silvertongue flared when shadows threw his father inside the portal to the underworld.

That was the night that Pike became Alexander Pike VI, slave and right-hand man of the Devil. That's when the rule had been made that he was to tell only enough of the truth to get by. And Pike had only then come to the realization that he'd told Cass his true identity.

His stomach clenched in that familiar way that anxiety always came.

"Did we scare you too much, Jay? You look a little pale." Ethan asked, eyebrows cocked up.

The two younger wrangles snickered.

Pike shook his head, swallowing hard. "No. It's obviously a legend," he tried to sound more at ease than he felt.

Ethan scoffed at him. "The story is true! Ask Watson yourself tomorrow. You'll see."

Benji started playing "Go Down Moses," eyes glazed and focused on the crackling fire.

"Well," Ethan stood with a grunt, "boss said we had one story then straight to bed. Long day tomorrow."

Ethan ducked into his tent. Benji stopped playing. "Jay, you can sleep in Watson's tent until he's off watch."

"You sure he'd be okay with that?" Pike pinched his eyebrows together, nervous knowing now that Watson was the man who'd gotten Pike's father killed. Pike's father still stood at fault for being reckless, but Watson had played a part in it, too.

"Boss would want you to be comfortable, even if Ethan and I don't agree with him."

Pike shifted uncomfortably.

"I don't like you," Benji's hawk eyes bore into Pike's own. "I don't trust you either. But I believe in the benefit of the doubt. We run off honor out here. And if you can't get behind that, you don't belong out here."

The crackling of the fire accompanied the faint whoosh of wind in the otherwise silent night.

"I'm not afraid of you." Pike squinted his eyes.

"Then that makes two of us." Benji twisted his mustache. "I don't think you're all that powerful. I think you're just another branch in some big tree with someone else calling the shots."

He started playing his harmonica, a signal that ended their conversation. All evening, he'd picked up on little mentions or phrases or looks. . . it all seemed oddly suspicious to him, like they knew his identity. And after that story. . . If they did know who he was, they were all doing a decent job at hiding it. If they didn't, paranoia had eaten at Pike's mind.

Pike cleared his throat. "Watson's tent?"

"That one," Benji paused, flicking a hand at the tent pitched behind Pike.

"Well. . . g'night," Pike said halfheartedly, waving a hand once to Benji who continued to play, "Go Down Moses" following Pike to bed.

As soon as the flaps of the tent fell closed behind him, Pike knelt to the ground. The weight of such a story pulled him down like gravity.

Watson is the one who'd ruined that night.

Did he know the Devil had returned? Was it Pike's time to die?

What happens when the Devil finds out that Cass knows?

As he lay there in the dark, his body trembled, though not from the cold. His limbs spasmed and shook while his breath grew shallow and his mind frantic. His mind tricked him, thinking he saw dark creatures watching him in the shadows like they had in the clearing in Greenwich. Tears streamed down his face without sound. His bones felt restless within him like they wanted to return to their Creator.

And despite every aversion in his being, Pike silently prayed. Unable to even form words, he groaned thinking, "*God, if you're out there, I want out. Please get me out. God, don't let me burn.*"

Time passed slowly as he tried and tried again to sleep. He knew he needed the rest, but it evaded him. So instead, he gave in to tears, completely alone in a borrowed tent trying to barter his way into heaven and begging God to save his tortured soul.

13

Every muscle in Pike's body ached. Pain radiated in his bones like knives piercing skin.

He wasn't sure what time he'd fallen asleep, but he had never been woken up to move. And on second thought, Pike wondered what had woken him up in the first place.

Blue light peeped in from the crack between the folds of the tent canvas. Pike pulled himself to a sitting position and brushed his unruly blonde hair back out of his face. Despite squeezing his eyes shut, that flare of silver flame still imprinted on the backs of his eyelids like a constant reminder.

His own personal nightmare.

There.

It sounded like some sort of pot or pan had been knocked against something, causing a hollow sound to interrupt the quiet morning in the wilderness. Pike slowly crawled to his feet and crouched to step out of the tent.

His senses were greeted with a multicolored sunrise, lighting up the sky like an impressionist painter. Orange cut through the sky, the edge of the sun still out of view but making its grand entrance, everything else still covered in the blue shadows of the morning.

By the fire, Ethan sat with something sizzling in a pan over the fire.

"I've made cowpoke eggs and beans," he whispered.

"Cowpoke eggs?" Pike matched Ethan's quiet tone and yawned and stretched. His body resisted him, still tense from whatever terrors that had assailed him in the night.

"Something I learned from Watson." Ethan shuffled the pan back and forth with quick motions, more sizzling sounds coming from the pan. "Scrambled eggs filled with anything you have lying around. In our case, a little bit of wild sage and leftover jackrabbit from that stew last night. I wish we had some cheese or salt."

"Jackrabbit." Pike frowned. He didn't think it had tasted much different than beef or chicken.

"Anyone else want coffee?" Benji climbed out of his tent, mustache still perfectly curled on each end like it had been the night before.

"Please." Pike nodded.

With a tense expression, eyebrows pinched together, Benji set about making coffee to start their morning for the long day ahead.

Pike didn't miss that the men appeared to be at least a little more friendly than they had been the night before. Had they simply needed to sleep on it to accept him as safe, to see that they survived the night with him nearby? Or had Watson talked to them again?

Though clouded by sleep, Pike felt jittery. His nerves were still on end, wondering if anything would come of the wranglers being friendly.

And where was Watson?

In the brief moments that the eggs sizzled on the fire and coffee brewed in its pot, the sky shifted, taking on more pink shades. The tip of the sun peeked over the horizon that stretched for miles, and without the trees that blanketed the mountains of the East, the sky seemed more vast.

"Where's Watson?" Pike asked, arms draped over his head. "He never kicked me out of his tent last night."

"He's meditating," Benji said a little awkwardly, like meditation wasn't the right word for it.

"A meditating wrangler?" Pike wrinkled his nose.

Ethan chuckled. "Sort of, yes. He'll be back for breakfast."

The three of them grew quiet, and Pike observed the ever-changing sky in contented silence. He walked a little ways back down the road to get an uninterrupted view of the skyline. Far in the distance, he could barely see the shape of mountains, pale blue breaking up the sky.

"Mountains in the plains. I think I've seen everything," Pike mumbled to himself.

Returning to their little campsite, he noticed Watson coming out of his tent in a second set of clothes, pulling his coat on.

"Morning, Jay," Watson muttered. "Hope you slept all right."

"I did. Thank you for letting me use your tent."

Watson grinned. "Don't get too comfortable. We'll get you your own today to borrow. And a set of boots. You can't be caught in those frilly shoes. They say only true cowboys die with their boots on."

Watson seemed to hold back a chuckle, and Pike joined him by the fire suppressing a grin. Benji passed out coffee in tin cups in addition to thin plates about the size of Pike's hand. Ethan split the cowpoke eggs between the four men, and each found themselves content in the quiet presence of the other men and the morning sunlight.

When the sun finally shone too bright to look at for long, Watson drained the last of the coffee.

"Pack up, boys." Watson stood and stalked over to the horses. "We're losing beautiful daylight."

Ethan and Benji downed the rest of their coffee and split up their tasks.

"Can I help at all?" Pike asked.

"Why don't you help Ethan clear up breakfast so he can pack his tent up."

Pike scraped off the scraps of beans and leftover egg and tried to dry out the cups as best as he could while he waited for the silverware to be sterilized by the dying fire. When Pike finished, Ethan quickly packed it all in the saddle bags of his horse and returned to his own tent to finish rolling up his bed mats.

"Can I help you with anything?" Pike asked Benji, who scrunched up his face, mustache twisting as he did so.

"I'm about finished here. Maybe you can attempt to saddle up Ocho over there?"

Benji pointed towards a horse that had the coloration of a cow, brown and white and big. He looked like he didn't want to be awake so early in the morning and Pike didn't blame him.

Pike also didn't blame the way Benji cut his sentences shorter around Pike. The tension seemed a lot less than the day before, but Pike felt like he might never get the other wranglers on his side. Not that he needed to, but it would certainly be easier to complete the assignment if they trusted him.

Watson tightened the straps on his own horse while Pike approached him. "I'm assuming that you don't know how to saddle a horse, Jay."

"You'd be correct."

Watson regarded him with a strange, seeing look that made Pike want to squirm where he stood. He almost couldn't look the man in the eye, and he nearly turned away when Watson moved to gaze at the sun.

"Well, you're about to learn. The next day or so you'll be doing this on your own, and by the end of your time with me, you'll be two steps closer to being a professional wrangler. Even old Bones here would be proud."

After patting his horse kindly, Watson met Pike's eyes with a jovial smile that made Pike sick. He attempted to return the smile, questioning whether or not Watson knew what was coming.

"Don't be nervous!" Watson slapped him on the back. "It's only a one-thousand-pound creature capable of breaking your ribs and more if you get kicked."

Watson laughed, walking to the other side of his horse where Ocho stood. Pike followed, watching each horse with a little more respect.

"This is Ocho." Watson gave the horse a light pat on the rump.

"He's a quarter horse." Here Watson pointed to Ocho's backside where the brown and white splotches were more pronounced. "He's also known as a Paint horse in broader terms, hence the paint looking markings. This is Benji's best friend. They go everywhere together. But today, just for about an hour, you'll ride together."

Pike nodded, reaching out to stroke the horse's nose.

"It's not going to be comfortable at all, sharing a horse," Watson said. "But it's all you have unless you want to walk."

Pike shook his head, furrowing his eyebrows. "I'll take feeling uncomfortable over being stranded any day."

"During lunch, I'd like to hear how you ended up way out here in the plains," Watson had that same seeing look that made Pike uncomfortable.

Pike swallowed trying to come up with a good enough excuse why he had mysteriously arrived at their camp.

"Enough chat. Let's get Ocho ready to go." Watson unwound a strap from the saddle that looped under itself. It buckled down under Ocho's barrel chest. Watson unbuckled it and gave it a swift tug causing the leather to squeak.

"You have to tighten them rather tight to keep the saddle stable to keep you and your horse safe." Watson refastened the buckle and relooped the strap so it stuck fast to the saddle. "Sometimes horses like to puff their stomachs out to avoid the straps, but Ocho's pretty good about being obedient." With one last quick pat, Watson walked to his own horse, where he tied up the saddle bags and brushed off the saddle.

"Ready to head out?" Ethan asked, siding up to his own horse and tightening the straps of his saddle.

"Ready as a rain in the spring," Watson chirped.

Benji tied his own things to Ocho's saddle. "I'll climb on first, then I'll help you up behind me."

With a swift push off the ground, Benji hauled himself over the saddle. He held his hand out for Pike. For a split second, Pike wondered if he could trust Benji, knowing how tense he'd been and that he controlled this massive creature. But at that moment there were no other options, so Pike carefully stuck his left foot in the stirrup, pushing up and holding on to Benji's hand.

Once seated on the rump of the horse behind the saddle, Pike cleared his throat. "Watson, you were right."

"About what?" he asked, astride his own horse, Bones, a dusty brown gelding with white accent marks.

"This is about as comfortable as wet denim."

This earned a low chuckle from each of the men. Ethan climbed onto his light gray and white spotted horse and rolled back his shoulders, pulling up his reins. "Am I leading this morning?"

Watson nodded. "We're following you."

Ethan clicked his tongue and pulled his reins to the left, turning Amigo's neck to the left and back on the dusty road. Bones followed next, and last Ocho carried both Pike and Benji, seeming not to struggle with the added weight, though Pike could already feel his legs growing sore where they rubbed against the back of the saddle.

As they walked in their slow pace further down the dusty road, Pike wracked his brain for ways he could pass off Watson's death as an accident. Maybe his horse bashed his head in when it got spooked. Or a sinkhole opened up and swallowed them both.

Instead, dread settled in Pike's stomach. He wouldn't be able to convince others to believe the stories. And if he couldn't pull this off, there would be dire consequences, maybe even the same his father had faced seven years prior.

14

The moment the party of men arrived at the ranch, Pike felt watched. Despite the gentle breeze, something caused the hair on his arms to stand. Ethan led them to the stables where other wranglers tied the horses to a hitching rail to be brushed.

"Jay." Watson beckoned him into a room attached to the stables.

Pike practically fell off Ocho, legs feeling tense and stretched. He tried his best to not look ridiculous while he followed Watson, walking almost in a waddle which he expected to be embarrassing. His calves felt like they were on fire, but he kept his thoughts to himself. He had a pretty decent idea of the teasing he'd get if he complained at all.

Watson brought him to a dimly lit room. Under the yellow tinted light, saddles and reins decorated the walls, the smell of freshly treated leather occupying every space. A chair sat in the corner next to a saddle stand.

"We need to get you fitted or at least decently set," Watson said. "Then you need a pair of boots, some real pants, and a horse to borrow.

Have a seat."

Pike took a seat in the small, straight-backed chair. Watson pulled one of the saddles off the wall and draped it over the stand.

"This will be yours for the next day or so. Before we leave this afternoon, let me know if it's uncomfortable at all."

Pike nodded, eyeing the saddle. The number eighty-two hung on the side where the flap met the leather.

"Go find Ethan. He'll get you your new accessories and all." Watson scratched his jaw. "I'll see you in the dining hall in an hour."

With that, he left the stables and wandered off towards one of the other small buildings on the property. Pike wondered if Watson lived there while he worked on property. He also found himself wondering if Watson had a family who would grieve him when he never came home.

Waving his thoughts away, Pike meandered around the yard taking everything in, making note of people and possible escape options in case things became dicey. Eventually, he came back to where they had first entered the ranch and found Ethan brushing his horse, Amigo, down at the hitching rail, joking among other wranglers.

"Watson told me to find you so I can become a proper cowpoke." Pike leaned against the post, squinting in the afternoon sunlight.

Ethan looked up at him, eyes shaded under his hat. "Clothes aren't what make a person a wrangler."

"Of course, I only meant—"

"Follow me."

As Ethan started towards the main building, Pike let out a deep breath. He wasn't getting very far at being likable. Following Ethan, Pike glanced around at the ranch. Little houses crowded in one section away from the main yard. In the center of the ranch, the bullpen and the stables filled the majority of the space in addition to the hitching post and the first part of a pasture. A few other barns were scattered over the land and rugged fencing closed all of it in. He didn't see cows anywhere.

"So what kind of operation do you run here?" Pike asked.

Ethan shrugged. "Your standard cattle ranch. The cows are in the southern pasture during this part of the year. Once spring hits, we'll have a cattle drive back to the western pasture out past those houses." Ethan pointed over to the cluster of small buildings.

"Did you grow up here?"

Ethan shook his head. "My father knew a man who keeps his horse here. Figured I'd like it more than being a teller at the bank."

Pike nodded. "Being a wrangler definitely beats staying in an office all day. Every day you get to see beautiful things."

Ethan furrowed his eyebrows, regarding Pike strangely. "I forget how much I take advantage of it. It is a blessing to be here." He walked up steps to a wooden front porch. "This is the heart of the ranch, where life happens."

The house, though a little bigger than his mother's house in Morville, had the same homely character, and Pike could tell it had been there for a while. A mix of chairs dotted the porch that overlooked the yard. There, a few wranglers sat picking at guitars and fiddles singing old western melodies.

Once inside the ranch house, Ethan slipped his hat off his head, and they took a right into what Pike assumed would have been a sitting room had it been outfitted like an actual home rather than a ranching business.

Boots in all sizes and colors covered the left wall floor to ceiling. Straight in front of them, a wall held hats, ties, and other western wear. To the right between the windows hung an old mirror, and against the wall under the windows were benches.

Ethan bent down and studied Pike's shoes. After a moment, he stood.

"Here." Ethan pulled a set of boots off the wall. They were a dusty brown with blue accent marks. "Try these and these." He passed another pair with darker brown accents.

Pike sat down on one of the benches and pulled off his ruined dress shoes. Clothing changes were a normal part of Pike's job, like costumes for a show. He had to play the role he was given and live up to each one. So he stepped out of elegant contractor and into western wrangler. He slipped on the pair of boots with blue accents then walked around.

"Should they be loose?" Pike lifted his right foot, and the boot slipped partially off of his foot.

Ethan shook his head, scratching his chin. "Nope. Try the other pair."

Pike sat again and slipped on the darker brown pair. His feet slid in and stuck. He stood again and walked around, looking at himself in the mirror.

"What do you think?" Ethan put his hands on his hips.

Pike regarded the boots. "They feel fine. Do you think these are all right?"

Ethan nodded. He walked over to the wall of hats and pulled off a dark brown one the same shade as Pike's new boots. "This will protect you from the sun and the rain while you're helping us out here." Ethan crossed his arms. "Welcome to ranching."

"When do I become a real wrangler?" Pike raised an eyebrow.

"You're a true wrangler when you start finding dirt up your nose." With a laugh, Ethan stepped back out into the main room of the building.

Pike followed, his heavy boots causing the wooden floor to echo beneath him. Ethan pulled a pair of pants and a heavy jacket off hangers in the main room and led them into a room with a toilet and a wash basin. He passed Pike the clothing. The coat was a deep brown, almost black, and the fabric felt soft to the touch.

"All of that is yours for now. Take decent care of it." Ethan grew silent. He seemed to be warring with something in his mind. "The boss likes us to wash up before dining. He says we can be wranglers and still have class."

Ethan pointed and grabbed a rag folded to the side of the basin. Dipping it into the water, he proceeded to scrub his dusty face. Pike followed suit, trying on his hat in the mirror.

"Don't forget to flick," Ethan knocked the edge of Pike's hat. Though the force shook the hat, it didn't budge, making Ethan smile, albeit a tight-lipped one.

"Fits perfectly." Ethan scrunched up his nose briefly. "I'll be in the dining hall. When you're finished, go out the back door. The hall is the long, flat building to your right across from the stables."

With that, Ethan left Pike alone.

Alone. Something Pike dreaded.

He supposed he had always been lonely, but it made things much worse when you couldn't escape your inner demons. Pike leaned against the edge of the counter, staring at himself in the mirror. It was haunting, meeting his own pale eyes.

The eyes of his father stared back at him, a ruthless man.

Icy. Cold. Distant.

"You are your father's son," he whispered to himself. "Don't mess this job up. You can't afford another mistake. You can't afford to be like him any more than you already are."

He splashed his face with warm water and groaned, exhausted from the previous night of strange dreams and fitful sleep along with the day's unfamiliarity of riding a horse, not to mention he had to ride behind the saddle. He hoped next time he rode alone. Despite hating to be alone, he did operate better when he only had to worry about himself.

After drying off his face and sloppily retying the scarf that Ethan had given him the previous night, he found his way to the dining hall. Ethan and Watson sat at a long table with other men and a few women, all chatting and eating. Luckily, they had seats saved by the end of the table.

"Ethan, you did good," Watson muttered with slight amusement. "He might pass for a wrangler after all."

Pike sat, shaking his head. "I only need to be good enough to help out for a few days."

"We'll take you where you need to go the morning after tomorrow."

Benji sat next to him. "Now all you need is a horse."

"If I manage to keep track of it without causing problems, I'll be impressed with myself," Pike tried to joke, humor tasting sour in his mouth.

They ate a meal of baked meat and potatoes with a side of green beans and bread. By the end of it, Pike felt stuffed. All the wranglers rose to split up, heading to their various jobs.

 115

"We get back on the horses after a meal that big?" Pike asked, eyebrows raised high.

The wranglers around him laughed.

"Just part of the job, sunshine." Ethan gave Pike a smug look.

Pike groggily followed the men back to the hitching rail where they resaddled the three horses they'd ridden that morning.

Watson pulled Benji aside, and they leaned in close like they were sharing a secret. Pike watched from under the brim of his hat as Benji straightened then glanced over at him.

Benji's body rippled with tension while he held his horse steady. It seemed like a hundred emotions passed over his face, though Pike could place none of them. What had Watson said to him to make him look so angry?

Benji hopped on his horse, still watching Pike with a strange look. He placed a hand on his hip and leaned over to say something to Watson that Pike couldn't make out. Watson shook his head before Benji, face set like stone, trotted out of the stable yard with Ethan following not far behind.

Watson sauntered over to Pike, still watching the two young wranglers riding out to their next assignment. "Ben and Ethan are headed back East to wrangle some cows back to our main pasture there. You'll come with me for a northern patrol. We won't be back until it's time for you to leave."

Watson watched Pike carefully. Something was definitely wrong. Did Watson know? That might be the only explanation.

What if he brought Pike out in the wilderness and killed *him* instead? Would Pike's mother be required to take over since Pike himself had no heirs? The thought of his sweet mother following orders from that fiend made Pike sick. She had never chosen this life, never known her husband's past until it had been too late when he took over from his father. She was already in too deep, a baby on the way.

"Is that okay with you, Alexander James?" Watson's voice pulled Pike out of his thoughts.

Pike's mind briefly flashed to his mother using his first and middle names. "I'm not sure how much help I'll be, but I'm always up for a challenge."

Watson nodded. "Let's get you a horse."

They walked over to another rail where about ten or twelve horses were waiting. Watson walked past the row of horses twice and glanced back at Pike several times before untying a horse.

"This is Beau. He's a stable horse with a mind of his own. He's curious but loyal," Watson said with that look in his eyes that made Pike uneasy. "A lot like you, I presume."

Pike felt like squirming under that gaze. "I'll go grab that saddle."

Pike stepped back into that dimly lit room, grabbing saddle eighty-two, much heavier than he expected. Pike carried it out to his new companion and heaved it over Beau's back, tightening the straps like Watson had shown him.

Watson came back towards him and passed him a holster strapped on a belt. "This is for you. If the belt doesn't fit, we can get you another one."

"You're giving me a revolver?"

Watson shot him a pointed look. "It's wild country out here. You may need it. And besides, it's mine. I'm only letting you borrow it."

Pike slipped the belt on, making sure it strapped tightly around his waist. This would be his means of completing his job. Things were falling into place without much work from him. It seemed altogether too easy.

Watson double-checked Beau's saddle straps and gave the horse a pat. He stepped over to his own horse, Bones, and mounted him. Pike climbed onto Beau, muscles groaning with the strain from the morning. The horse shifted ever so slightly, turning around to gaze at Pike.

At least he rode alone.

"Ready?" Watson asked, that strange look starting to fade from his eyes.

After nodding, Pike held the reins loosely in his hand.

Plenty of people ride horses. Surely it can't be that difficult to learn.

With what he hoped looked like a natural nudge, Pike heeled the horse with his boots and set off to follow Watson out to the wilderness of the north.

15

Hours passed before they were in closer range of the mountains in the north. Once they'd left the ranch property, Watson had taken about thirty minutes to teach Pike how to post a trot; otherwise, Pike would supposedly have been miserably sore later that night.

Not that he wouldn't be sore already.

Pike started to tire of the heat of the sun on his back and was grateful when clouds started rolling overhead. But now the wind had kicked up, sending chills down Pike's spine.

The witching winds.

His ever-present companion.

A reminder why he was here.

Dread settled once again in his stomach as he tilted his head down to avoid getting dust in his eyes. He knew he needed to think of something soon, to form some sort of plan. He had the weapon, the skill, the isolation, but was there a way to twist it to look like an accident? Surely Benji and Ethan would go looking for Watson once he'd disappeared.

And you told them where you were from, Pike cursed himself mentally. Another slip up.

"So, Jay," Watson turned around in his saddle to look at Pike. "What brought you out here to the great Oklahoma Territory?"

"I must seem pretty foreign to you. . . all northern and cold." Pike chuckled half-heartedly, hoping to deflect the conversation.

"You certainly aren't from Jovy."

"No, sir, I am not."

Watson grew silent while that same look of seeing right through Pike's ruse rested in his eyes. Pike couldn't look at him for long, so instead he watched the looming mountains ahead, focusing on trying to maintain posting the trot rather than sitting it. It was constantly up and down, up and down. Sometimes he felt wildly out of control, other times he wondered how he'd even gotten to where he was in life.

He often wondered if his father had traveled to as many places as he had. Pike had never had the chance to talk to his father about the job. He'd assumed one day, when he grew older, that his father might have talked to him about it. But he'd never gotten the chance. He'd died and left Pike to pick up the pieces, stumbling his way through paying off this debt. Pike had been dropped into the depths of the sea, and he still wasn't sure whether he swam or drowned.

The sound of Watson coughing drew Pike's attention back to the present moment. Pike hoped that his inward tension wasn't outwardly visible.

"Beau there doesn't love trotting," Watson turned slightly to face the mountains. "He's a big fan of loping. It's not sustainable for the long haul, but it gets his blood pumping, his heart racing." He paused and gave Pike a deep stare. "He runs as fast and as far as he can, outrunning whatever is behind him. Never looking back. Never dealing with what he's passed by."

Watson stopped talking but continued to watch him. Pike assumed that the wrangler wasn't talking about the horse anymore.

He knew.

The realization hit him like a weight thrown against his chest.

Watson cleared his throat and continued. "What do you say we have a little race, Jay?"

Was that purely imagination, or did he put too much of an emphasis on Jay?

"A race?" Pike swallowed a momentary bout of fear. "I-I don't know anything about loping."

"No," Watson agreed. "But Beau does."

Pike met Watson Moore's eyes. The man's wild rag fluttered in the November gale, his hat casting a low shadow over his wizened eyes.

Pike nodded once. "Okay."

Watson smiled slowly. "When I shoot, give Beau a big ole kick and a shout."

"When you *shoot*?" Pike repeated.

Watson pulled his pistol out of his holster. "Three."

Pike's heart began to race. It pounded painfully against his ribs. It jumped out of his chest and into his throat, restricting his breath entirely.

Is this what my victims feel like? Pike's heart shuddered again.

"Two." Watson cocked the gun, holding the tip of his finger on the trigger. He brandished the gun in the air with a wicked, mischievous smile.

Everything around Pike felt like it slowed to a creeping pace. All of the sound around him felt muted like he was underwater. The horses' hooves beating against the earth matched pace with his beating heart. The wind rushing through the trees slowed, Pike's scarf blowing back behind him. The dust slowed. Pike glanced up at the blue-tinted mountains ahead before meeting Watson's eyes, adrenaline coursing through his veins, vying for control to snap into action.

"One." Watson fired directly upwards.

Time resumed its normal pace. Pike shouted and gave Beau a swift kick. Without hesitation, Beau shifted into a full lope, and Pike slid nicely into the rocking motion of the saddle. The world whizzed by him while he left it all behind. Brambles, rock formations, sage bushes, all of it flew by before Pike could even register them. His original panic melted into bubbling joy. To his own astonishment, a laugh slipped out of him.

Beau responded to this by adding speed to his gait. Pike glanced backwards and saw Watson a pace or two behind, grinning from ear to ear. Watson clicked his tongue and his horse caught up to Beau with ease, siding up beside them.

"Having fun?" he called.

The horses seemed to understand their riders were racing, each pushing the other to a new speed.

Pike laughed in response, exhilarated by the whole experience, not sure he could figure out how to speak while maintaining the gait. Bones pulled ahead of Pike and slowed to a trot. Beau slowed to a trot without following a cue from Pike.

"How was that for an adrenaline rush?" Watson asked, panting heavily like Pike and the horses.

They slowed to a walk while Pike gathered his thoughts.

"That was incredible. I don't even have words to describe the feeling."

Although Pike *did* have words for his irrational fear that Watson might have shot him. His paranoia had gotten the best of him again. Watson was only a kind, old man. Pike turned to the mountains, hoping to hide the shame on his face.

"Horses can only keep that pace up for so long. The trot is their most efficient pace." Watson sniffed, wiping his nose from the harsh winds. "It makes you feel like you're flying."

"Flying. That's a great way to describe it."

They grew silent again, comfortable watching the horizon, mountains casting their shadow over the land in front of them. In his heart, Pike knew that's where he would complete his job. He cleared his throat, trying to push away the anxiety he felt building inside of him.

"Jay, let me ask you something." Watson shifted in his saddle. "Why are you here? And I don't want your fabricated answer. I know you've been lying to me. Not about everything, but you haven't told me the truth either."

Pike swallowed. His throat felt dry, and that same uncomfortable lump stuck, making speech difficult. "Oh?"

Watson nodded. "I'm old. I know when I'm being lied to."

Pike bit the inside of his cheek before answering. "I'm here for business."

"What kind of business do you do, Jay?"

"Contract work."

"What exactly are you contracted to do?"

"I solve problems."

"Whose problems?"

"My boss's problems."

"And your boss is. . . ?"

Pike hesitated. He swallowed again, trying to get that dry feeling to go away, but nothing worked. Flashes of silver flame blotted his vision when he responded quietly and truthfully. "Terrifying."

Watson grunted but said nothing.

For a long time, Pike thought he'd given up on the conversation. At least, he hoped Watson had given up.

But Pike wasn't that lucky.

"I know who you really are, Jay."

Pike froze in the saddle. His heart pounded so loud it sounded like horses were racing in his ears. A sharp pain radiated from the center of his chest, and for a moment, he wondered if he'd been somehow injured by the riding after all. His hands slipped on the reins as he struggled to breathe evenly.

Watson pulled Bones around in front of Beau, stopping them both.

"I knew your father," Watson stated plainly.

Pike didn't think his heart could beat any louder. It seemed like the only thing he could hear at that moment.

"I met him about six years ago."

Pike closed his eyes. "Seven."

Watson watched him, not giving any emotion away. "So you know?"

Pike swallowed his panic. "He died that night."

"I'm sorry to hear that."

"I only heard your side of the story last night."

Nodding slowly, Watson pulled off his hat, showing gray hair underneath. "I figured the boys told you that one. It's their favorite."

"It doesn't exactly bring up pleasant memories for me," Pike mumbled through gritted teeth.

Watson tilted his head. "I'm sorry, Jay. I—"

"I don't think you are sorry." Bitterness filled every crevice in Pike's partially calloused heart. Despite still hating his father for who he had been while he was alive, Pike still loved his memory. And now he understood what position his father had been in years ago. "You had no idea what you were getting into, and it caused so much irreparable damage." Pike met the old man's eyes. "I was fifteen, Watson."

Watson sighed. "I'm sorry you had to grow up without a father's love."

"My father. . . love wasn't something he showed much. Which is why he was good at his job."

Watson grunted. "I figured he was powerless, forced to do things against his will."

"Well, he was. But that doesn't mean he was innocent either."

Watson shrugged. "You may be right. . . But you took over? That night?"

"Cursed family."

They grew silent, the only sound was the wind in their ears rolling over the mountain's edge. They were in the shadow of the mountain now, sunlight blotted out by the climbing hills around them.

Pike felt hollow. The Jovy job had been jeopardized now that Watson knew the truth. Truth was the last thing Pike needed him to know. But apparently there was no escaping the truth.

"Alexander," Watson started.

"Call me Pike," Pike answered, dully refusing to look the man in the eye. He felt his throat tighten. "Alexander was my father."

"Since you took over the family business," Watson cleared his throat, "has my time finally been called in?"

Pike paused then nodded slowly.

Watson sighed heavily. "I figured. I knew it would come someday. When you stumbled into our circle and I saw your eyes. . . You look so much like him, you know."

Pike's head shot up. "You knew this whole time? Do the others?"

Watson assented. That at least explained the strange look Benji had given him before they'd parted ways at the ranch.

The two men grew silent again, and Pike's hands started to shake. He practically felt his nerve breaking while they sat there.

"How long do I have?" Watson asked after a while.

"Until tomorrow night." Pike turned to Watson.

Watson shrugged. "There's no sense in worrying too much about it."

Pike's eyebrows furrowed. "Worrying? Watson, I'm not innocent. I know I'm young, but I've done my fair share of evil."

"I know you're innocent, Pike." Watson surveyed the horizon, hand on his hip.

Words spilled out of Pike's mouth before he could stop them. "But I'm not. I'm not innocent. You don't know the things I've done, how I've hurt people. How I've ruined families and futures. You saw me yesterday. Someone else's blood stained my clothes."

"You said he deserved it."

"But what if he didn't?" Pike's eyesight blurred as he remembered Mrs. Benson's limp form in his arms hiking to the crossroads. "His wife didn't deserve what she received. She'll die because of him."

"Sometimes that's how life goes. But Pike, it's not your fault. I know who owns you. We all make our own choices. Letting your own nature control your mind leads to death. But letting the Spirit control your mind leads to life and peace. That man—the one whose blood covered your clothes—he chose wrong, nothing more."

"But what did I choose?" Pike asked desperately, knowing there wasn't a good enough answer to calm his fears. His voice cracked with emotion. "What can I choose even now? Nothing. I choose nothing. I have no free will."

Pike met Watson's eyes. He hated crying, but the tears came out in a rush. He couldn't see more than blurred shapes. His life crumbled around him.

How could he finish this job?

And if he didn't finish the job, he wouldn't survive past tomorrow. He would be beaten, tortured, then thrown into that horrible silver flame exactly like his father. His mother would have to take over and be forced to do despicable things. Pike would do anything to protect her from that fate. That was the only real leverage that the Devil had on him. Pike would voluntarily give up his own life if it meant his mother's freedom.

The thought of his mother having to harm another human broke something inside Pike. Sobs wrenched through him, and he shook in the saddle. Beau shifted his weight underneath Pike and flicked his ears back and forth.

In an instant, Watson slid off his horse and moved to Pike's side. Grabbing the reins from Pike, he tried to steady Beau, who began to snort and stamp.

"Pike, step out of the stirrups," Watson held Pike's arm.

Pike's brain told him that Watson couldn't be trusted. Pike needed to kill him. He knew that this assignment was life or death for both of them, depending on their choices in the next twenty-four hours. But Pike's brain didn't register much else, being preoccupied with the image of his sweet mother dancing with the Devil.

In his mind, he saw the creature's suave human mask bowing like a gentleman to Pike's mother, dressed in her simple floral dress that she used to wear to church. She looked brave taking the Devil's hand. And they began to dance to a terrible song, a screeching melody that made Pike's hands tremble. During each turn, the Devil's carefully crafted disguise melted into more of the truth. An evil form began to appear beneath the dripping skin, black like tar, darker than night itself, and his beady red eyes stared into the depths of Pike's soul. Still yet, the Devil's limbs stretched and cracked until his body malformed into the pure evil being that Pike knew.

Watson tugged on Pike's arm, causing the mental image to disappear like smoke in the wind. Pike obeyed Watson's silent plea and slid out of the saddle into Watson's arms. Entire body shaking, Pike let himself be held up by this stranger.

Before that month, Pike hadn't cried in years. Not since his last beating when he'd failed to kidnap a young boy no older than five. He'd had to harden his emotions over the years, compartmentalizing in order to survive another day. He couldn't afford to have feelings. There was too much at stake. And yet here he was, being comforted in the middle of nowhere by the very man he was supposed to kill. He buried his face in Watson's shoulder, unable to control himself any longer, overwhelmed by mental anguish.

Watson Moore held Pike until there were no more tears left to cry, until the shaking turned to occasional tremors, and until the sun dipped just below the horizon, eerie shadows cast over the wasteland surrounding them.

When Pike stepped back to wipe his eyes with the balls of his hands, Watson's own eyes were red and puffy. Pike felt his skin grow hot when he realized how long he'd been crying, how long he'd bared his soul to this man he didn't even know, to this man whom he had to eliminate. Pike rubbed his sleeve on his nose, swallowing hard.

"Watson, I'm sorry. I didn't mean—" Pike's hoarse voice broke.

"I know, son." Watson gently patted Pike's shoulder. "Let's start a fire and warm up. These witching winds are hell."

16

The fire was built, a meal was made, tents were pitched, and nods of thanks were passed between men. Wind snapped the fabric of the tents back and forth, the night thick around them.

"I'll take the first watch," Watson whispered—the first words spoken since Pike had stopped crying.

Pike's head shot up at the sound of Watson's voice. The old man looked at Pike like he was trying to answer some sort of riddle.

Shaking his head, Pike stared at the ground. "I want you to know, I'm not going to do it tonight. You don't need to worry about me."

"I'm not worried *about* you, Pike. I'm worried *for* you."

Pike stared at the man's dusty boots, old and weathered. Watson hesitated for a moment, maybe hoping Pike would respond, but he walked away, out of the circle of light, before Pike could gather the courage to speak.

Pike stared into the fire for quite some time. He liked fire. *Normal* fire. Orange and red and yellow tendrils dancing together. It was natural.

A person could create it and build it and manipulate it. He could put it out, no problem.

But those silver flames.

They weren't natural. Only the Devil and his closest servants could make it and manipulate it. Only the Devil could put it out. And those flames ate everything thrown into it.

Year after year, Pike wondered if his fate would be those silver flames. Nightmares about them haunted him day and night. But if he was exhausted enough or intoxicated enough, he could at least black out for one night of cheap rest.

He didn't want to go to sleep even now, even with how tired he felt. He was empty.

"Maybe I should kill myself instead," Pike mumbled to the fire, his lone companion in the night.

Dying didn't scare him. But death. . .

He mostly wondered what happened after death. Would he feel pain or was it so quick that it would pass him by? Where would he end up? Would the Devil be shocked if they accidentally met in hell? He wondered about the truth, if he would still have to stand at Heaven's gates before he'd end up in his eternal resting place, staring judgment in the face.

Or maybe death wasn't as bad as people thought.

He fiddled with the trigger on his pistol, what-ifs echoing in his mind. The world would be better off without him anyway.

Instead, Pike crawled onto his sleeping mat in his tent and fought his restless sleep.

Dark dreams haunted his mind. Eerie shadows grew up from the branches dancing against the light of the full moon. Once again, he stood in front of a burning building. A house in the woods, filled with screams. A young girl trembled next to him, the firelight reflected in the tears streaming down her cheeks, her father screaming her name into the night.

She sprinted towards the flame, shoulders set and resolute. Pike ran after her in a moment, wrapping his arms around her waist, pulling her back. She kicked against him, sobbing.

"I have to save him," she cried. "He doesn't deserve it. He could change. He could—"

"You did what you had to," Pike whispered as kindly as he could into her ear.

She crumpled back into his chest. He held her up with his arms but loosened his hold slightly. She shook and cried, and they watched her family burn in the house that wasn't a home.

The picture of the house swirled into the shape of a red maple leaf landing on the surface of a still pond. The blue face of a drowned girl, lifeless and beautiful, looked up at him from under the surface. She could have been sleeping.

A woman stepped out of a nearby house to put the laundry out to dry. Pike left a single white chrysanthemum by the pond, with the girl's engagement ring and a note, before slipping into the shadows.

The picture changed once again, and this time, he stood in the garden in Greenwich with Cass. But the light that had danced in her brown eyes had dulled, the warmth in her skin had since gone cold. She slumped before him, a corpse, only a fragment of what she had once been.

Shadows curled around Pike's feet and floated around his arms in inky black smoke. He heard their raspy whispers, despite not being able to see their deformed faces.

"You did this, Alexander," the demons whispered. "You took away the innocence, killed the pure girl that you loved so dearly."

"I barely knew her," Pike breathed, suffocating under the pressure of the demons surrounding him.

"You killed Cassidy Jackson," they hissed.

Her body lifted in front of him, her debutante dress caught on the end of a crooked black finger. The Devil stepped out of the shadows, dangling Cass's body like it weighed nothing.

"You know you can stop at any moment, Alexander," the Devil's grating voice cracked in the silent night. "You can choose your life of quaint American dreams. But you will never be able to run from the demon within you. She will be corrupted. And she will fall because of her love for you. Do you really want to ruin another perfect soul?"

"No." Pike swallowed. "I would never hurt her. I wouldn't—"

"Even now, Alexander, are you really in control of yourself?" the Devil snarled. "Do you even know what your body is doing right this second? You have no control over the demon within."

"No," Pike breathed, taking a step back. Claws pushed back against him, and he stumbled forward, falling to a kneel in front of Cassidy's body.

The Devil lowered her onto her own two feet again. She looked down at Pike, eyes emotionless. "You did this to me. How could you?"

Pike began to weep. "Cass, please."

He reached up and wrapped her cold hand into his. She merely tilted her head the same unnatural angle as the Devil's.

"Please, Cass. I told you to forget me. I didn't want this."

"I loved you, Pike," Cass stated. *"And look what I got in return."*

A hand clasped his shoulder. Pike tried to swat away, not wanting to succumb to the demons. The hand shook his shoulder again.

As Pike turned, he met Watson's gaze. He was awake. He was trembling, drenched in a cold sweat. He was alive. But was Cass?

Watson raised an eyebrow. Pike shook his head when he stood, grabbing his gun and the coat he'd taken from the ranch. The winds were whistling through the brambles like in Pike's dream. He jerked his head to the side where low bushes rustled in the night, expecting the shadows to reach for him. It sent chills down Pike's spine.

Still on high alert, Pike moved about twenty or thirty yards from the tent. With the night clear above him, the solar system had erupted in a work of art, stars settling like dust amongst the constellations painted in a light green hue. It made him feel small, but in a good way. The same way standing on top of a mountain makes you feel awed and insignificant. Pike needed insignificant after the nightmares.

Crossing his legs and gazing at the stars, he made himself comfortable on the ground, trying to shake the feeling of being watched. His thoughts drifted to the man not too far away from him. He wondered about Watson's faith and if maybe he could use that as his last resort.

Maybe he could have a better life if he only tried.

Pike cleared his throat. "I don't know if you can hear me. I don't know if you'd even care about me, knowing who I work for. I'm not even sure if you could help me at this point. But. . ."

Pike hesitated. He'd kept his dreams locked safe inside for so long, knowing he might never have the chance to make them come true. He'd hinted at dreams when talking with his mother, but he'd always been afraid to jinx himself by stating it all out loud or risk the Devil hearing. And it was vulnerable. Vulnerable was difficult for him.

"I want—"

A gust of wind hit his back, and a flash of silver light nearly blinded him. Pike raised his arm to cover his eyes, wondering if God had sent an angel like He had in the past for other people.

Instead, a sickly smooth voice crooned, "Well, this is unexpected."

Pike blinked rapidly as he scrambled to his feet, trying to regain his sight.

"Really, Pike," the Devil stared at him in amusement, outfitted in his usual suit and styled dark hair. "I thought prayers were beneath you. I mean, you of all people. It's surprising, really."

"I still have one more day," Pike stuttered, panic filling every part of his soul.

Even though Silvertongue stood in front of his silver flame, illuminated, sharp white teeth glimmering. "You do. I was checking in, seeing how things were going."

"Checking in?" Pike tilted his head to the side, trying to mask his heavy, panicked breathing. "I always finish my jobs. You know that. You've never needed to check in on me."

"Until now, Alexander. Things change. *You* change. Your poor, fickle, *human* heart can't help it. It pines for another person or a dream that you'll never accomplish."

Pike stayed silent, looking to the side away from the Devil's piercing gaze. He hoped that he could hide the reddening of his face and the way his hands still shook after his dream. He bit his tongue to hold back his emotions, all his feelings for Cass, and their imaginary future.

"Oh, dear," the Devil mocked. "Do you really not remember the discussion we had moments ago? What about that darling girl, Cassidy? Or that cabin you've been wanting in the mountains all alone to yourself and your nonexistent family? Please, Alexander. Don't play dumb. It doesn't suit you."

Silvertongue stepped next to Pike, shoulder to shoulder but facing the opposite direction, and leaned over to whisper in Pike's ear. "Do you think your mother would approve of her? Do you think little Cass would care about the real you, the human slave? Would she appreciate your status? Right hand man of Satan himself?"

Pike's ears started to ring. He tried to ignore what his boss had said, but the words hit their mark. She would never love him if she truly knew him. He was poor—less than poor. He was worth more dead than alive at that point. And she wouldn't want anything to do with Pike if she found out the truth. Silvertongue laughed, a devious sort of laughter that echoed and folded in on itself all at once.

How could he have ever thought that his dream life could be possible? He still didn't know how much debt his family owed, much less what his great, great someone or other did in the first place to owe such a tremendous debt to the Devil himself. And how could he believe in a brighter future when his consequences had already done their work inside of him?

"Dearest Pike," Silvertongue tutted. "It doesn't do to dwell on dreams. Much dreaming and many words are meaningless as the great King Solomon once said."

"You're quoting the Bible at me?" Pike asked, furrowing his eyebrows.

The man shrugged and made a face. "I've been doing this for millennia, my friend. It's what I do." His smile turned into a sneer. "Get the job done. If you fail, there are consequences. *No* sentiments. *No* dreams. You work for me."

As the Devil started walking away and the silver flames followed, he began to whistle a jaunty tune. However, before getting more than a few steps away, he paused, head inclined to the side. He turned his head

133

ever so slightly toward Pike, looking at him from the corner of his empty eyes. "And Pike?"

"What?"

"Do tell your old friend that he won't be seeing his daughters for Christmas this year."

And with another gust of witching winds, the silver flames swallowed the Devil, and left Pike standing alone in the dark feeling very, very small.

As he turned around, he saw a body silhouetted by firelight. Pike sighed heavily from the weight of the conversation. With a shake of his head, he picked up his pistol from where he'd dropped it in the dirt. He trudged over to Watson who stood like a statue on the edge of their campsite.

Pike swallowed, his throat feeling constricted and tongue dry. He shook his head in response to the silent question that loomed over them.

Watson barely nodded. He beckoned Pike back towards the fire, nearly embers at this point, and took a seat. He poked at the embers, and a few reddish-orange flames perked up.

"What did our *friend* have to say tonight?" Watson asked like he talked about a mutual friend.

Pike shook his head. "Nothing particularly kind, except he did quote the Bible at me."

"Oh?" Watson raised an eyebrow. "And?"

Shrugging, Pike stared into the fire. "Something about dreaming being meaningless."

"Ecclesiastes," Watson grinned, pulling a small book out of the inside pocket of his coat where it had rested against his chest. He tapped the cover and held it reverently in his hands.

"What?"

"Well," Watson thumbed through the yellowed pages, "the man who wrote that book was very rich and very wise, but he lost himself for a while. He indulged in many things, and in the end, he declared everything meaningless."

"Sounds like depression."

"Maybe, but at the end of chapters worth of meaningless things and what *not* to do based on his own experiences, he comes to one conclusion." Watson pointed at Pike with the old book. "Fear God and obey Him. That's our whole job as humans."

"Fear God? Is He worse than the Devil?" Pike asked, slumping his shoulders and looking away. "The Man upstairs feels like a killjoy."

"Sometimes it seems that way, but He's far from it." Watson grew silent, adding another small branch to the fire. "We don't quite understand the full picture like He does, so sometimes He says no to our dreams. But it also says if we trust Him and do good, that He grants the desires of the righteous."

"And if you're not righteous?"

Watson shook his head. "No one is righteous. Knowing Him, walking alongside Him. . . that brings you closer. But you can't earn it. It's a gift."

Pike cleared his throat. "Do you think He knows who I am? And if He does, why would He give me anything? We both know that I don't deserve mercy."

Watson sighed. "It's something I've struggled with myself, but there's always hope for men like us."

Pike hesitated in his answer, wondering what Watson meant by the words *men like us*.

What has he done worth eternal damnation?

"I think I'm too far gone for forgiveness." Pike finally said, wiping his nose on his coat sleeve. "I've done too many terrible things. Even now—" Voice breaking, he turned away.

Watson shook his head. "No one is too far, Pike. Not even you. You've made mistakes, sure. But you are not a mistake." He stood and replaced the book in his coat pocket. "I think we're pretty safe out here now that our friend is gone, don't you think?"

Pike didn't answer. He couldn't even pull his thoughts together enough to give one.

"Pike, you need some rest."

Despite not wanting to lay down again, Pike shuffled to his tent, curling up on his sleeping mat, thoughts jumbled and confusing. One tent over, Watson sang a hymn about a story and blood. Something twisted in Pike's gut thinking of how Watson's blood would spill.

That will be the end of his story.

It was odd, laying there in the dark listening to words that sounded so foreign yet so familiar. He thought of his mother. Of his childhood before his father had died. Of hope. And he found himself drifting to sleep easier than he had in seven years.

And he dreamt of Cass, alive this time, the only woman who had ever made him believe in love. The only woman who had ever made him feel like it was something he could have.

She laughed in his dream, so full of light, alive in every way. And they had children. Three. Two daughters and a son. But something told him that his son wasn't Alexander Pike VII.

One way or another, the family business would end with Pike.

17

When Watson woke him before the sun rose, Pike—bitter that his good dream wasn't a reality— was grateful that his nightmares weren't true. Watson's words from the night before rolled in his head like waves on the shore. Back and forth.

No one is too far. Not even you.

Low-covering clouds that threatened rain blanketed the sky. The air felt wet in Pike's lungs, and the cold sank through to his bones. He shivered involuntarily, though he wasn't sure if the cold had gotten to him or the reality of Watson's imminent death.

They'd quickly packed up camp in the blue hour of the morning and set out on horseback, trotting further north. The riding felt easier than the previous day, and Pike hoped he might not be so sore after riding so often.

As the sun rose and lightened the clouds around them, Watson pulled Bones back to a walking pace. "What a beautiful, misty morning. Don't you think so, Pike?"

"I don't understand how you can have such a happy outlook on today," Pike whispered. "I feel sick. The time is seeping away."

"Oh, come on." Watson swatted the air. "None of that kind of talk. We're going to have a great day. What could be better?" Watson smiled then clicked his tongue. Bones began climbing, starting their hike into the mountains.

Pike welcomed the distraction of guiding Beau around bushes and through the rocky paths. They stopped for a quick lunch of dried meat and bread and to let the horses rest for a bit, sheltering from some of the drizzly weather of the morning. Then they started off again. They didn't talk much, but Watson sang most of the way up the mountain.

"Usually," he had explained, "Benji is playing songs, keeping us entertained. And while I enjoy it, I also think that singing is the truest form of music. Just my thoughts and my words."

And he went back to singing again.

Pike hummed along occasionally, recalling deeply hidden memories of hymns and church services he'd attended as a child. But he never sang. Something about the weight of the lyrics made him hesitant to say them out loud.

Once they found themselves near the top of the peaks, they stopped. Watson slid off Bones and left him snacking on some brush. Pike followed suit and found the older man overlooking the valley below them, horizon muddled by the rain that they had thankfully missed for the most part. Bits of the view were curtained by clouds, though you could see the effects of the wind blowing them quickly to the east.

"What a beautiful view," Watson whispered. He glanced at Pike. "Where do you want to be?"

"Sorry?"

"Tonight," Watson answered. "Where do you want to be? The sun will start to set in an hour or so. I could forage for some things and make us a nice dinner."

"Watson, do you hear yourself?"

Watson raised his eyebrows. "I haven't suddenly gone deaf, so yes, I hear myself loud and clear."

"I can't believe how calm you're being about all of this!" Pike motioned in the air. "You're talking about making your last meal."

"And?" Watson stared Pike down, his dark eyes steeled beneath his graying brows.

"I don't understand what you're trying to do here. I can't not kill you."

"I don't expect you not to kill me. I fully intend to die on this mountain. Ethan and Benji will come bury me up here and set up a memorial at my favorite spot."

Pike put his hands on his hips. "Pardon?"

Watson gazed down at the dirt beneath their feet. "Pike. . . There wasn't any work to do out here. I rather like this mountain and preferred something a bit more secluded for the task at hand. I'd hate to cause a ruckus in town or at the ranch when you. . ." He swirled his hand in the air.

"I cannot believe you." Pike shook his head. "You are joking with me, right? You're not serious."

Watson raised his hands. "Pike, I'm not upset about this. I knew it would come eventually. I am at peace. I had to let the boys know where we were going and why, so they'd be able to bring news and closure to my family. I promise, all is well, Pike."

Pike met the old man's kind eyes. He sighed heavily and glanced away again. He could've been upset with Watson, but instead he was angry with himself. He should've known. Watson had been too accepting of him, covered in someone else's blood. From the beginning, he had stood his ground, all the while planning his own funeral.

Watson stepped toward him and patted Pike on the shoulder. "Why don't you set up camp like we usually would. Clear out a space and start a fire."

Watson untied a leather satchel from his saddle and threw it over one shoulder, setting off away from Pike, whistling while he walked.

Standing there on the mountain, overlooking what seemed like the entire world, Pike felt small again. He was helpless to the events unfolding before him, helpless to control any part of his life.

Despite their tense situation, Watson had been nothing but gracious to him, even knowing their relationship would end among blood and gunsmoke. His kind demeanor had won Pike over, but what did that leave them with? Watson would still die, and Pike would still be a monster.

Pike exhaled deeply and looked at the horses. "I guess it's the three of us now."

He unloaded the horses' packs first and loosened their saddles a bit to help them be a little more comfortable. He then gathered as much dry kindling and sticks as he could find to start their fire, now that the damp weather receded. Digging through Watson's belongings, Pike found his matches. Striking one, he carefully lit the kindling and tended to the fire until it crackled all on its own. He placed a few logs here and there for the fire, then went to set up tents.

By the time both tents were pitched and furnished with their mats, Pike's stomach rumbled. Regret kept resurfacing in Pike's mind for meeting Watson under these circumstances. He had a feeling that they would have been great friends any other time.

Stepping to his own tent, Pike pulled out and examined his pistol. It felt heavy in his hand and colder than the winds around him. His stomach turned, his mouth watering.

He laid the gun down inside his tent, burying his head in his hands.

As a child, he knew he'd take over his father's job, but he figured he would've been much older than fifteen. Now at twenty-two years of age, Pike felt like nothing that he did after this night would mean anything. Did he have a choice? But there was no good option, no good alternative.

He thought back to Watson's words about Ecclesiastes.

Meaningless.

How was he going to go through with this? Watson said he was at peace, but how could Pike look this kind man in the eyes and end his life?

Pike's head snapped up at the sound of a voice drifting in the air. After several moments, Pike relaxed a little. Watson sang to himself again. He carried the satchel like before, but it looked weighted now.

Watson sighed with a smile. "We were lucky enough that the birds

haven't gotten to the persimmons yet. And plenty of greens. Oh!"
Watson brightened and dug a handful of pecans from his pocket. "I found these too!"

"With the rest of the dried meat that we have, it looks like we'll have a decent meal tonight," Pike tried to feign a little bit of happiness.

"Come on, Pike." Watson tucked the pecans back in his pocket. "I'm famished!"

Pike pulled out their campware and boiled a bit of water. He soaked the dried meat while Watson rinsed the greens and stuck them in the hot water. While Pike watched the pot, Watson searched the ground around them.

After a few minutes, he returned with a handful of a yellowed-tinged small plant that resembled a bristle brush. Watson stripped the stalk and tossed the seeds into the pot with greens.

"What's that?" Pike asked.

"Wild mustard." Watson passed Pike a small stalk then bit the top of one right off, chewing up the plant. "Go on, try it. It's spicy."

Wary and a little perturbed about eating a weed that could've been eaten by the horses, Pike nibbled off the top bit of the wild mustard plant. At first, it tasted like dry grass, but the flavor quickly melted into a spicy sweetness that almost tasted like sweet peppers.

"This isn't terrible," Pike said.

With a laugh, Watson stirred the pot of greens. "Fidei sicut sinapis sedis, Pike. That's all it is."

And before Pike could ask what it meant in English, Watson went back to singing. He passed Pike the leather satchel and a knife. Inside sat the bright orange persimmons, a sunset captured in a bag.

Pike had never seen a persimmon eaten before, but he figured maybe you could cut it like a date or a fig. He wasn't even sure if it had a pit or seeds in the middle, so he started by cutting the first one in half. Instead of finding tiny seeds, the meaty flesh of the fruit along with a few long seeds sat in his palm.

"They taste almost like apricots," Watson commented.

Pike's eyebrows pulled together as he scooped out the seeds with his knife and set the rest of the fruit on one of the camp plates they'd brought. He did the same with the other half and cut the rest of the persimmons the same way. They smelled sweet, but they were unlike anything he'd eaten.

"Pecan?" Watson asked, tossing one in Pike's direction. Pike crushed it under his foot and ate the inside of the nut like he used to do with his father. At the remembrance, his throat tightened, and he quickly set back to work.

Finally, they sat down, camp tins in hand.

"Thank you for this food," Watson beamed at the hazy view behind them. "And bless all of Pike's endeavors."

Pike choked on a bite of fruit. All of his endeavors included Watson's death. All of his endeavors meant obeying the Devil. There's no way that his endeavors would be blessed.

"So, Pike," Watson took a piece of persimmon, "where are you off to next? Back to the wilds of the Washington Territory?"

Shifting, Pike replied, "I think we're going up to Lankin in the Montana Territory. I don't know what my job will be up there. But I'm hoping to go back home for a while after that. I'll have to convince. . ."

In Pike's pause, Watson grunted. "If you do get to go home, where is that? Seattle?"

"Morville. A ways northeast of Seattle."

"Washington is a place I still haven't been." Watson closed his eyes. "I'd like to go someday."

He began to sing a song while Pike ate his dinner. Watson's words carried on the wind and through the sparse trees.

When peace, like a river, attendeth my way,
When sorrows like sea billows roll;
Whatever my lot, thou hast taught me to say,
It is well, it is well with my soul.

"I love that song." Pulling out a handkerchief, Watson wiped his face and patted against his chest where he'd slipped that small book into his coat pocket.

Pike watched Watson from the outside, like he wasn't truly present.

"My daughters used to sing that with me," Watson continued. "They're visiting family out East until the new year."

"They're very lucky to have a father like you, Watson."

The old man beamed with pride. "I am blessed to have them. No doubt they'll sing that song during Christmas this year for me." He nodded, a smile still on his lips. "But I think it's high time I head home."

Pike was about to ask what he meant when Watson cleared his throat and placed a hand on his hip.

"Pike," Watson took a shaky breath. "I need you to do something for me."

As Pike looked up, Watson bent over his saddle bag by his tent and dug until he found a small rectangle. Watson passed him a cheaply framed tintype photograph of a family. Watson looked back at him only without gray hair, and straight-faced as the custom, standing with three elegantly clad ladies.

Watson cleared his throat again. "I want you to keep this. And if you ever find yourself back east again, up in Boston, ask around for the Moore family. I know you'll find them somehow. Tell them that I love them dearly."

Pike shook his head. "Watson, I can't do this. I'm not—"

"It's your job. And besides, my time has come." Watson pressed the frame into Pike's hands. "Please."

Pike slipped the frame into the inside pocket of his coat, shoulders slumping while he tried to stop his hands from shaking.

"Well," Watson glanced back at the dying light breaking beneath the cloud line, "I think it's almost time, don't you?"

He stood and walked over to Bones, his old friend. He whispered in the horse's ear and stroked his nose with affection. Giving the massive beast a hug, Watson kissed Bones's nose gently and scratched his ears in a final goodbye.

18

They moved away from their camp and horses. Pike's gun now hung weighty in the holster strapped to his belt, seeming to grow heavier and heavier until he almost couldn't bear it.

Though they were already high up, Watson led him up a path leading eastward, and they wound their way to the true peak of the mountain.

Watson finally stopped their excursion where it felt like one could see both sides of the world. The eastern wind whistled in their ears, desperate to carry the sound of death on its back. The horizon slowly revealed itself in the last light of day, flat land stretching into infinity, half-digested hills dotting the countryside.

In any other circumstance, Pike might have enjoyed such a view. But the wind and the openness of it all made it seem like eyes were watching them. The idea settled heavily in Pike's mind.

"Is this suitable enough?" Watson asked.

Pike shook his head, afraid to speak.

Nothing would be suitable for this.

Watson smiled but didn't reply. He stepped close and pulled Pike into an embrace. The two men stood, Pike holding on to the moment for as long as he could. When Pike pulled away, the last light of the sun fell in his eyes. He knew that Watson could see the tears streaming down his cheeks.

"Pike, I want you to remember me this way." Watson placed a dark hand on his own chest. "No matter where you are, picture me singing and trekking through the brush. Can you do that?"

Pike shook his head again.

This isn't right.

Why would God allow this to happen? It didn't make any sense. Maybe He could provide a way out.

Pike could prolong it, waiting until midnight to fulfill his job. They still had a little more time.

Watson must've seen the look in Pike's eyes change because he shook his head. "We do this now. I want to die while the earth can still see me."

Pike swallowed and choked back his emotion, furiously wiping his tears away. He stumbled a few steps backwards. The fading sunlight outlined Watson, the picture of a true cowboy. He faced Pike with a smile, eyes glistening.

"Whenever you're ready, Pike."

Pike took in a shuddered breath, body shivering from the wind that whipped around them. His hands trembled, and he prayed that the bullet would hit its mark rather than miss and cause a prolonged, excruciating death.

The wind kicked up, blowing both of the men's scarves and Pike's hair. Dust swirled at their feet. Pulling off his hat, Watson turned to gaze after the wind into the sunset. Pike recalled his own words to Hank in Jethro, Alabama, at the beginning of November, seeming like ages ago though it had only been ten days.

Death comes for us all, he had told the young man. *In the end, we are not cowards for facing it. We are brave. Death is nothing to fear.*

But here, now, facing a man who was truly brave, Pike felt like a coward. A coward who ended lives without thought in order to save his own neck.

"Watson?" Pike called out over the roaring wind.

Watson said nothing but turned back to the tortured young man.

Pike's dirty blonde hair blew in front of his ice blue eyes, scarf whipping in the wind. His hands shook involuntarily, and his face twisted with anguish.

"I won't forgive myself for this," he cried.

Watson didn't respond immediately. He looked once more at the painted skies that stretched for forever. When he faced Pike again, something had changed in his demeanor, more set, more resolute.

"I forgive you, Pike."

A sob wrenched from Pike's throat. He bit his tongue in hopes of holding himself together for a moment longer and cocked the gun. Every muscle in his body screamed in protest. He should've been glad to kill the man that had forced him to inherit his father's job. The man who had taken everything from him. But instead, Pike's heart sank from the weight.

"I'm sorry, Watson. I'm so sorry."

Watson smiled.

The gunshot echoed across the valley.

People must have heard it for miles, a gunshot echoing on the November winds. But no one could have known that a broken young man crumpled to the ground seconds after an older man fell and laid silent. No one knew that the words "I forgive you" could do so much damage to an already fractured soul.

The sun sank below the horizon while Pike sat back on his heels and screamed. If Silvertongue showed up now, Pike would beg for death because it had to be better than heartache.

If he could go back, he'd take Watson's place. There was no use living a lie. And if anyone deserved to live, it would be Watson Moore. The weight of Pike's borrowed gun, though lighter by one bullet, felt heavier as he slid it back into its holster.

He pulled himself to his feet, vision still blurred by tears. He couldn't bring himself to look at the body, to see Watson's eyes lifeless. So instead, he stumbled back to their campsite where the horses seemed to think nothing had changed.

Bones lifted his ears when Pike approached. All Pike could do was shake his head. The horse's friend would not return.

Pike fell to the ground by his tent, hot tears still running down his cheeks. It stung the wound nearly healed on his nose, reminding him of how much he'd been hurt, broken, left to pick up the pieces. Scrubbing his face, trying to stop himself from spilling anymore tears, Pike looked around. He needed to leave. He didn't want to be near their camp, afraid of seeing the memory of Watson roaming the hills.

He rolled up his mat first and disassembled his tent, packing them away. Pike felt for the tintype in the photo frame in his coat pocket. The flat, hard object sat against his chest near his heart. He'd carry this until he found the Moore family or until he died, but it would always be special.

A reminder.

He thought momentarily of the book Watson kept on him and cursed. He should've gotten it before he'd left. But he couldn't bring himself to face Watson's body again.

Instead, Pike set off down the mountain, leaving the horses next to a dying fire in the dark. Ethan and Benji would be there in the morning to take care of Watson's body, and they'd take care of the horses then. He shook the thought from his mind, hoping to forget how heavily Watson's body had hit the ground.

The way it didn't stir.

In the dark he lost his way several times, having to double back and find the path again. He slid down rocky portions, scattering pebbles down the mountainside. But finally, he made it to the base of the mountains, stars hidden from view by the incoming clouds. The wind still whistled in his ears, still hungry for more.

He wished it away. Pike hated its constant company.

A blur of time passed before he made it to a crossroads, but the Devil already awaited him.

"You finally made it," the Devil sighed. "It took you long enough. I trust you finished the job?"

Pike simply nodded. His throat was dry, and his lips felt like they were glued together. He didn't have much to say anyway.

"Are we ready for Lankin then?" Silvertongue tilted his head to the side, the movement unnatural, enough to put any man on edge.

Pike nodded again.

"I take your silence as a good sign."

The Devil squeezed Pike's shoulder, and the world spun once again. But this time Pike's vision grew darker and darker, and the entirety of his senses disappeared into nothingness.

Everything was meaningless.

Everything was dark.

He was formless and empty.

19

D reams, ceaseless dreams.
Dark hands.
Shadows.
A blinding light.
Silver flames.
Pain.
Nothing.

When Pike woke, it took him several minutes to fully return to awareness. He lay in a hospital bed. Alone.

I'm not dead.

And then the crushing weight of grief hit him again. But no tears came. He felt empty, numb.

He fell back into oblivion.

Floating in and out of consciousness, Pike waltzed between night-mares dancing with the Devil and watching Watson's body fall again and again.

Eventually, a nurse walked in and noticed him stirring. She quickly left the room and brought back a doctor who ran some tests and checked vitals. Unaware of the passing of time, Pike pushed down thoughts and memories of Watson. His kind demeanor, his last words.

I forgive you, Pike.

Coming to again, Pike saw a blurry shape next to his bedside. The nurse made notes, most likely about Pike and his progress. Pike wondered what had happened, if this sort of sickness came from the Devil or some natural occurrence.

"Miss?" he croaked.

She turned towards him, surprised. "I'm glad to see you awake!"

"Where am I? What happened?"

The nurse smiled sadly. "I'll send the doctor in, and he'll explain everything for you."

Apparently, Pike had fallen to some sort of fever in his travels. The doctor told him that his *friend* had brought Pike to the hospital in urgency, and they'd caught whatever it was in time. They were able to keep Pike stable while his body recovered from whatever ailed him.

If that story happened to be true, then the sickness wouldn't have been caused by the Devil no matter how much Pike wanted to put the blame on him. No, this was something different, something metaphysical.

"What day is it?" Pike asked, voice hoarse from not using it for a while.

"November 22nd," the doctor answered with a smile. "Welcome to Lankin."

Pike had lost twelve days.

They wanted to keep him overnight one more night, but they said his friend wanted to visit him first. After helping him bathe and feeding him, the doctors let the Devil in to see Pike. Instead of his usual dark evening suit, he wore a walking suit, looking like a businessman.

"Alexander, you are looking much better." He raised an eyebrow. "Twelve days. You gave me quite a scare."

Pike glanced around and noticed a few nurses close enough that they might be able to hear. He had to be careful with his words.

"I didn't think you could get scared by anything," Pike replied.

Silvertongue shrugged. "I would hate for you to get sick on my watch. It must've been all that dust and wind further east."

Pike nodded. "Maybe so."

He felt so empty.

Silvertongue patted Pike's shoulder like an old friend despite the tension between them. "Well, hopefully you'll feel well enough tomorrow that we can get on the road back home. No sense in lingering too much after that funeral."

Pike's heart sank. He wondered if this *disease* would flare up from now on. He wondered if something inside of him had changed. Seven years, hundreds of faces, yet one atrocious month and everything fell apart. Would he slip into a fever the next time he had to kill someone? Would he even be able to complete his assignments if his body reacted this way?

During the night spent in the hospital, tossing restlessly, Pike drifted in and out of consciousness, sleep coming close and blowing away like smoke. Fragments of dreams came clear only to melt away soon after.

Faces.

Never-ending faces.

If he had to put a number to how many people haunted him, he would have guessed more than three hundred. Some were dead, some long since calloused to joy, and others only mourned the lost innocence of childhood. But all of them felt like failures to Pike.

Each moment, a chance for him to say no.

Each one a reminder of what he had become.

The next morning, the Devil returned.

He'd handled all forms of payment, so they only had to collect Pike's things. As soon as he received his coat, Pike felt for the Moore family photo. It still rested in its pocket, safe and sound. And his pistol still hung in its holster.

The two set out on foot away from the hospital, down the main road covered in a layer of snow, and out of town before speaking a single word.

"The Lankin job," Silvertongue started. "It's an odd job. I need you to talk to this man."

"Talk to him?"

"I need you to convince him that God isn't real. Make him doubt."

"That's it?"

"That's it."

Pike walked along in silence for a while before asking, "What if I can't?"

"You kill him. But he doesn't need to know that."

Pike shuddered internally, knowing that he'd have to kill again. A week or two ago, that might not have bothered him so much. What if he fell into a fever again? Maybe he wouldn't get so involved this time.

"Where?" he asked, cowboy boots crunching in the snow.

"A river up north. There are some loggers that can take you up the mountain. Explore the area."

"Name?"

Silvertongue turned. "Hickory."

"Sorry?"

"He goes by Hickory."

Silvertongue stopped walking and squinted back down the road. Pike stopped and watched his boss. The snow began to fall in soft flakes, a contrast to the sharp man who stood before him. Despite the years of working by the Devil's side, it unnerved Pike how suave, how normal the Devil could be. And really, how little Pike knew about him.

Pike swallowed down fear while he mentally pushed away the flashbacks again, watching Silvertongue carefully.

"Alexander. . ." the Devil began, shoulders slouching slightly.

Pike raised his eyebrows. This was a new tone of voice from Silvertongue. Was it sympathy? Doubt? Exhaustion?

"I've known your family for centuries. Well, a century and a half at least. But the sun is setting on our time together."

"I don't understand." Pike's heart pounded.

"You have one more job after Lankin. One more."

Pike hesitated. "And. . . I'm done?" He tried to push away the hope that fluttered in his chest. Surely it had to be some twisted game.

The Devil straightened. "The clock is striking twelve. After you complete this job at Lankin, I'll give you your final job."

Pike nodded eagerly. "Thank you."

"I'll see you when I see you." Silvertongue turned on his heel, whatever emotion that had weighed on him fading away as quickly as it had arrived.

"No time limit?" Pike called after him.

Silvertongue tilted his head. "Do you want a time limit?"

Pike shrugged. "You've never not given me a time limit. . . So I talk to this guy?"

"Or kill him if he doesn't recant."

"No time? Just find him?"

The Devil rolled his eyes. "I'm starting to get very impatient. Yes! Find him, have a little chat that ends in blood, and be done with it! You have a name, you're in the town, you have a pistol. Now go!"

Silvertongue disappeared before his shout had even finished. Something inside of Pike told him to doubt the Devil, that he couldn't possibly let Pike go. The debt couldn't have been paid. And even if it was, why didn't the Devil lie and tell Pike it wasn't?

There's a trick somewhere to find.

Pike shook those thoughts away.

November 23rd ticked on minute by minute. He had a job to do.

He walked back into town alone.

As he walked through the snowy streets, he took notice of the drifts and shoveled piles on each side of the road. They were all tinted brown by the dust and dirt and muck. Pike buttoned up his coat, counting his steps.

One. . . Two. . . Three. . .

He made it to six before his mind slipped back to Oklahoma.

Again.

One. . . Two. . .

That damned song flitted through his head.

Again!

One. . .

Watson. He couldn't get rid of that smile.

Pike tugged his hat closer and tucked his nose under his wild rag. It was too cold. It was too still.

He remembered the stillness of the body.

The stillness of the night.

How the gunshot echoed.

Get it together.

Ragged breaths came to Pike now while his eyes flicked from building to building. Lots of their windows were decorated with boards, sheltering from the harsh winter. Some had glistening yellow lights peeking out into the gray day.

A drink.

He glanced over his shoulder down the empty lane before crossing over to the saloon. A fiddle melody drifted out the doors when Pike stepped inside. The warmth hit him with such force that he stood still for a moment. His clothes stuck to him as he slipped off his hat and into a chair by the bar.

"It breaks my heart to think of her now," a bearded man sang from the corner. "She has curled these locks, she has kissed this brow."

A moment passed before Pike adjusted his eyesight to see the room fully, musicians looking like Watson's wranglers.

"Oh bury me not," the bearded man sang. "And his voice failed there. But they took no heed to his dying prayer. In a narrow grave, just six by three they buried him there on the lone prairie."

"Can I get you anything, darling?"

Pike shot his head to where a woman stood behind the counter pouring a drink. She wore a long cream colored dress with colorful embroidery and fringe. Her dark hair, braided and pinned low, peeked out underneath a beige stetson. And she watched him with bright and piercing eyes.

"Something warm," he mumbled, turning his eyes down to the bar where his hat lay.

"All right. Are you passing through?" She turned away, pulling a bottle and a glass from the shelf.

Pike wondered how small Lankin was, if this woman who heard all would know of him. "I've been in the hospital for the past twelve days."

"So you're the stranger," she narrowed her eyes at him then pulled a jar of something cloudy brown out of the cabinet below the counter. "Are you feeling any better?"

Pike hesitated then shook his head. "Still not quite myself."

"And who exactly are you?" She unscrewed the lid on the jar and set it down. It read *honey* in curly lettering. She spooned some into the empty glass then screwed the lid back on.

"Alexander," he offered a small smile.

"Phoebe," she smiled back. After dosing it out, Phoebe poured what looked to be rum or maybe whiskey over the honey.

"Alexander," she hummed when she turned her back on him again, pouring water into the glass from a pitcher. Making her way back to where he sat, she grabbed a toddy iron from the fireplace. "Where are you headed?"

The drink sizzled and steamed as she submerged the tip of the rod into the beverage, swirling it slightly. Pulling the rod out and setting it to the side, she grated spices over the top of the drink.

Pike shrugged. "I'm not sure. I've been sent to talk to a man up in the mountains, but I don't know these parts very well."

Phoebe slid the drink to Pike. "See those men over in the corner?"

Pike turned around to where the men sat picking their instruments. The bearded man bounced his head along to the beat.

"The musicians?"

"Loggers," Phoebe corrected. "They'll be leaving soon."

Pike watched the bearded man singing once again. "And the cowboys now as they roam the plain, for they marked the spot where his bones were lain. Fling a handful of roses o'er his grave with a prayer to

God his soul to save."

Pike swallowed, thinking of Ethan and Benji who must've buried Watson's body on the mountain. "And these loggers can help me?"

He turned back to the woman who nodded. "They'll get you to where you need to go. Keep in mind that it'll be below freezing out there tonight. Snow storm could be blowing in soon."

Pike held the hot drink in his hands, smelling the spices. "Don't tell me that. I won't want to leave the warmth of the saloon."

Phoebe laughed a laugh as piercing as her gaze. It fell oddly flat in his ears. He loved making women laugh, but none compared to the one he left behind in Greenwich whose laugh felt like fire on a cold night.

"Angus is my brother," Phoebe pointed to one of the loggers. "He can help you."

Pike laid his payment down and raised his glass in thanks. He made his way over to the musicians in the corner.

"Afternoon," he put his hat back on. "Phoebe said to talk to Angus."

"That would be me," the banjo player said. "What can I do for you, stranger?"

"I need help navigating up the mountain."

Raising an eyebrow, Angus smiled. "You're lucky we haven't left yet. Where are you headed?"

"To a man called Hickory's," Pike drank deeply of the warm beverage. It filled in all of the cracks in his spirit that had opened up over the past few weeks. Despite the darkness sinking in his soul, the drink made him feel warm and safe.

"Hickory's," Angus repeated.

"Yes, sir," Pike glanced at the other men who were chuckling.

Angus sighed. "We can get you there if that's what you really want."

"Thank you. I'll help out any way I can."

They began their trek after a small lunch at the saloon and didn't stop until late that evening after the sun had sunk below the horizon and the gray clouds turned charcoal like a smothered fire. Pike had spent the hike convincing himself that all he'd done would be worth it with his debt paid in full.

It will all be worth it.

"We'll set up camp here," said the bearded man whom Pike had come to know as Chief. "Angus, start a fire. It's looking to be a cold night."

They all dropped their gear and began working on a campsite. Without having much to do, Pike dusted the snow off of a partially buried stone and sat breathing hard. The snow proved a challenge for Pike's cowboy boots, but he managed well enough to keep up until they stopped.

Pike shivered despite his coat and hat. Luckily, the loggers came prepared, and he tucked into a canvas tent with a few other men and plenty of blankets. They all bedded down, Pike included, cozied up for the night.

While Pike didn't sleep soundly in fear of having nightmares in front of these strangers, he fell into a sort of daze. Between the sounds of the forest and the quiet hum of breath coming from the loggers, Pike felt a sense of peace and community.

The next morning, the loggers were up before dawn, cooking breakfast and planning their cutting spots for the day. Pike took the opportunity in the quiet moment by the fire to ask about Hickory. At first, he got a few strange looks from some of the men, especially Chief. He'd received the same reaction the day before in the saloon. Thankfully Angus happened to know where Hickory's cabin might be.

"You don't want to be hanging around him too much," Chief said.

"No, you don't want to catch the contagious insanity," another man laughed.

"What are they talking about?" Pike asked Angus.

He shrugged. "He's a little off his rocker. Sometimes people see him in town hauling a wagon full of boxes. But he doesn't talk to people very much. He used to play music in town weekly, but now. . . It's rumored that one time he tried to befriend a grizzly bear. He's lucky to be alive, that one."

Angus sipped his coffee.

"But why do they call him Hickory?" Pike rubbed his hands together.

He shrugged again. "No one really knows. No one cares to get close enough to ask. I don't think the light is all the way on, if you know what I mean."

Pike nodded. "Well, I have to find him. I'm contracted to work out here and he's involved. Do you think he'll be at his cabin?"

The man tilted his head side to side. "Like I said, no one cares to get close to him. No one really knows what he does on a daily basis. There are rumors he does business in town on occasion. But if you're going to hike there and back before tonight, I suggest you start now. You wouldn't want to be caught in the open at night out here in the wilderness."

The man pulled a notebook out of his bag and ripped a sheet out. He scribbled several lines on it and circled a small house-like square that he'd drawn.

"That's old Hickory's cabin. Best route is following the river up north and branching off once you hit this rocky patch here." He indicated little circular scribbles he'd made. "There should be a service road out there somewhere, and if you keep following that road, old Hickory's cabin is off a side path that's tucked in the trees."

"Thank you." Pike accepted the rudimentary map. "You have no idea how much you've helped me."

"Right, well you need to get a move on. Take these." The man tossed a pair of thick leather gloves at him.

"Thank you." Pike smiled. And off he went with a hand-drawn map, a pistol, and a name.

In the grand scheme of things, Pike could at least appreciate how many places he had seen thanks to his job.

He'd stumbled through deserts in the great expanse of the southwest, hunted bison running through the plains, foxtrotted among the higher society of Manhattan, shivered among people in the harsh temperatures in the north, strolled along beaches as the sun rose. He had seen and done so much in such a short amount of time, and he often forgot about it when compared to the more difficult and soul crushing parts of his job.

Now, trudging his way through the expanse of the Montana Territory, snowflakes drifted down in waves. It reminded him of the time he'd gotten caught in a snow storm in Vermont in the middle of February, but that time he'd be inside. This time, he was alone in a very vast forest.

The forest grew quiet around him as creation hushed to listen to the beauty. Only a slight breeze and the sound of snow hitting branches interrupted the tranquility. Pike stopped in his path and gazed up at the branches high above him.

The sky had adopted a hazy gray color, faded by the snow obscuring the view of the mountain peaks ahead of him. Snowflakes melted on his hands and cheeks, sending a chill down his spine. He quickly pulled on his borrowed gloves and headed further into the chilly wilderness.

After stumbling around the rocky terrain for a while, he tripped upon the service road blanketed in snow and continued onward. His fingers and toes had gone numb and his cheeks were whipped raw by the wind.

By the time he smelled smoke and something delicious cooking on a fire, he didn't care about Hickory so much as he did food and warmth. So he bolstered his strength and pushed on, leg muscles aching and body desperate for shelter.

A small dirt path appeared when Pike rounded a bend in the road. The smaller path cut off from the side of the main road. It roamed deeper into the depths of the forest into the dark. He carefully approached the cabin, letting off an amber glow like a lightning bug cupped in a child's hands. It looked like a place he could get warm and dry off his clothes, warding away the cold that clung to his bones. Smoke rose from the chimney and a faint, hollow sound came from behind the house.

"Hello?" Pike called out, not intending to frighten the old man. "Is anyone there?"

Pike made his way around the corner to see a man in faded overalls, a plaid shirt, and heavy work boots chopping wood. The man turned to look at him with striking blue eyes, almost like Pike's own. Pulling off his wide brimmed cowpuncher hat, the man wiped his forehead with a handkerchief.

He leaned on his ax and stroked his beard. "Evening. How can I help you?"

"I'm looking for a man called Hickory?" Pike swallowed, making his cover story decision on the spot. "My name is James. I've been hired to talk to him about God."

The man's face split into a grin while he scratched his chin. "I know all about Him. I'm the one you're looking for. Would you like to come inside and wash up? You look like you've had a rough day in this snow. I have coffee, tea, and water. Anything that might interest you. Supper is still cooking."

Pike nodded. "Thank you for your kind invitation. I would love to sit down."

Hickory lifted his ax over his shoulder and walked towards Pike. "Come on in, I'll show you around. I don't get many visitors out here."

Pike wondered if Hickory had been misjudged. He seemed mentally stable, only a little strange for living so far out all by himself, but many families did that.

They made their way to the front door where Hickory scraped his boots and leaned the ax against the front wall. Pike followed suit with his own boots then followed Hickory inside. Their footsteps thudded against the wooden floors and echoed down the hall. The cabin matched what Pike expected, sparsely furnished with comfortable seating and a matching table. A fireplace tucked inside the far wall instantly made Pike feel safe and warm. But Pike's attention focused most on the instruments that covered every inch of available wall space.

"Did you. . . collect all of these?" Pike gazed up at a row of beautifully unique fiddles.

"I made most of them. Some of them were gifts. I supply the general store down in Lankin and even some other towns farther away." Hickory held out a glass of water and a mug of coffee. "Pick your poison!"

Despite his long hike, Pike picked the coffee, aroma almost as intoxicating as alcohol. The heat from the cup burned his chilly hands, but it was a nice kind of pain. One that promised comfort whenever you adjusted to it.

"Thank you very much, Mr. Hickory."

Hickory waved his hand as he sat down on the far end of the couch facing the fire. "Oh, it's just Hickory. It's not my real name anyway."

Pike lowered himself into one of the smaller chairs. "How did you come across the nickname? I admit I was very curious when I learned of you."

Hickory chuckled. "Do you want legends or truth? I've got both, though the legends are far more interesting."

Pike smiled. "I wouldn't mind hearing both, but preferably the truth."

"Oh, I suppose it started when I moved out here to make instruments. I've always felt more at peace away from the hustle and bustle of a town. Submerged in nature is where I feel God the most. This is how life is supposed to be. Peaceful."

Hickory paused for a moment. The sounds of the winds outside were a harmony to the melody of the crackling fire and the tinkling of ice against Hickory's water glass.

The peace was palpable.

Pike leaned forward in his chair, holding the hot coffee in his frigid hands. His feet tingled from the warmth of the cabin and his mind drifted off to some distant past in the wilds of Montana.

Hickory sipped from his glass before he continued. "My mama always told me that God had something grand in store for me, something He'd like to give me if I only had open hands to receive it. I held on to small things."

Hickory stopped talking and stared into the fire, sipping his water. Pike watched him carefully, wondering what thoughts were running through the man's head.

"I'm sorry, I don't think I understand," Pike murmured, afraid to interrupt whatever memory had washed over the man in front of him.

Hickory took a deep breath. "When you're sitting in nature, truly being a part of it, you start to notice these cycles. Birds molting feathers, trees losing leaves, snakes shedding skins. There is a process of letting go, like a hickory tree lets go of its fruit and its leaves. By seeing those patterns and understanding them, we get a sense of how letting go and trusting God permits us to grow.

"One Sunday after church, one of the older men handed me a fiddle." Hickory's eyes practically lit up with joy. "An instrument, the best thing you could've given a young boy with nothing else to occupy his time. I learned as much as I could, playing by ear to the tunes I heard. I even played in several local bands. But then I started making instruments for other people right before I married my beautiful wife."

Hickory stood and stepped over to his mantle where a carte de visite of a smart looking couple sat on display. He picked up the framed photo and handed it to Pike. A younger version of Hickory gazed out from the photo, eyes still blazing blue, but with a shorter beard and dressed in his best. The woman, equally striking, had beautiful hair and a modest figure, but her soul laid bare in her kind eyes.

"Caroline was the best thing that happened to me. I made her move out west with me. We traveled for a bit. A little bit strange, but we loved it. And then when we found out she was expecting a child. . . We settled down rather quickly. We had a house down closer to Lankin, not far from the main street. It's still standing, though now a growing family lives there. I worked tirelessly making instruments and fixing up the baby's room. We went to church every Sunday and prayed for the sweetest child. I hoped the child would look more like her, but. . . I never got to hold it."

Another memory overtook Hickory, a shadow passing over his eyes. His voice scratched with raw emotion when he spoke again.

"I lost both of them during delivery. I stopped going to church for a time. I even stopped playing music. I hated God for what He did. He extinguished my light. I sold the house, gave away all the baby things I would never need, and I moved out here on my own. Isolated. . . I think originally it was an escape. But I have found peace out here. I eventually started going to church again, and I still attend every Sunday. I play music there, too. But past that, I don't see many people. Mainly the general store owner when I drop off deliveries and the occasional outdoorsman who braves the rugged country out here."

Hickory grew silent again, setting his water glass to the side. He took the photo from Pike and placed it back on the mantle with such gentleness. He looked older than before, and much more sad.

"And that's why they call me Hickory," the old man exhaled.

"Because you had to let go of your wife and child?"

"Because I let go of control, much like the nuts and leaves off a hickory tree. And I withstand the trials I've been given, like a hickory tree can withstand any storm. Nothing I do can stop His great plans. And it's not my job to figure out what happens next. I let go and follow what He has for me."

Pike grew still, contemplating Hickory's words.

Let go.

Impossible.

It was impossible to let go. There were so many things Pike had lost. If he let go now, what did that leave him with?

Hickory added another log to the fire and sat back down. They grew quiet listening to the gentle crackle of the fire and the wind whistling lightly at the windows. Pike's shoulders slumped at the sinking weight of his assignment. How could he possibly go through with it?

"You came here to talk to me about God. What is it you're wanting to talk about?"

Pike's throat dried. He doubted that he could ever convince Hickory that God wasn't real. Not at this point anyway. Not after hearing his story. Which left him no choice.

"I'm sorry, would you excuse me for a moment?" Pike stood and quickly walked outside of the cabin to the front porch, letting the door slam behind him. The wind made the air seem even colder somehow and the smell of snow hung on the breeze. A layer of powder blanketed the grass.

For seven years, Pike killed people without a second thought. Maybe it was a survival instinct that kicked in. Or maybe he hadn't been mature enough to know right from wrong. But after all that time, each job had become more and more difficult to complete than the last. And now all that stood between him and freedom. . . Hickory and one more job.

It has to be done.

Otherwise, Watson's death meant nothing.

Hickory opened the front door and peeked out. "Did I say something to upset you?"

Pike shook his head. "Hickory, what if you had to do something despicable to someone that is beyond kind to you?"

Hickory frowned. "It certainly depends on what you believe. Will it benefit anyone?"

Pike shrugged. "Two people. Maybe more."

"Will it harm anyone else?"

"Directly."

"Then why do it?"

Pike hesitated before answering, "I have a job to do. And unfortunately that relies on hurting someone. I am legally bound to do the job."

Hickory sighed with understanding. "So you have to do it, or you're fired."

"Something like that." Pike swallowed hard, his mind flashing to the silver flames that haunted his sleep.

"My advice would be to follow your gut. Where do you think you're being led?"

Pike shook his head. "I don't know."

Hickory looked at him with the same knowing look that Watson used to give Pike. It made the ache in his heart even worse.

Hickory smiled. "Why don't we take a walk?"

"Isn't it getting too dark? And cold? Aren't there bears and other creatures in the forest?"

Hickory chuckled. "Haven't you heard the legend of when I supposedly tried to befriend a grizzly?" He waved his hand in the air. "Follow me. I'll show you the best spot for making big decisions."

Hickory started down the porch stairs and back around his house again. They passed the wood pile that he'd been chopping earlier and veered left down a small path through a pine needle forest floor. At first, the trail lay relatively flat, but then it sloped and became much rockier and extra slippery in parts that were touched by the snow.

The sun had reappeared, but it sank deeper in the sky, and the gray color faded to a light pink between the pines. Pike almost suggested they turn back before it got too dark when Hickory stopped.

"Here we are, Mr. James." He gestured for Pike to take the lead.

Pike moved around Hickory and stepped onto the edge of a steep cliff overlooking a lake. Pike's eyes didn't know where to land. Mountains in the distance, trees, a curling river, the pink of the sunset reflecting on the fresh snowfall, and smoke plumes swirling up from the town of Lankin in the valley far below.

"I try to make all of my big decisions here on this mountain." Hickory sat on a small rock formation jutting out of the ground below them. "It makes you feel like the world doesn't depend on you. That one decision isn't that big of a deal."

Hickory had a point. The only deterrent being that Pike's problem was a massive deal, at least as far as Hickory was concerned. How could he tell the old man that?

He sat next to Hickory. "I don't think I'm going to do it."

"No?" Hickory raised an eyebrow.

Pike shook his head slowly. His words had surprised him, but he was more surprised to find the truth in them as well. "I've done enough damage. But even by doing the right thing, I still think another person is going to get hurt besides me."

His breath caught in his throat thinking about his mother. She was too pure and old for this job. But maybe she'd only have to do one job. But for what purpose? Everyone she loved would be gone.

Hickory smiled. "I rather think she'll forgive you for it, *Pike*."

Pike met Hickory's eyes in an instant. He tried to pull himself together, wondering if he'd voice his thoughts out loud and let his real name slip. "What?"

Hickory turned away, gazing at the dying sun. "I was warned about you. In a dream actually, a little more than a week ago. All I knew were the eyes and those boots."

He inclined his head to Pike's boots, the ones Pike had received from the ranch while getting a change of clothes with Benji.

Hickory cleared his throat. "I knew you were mixed up in a lot of trouble. I knew that my life was on the line, but more importantly, your life was and is on the line. I knew you'd be coming along, Mr. Pike."

"But why did you pretend not to know?"

Hickory shrugged. "I figured it was best this way. Maybe you'd listen better if you thought I was only a sad, old man."

"But you knew why I came!"

"Did you know the outcome when you first walked up the path to my doorstep?"

Pike shook his head. "No, sir."

"And do you know what the outcome will be even now?"

"No, sir."

"Then we leave it up to God to decide. But despite all this, we still enjoy this sunset like it's our last."

Pike's heart cinched. A vision flashed in his head of the dark-skinned man, silhouetted, wild rag blowing in the gnarly winds. Watson had been so at peace.

Hickory grew silent watching the sunset. Pike had reached a dead end in his plans. He couldn't do it. How could he when Hickory reminded him of the gaping hole left after killing Watson?

How would he explain this to the Devil? He wouldn't care about sentiments. Pike couldn't complete the job, and there were always repercussions to disobeying Silvertongue.

"I don't know what to say to him," Pike mumbled.

"Tell him the truth," Hickory stated. "The truth is always the best option."

"You don't know him like I do," Pike huffed.

"You may know him on a more personal level than I do," Hickory started, "but I certainly know what a coward he is. And I'm not afraid to tell him that myself."

Pike grinned, turning to look at Hickory but paled when he saw silver flames trickling up the path in his peripheral vision.

"You're about to have the chance," Pike hissed when he stood, backing to the edge of the steep cliff.

"Well, isn't this a quaint meeting," the Devil purred, emerging from the unearthly flames.

Hickory stood with the kind of groan that comes with old age. "I don't believe we've met. They call me Hickory."

With confidence, he stuck out his hand, ready to be polite even to the Devil himself. With disbelief painted on his face and perfect eyebrows raised, Silvertongue eyed Pike and then Hickory with a cold glare that could kill.

"I don't shake hands," he stated plainly.

Hickory pulled his hand back and stuck both hands in his overall pockets with a genuine smile on his face. "I take it you've been bothering my friend here. We don't want you here, so please leave. We're doing fine on our own."

"I'm afraid that isn't going to happen," the Devil said.

"Silvertongue," Pike started.

The Devil turned to Pike with such fury that his human mask evaporated instantly, leaving his true nature on display. Instead of his typical soulless dark eyes, a red fiery glow remained. His skin rippled like a still pond hit by a pebble of a troublesome servant. Pike hid behind his arms, knowing he would almost certainly die.

"Do you think you're in a place to argue with me?" The grating voice rattled Pike's bones.

"How can you hate someone who is so kind?" Pike shouted.

"He may be kind, but he is gullible," the Devil hissed. "Can you really believe in a God who allows good men to die?"

Pike clenched his teeth, refusing to let his chin tremble thinking of Watson. It was his fault. And he couldn't take back what he had done.

When Pike didn't answer, the Devil moved towards him, back in his composed, human state. "Honestly, Alexander, look at yourself. Do you really want your mother taking over? She won't even have the strength to bury her only son."

Pike's heart sank, mind flashing to his mother kneeling next to his grave, weeping. Would she survive that kind of heartache and loss? What would she have to live for after that? Every muscle in his body tensed.

"But I would have her all to myself." The Devil circled Pike now, leaning in to whisper in his ear. "And she would be *delicious* to torture."

"No," Pike breathed.

"Finish him, or I will."

"No." Pike assumed his voice came out inaudible, especially with the pounding of his heart.

"No?" The Devil repeated. "No? How *dare* you refuse me you vile, incompetent—"

His next words were incomprehensible, the language of the underworld, so evil it sounded like screams. Pike was knocked back, his head and shoulders nearly dangling over the edge of the cliff.

This was the moment.

He was about to die.

He squeezed his eyes shut while he grasped for anything, any hold that he could cling to. His hands found a cleft between the stones that made up the cliff. Leaning sideways he pulled himself away from the cliff edge, scrambling back to safety.

His heart throbbed wildly in his ribs, his chest tightening. Pike's hands shook as he tried to find Hickory.

The old man had been knocked back against a pine tree, the shadowmen crawling at his feet. Hickory slumped to the ground in a daze. With little effort, the shadowmen, stiff and tree-like, grabbed Hickory by the straps of his overalls and dragged him into the silver flames behind the Devil.

"No!" Pike shouted, though he didn't think it had been heard.

A shrill grating sound erupted from the flame while sparks exploded from it, much like it had done when hands threw in Alexander Pike V seven years previous.

I failed.

Again.

His chest ached even more, sharp pain emanating from below his sternum. Pike had barely gotten to his feet before the Devil had him pinned to the rock formation he had been sitting on only moments ago.

"Not a single word from you!" he bellowed. His eyes flashed red. The places where his blackened flesh touched Pike's skin burned like fire.

Every part of Pike's body erupted in searing pain. A scream ripped out of his chest. His vision had turned white around the edges, and he could see the forest slipping away.

This is the moment.

I am about to die.

And with a gust of wind, they disappeared from Lankin.

21

It had been three days since the Devil, in all his rage and fury, had thrown Pike to the ground in Morville, Washington. It felt so similar to his father's last night that Pike knew he would die.

Pike lay there in the cold wet grass, the Devil shouting in his language that Pike couldn't understand. Silvertongue's looming figure filled every part of Pike's vision. He squeezed his eyes shut, afraid to look such evil in the face.

He didn't find any solace in his mind. Instead, visions of Hickory's body slumping against that tree swam in his head. The shadowmen creeping closer. The way the silver flames sparked, that sound of grating screams that cried in triumph. . . He was haunted even then.

The Devil let out a howl that caused the roosting crows in the neighboring trees to fly far away. Pike swallowed and held his breath.

One. . . Two. . . Three. . .

He counted beats, feeling no attack. There were no hands pulling him to the underworld, no dogs nipping at his heels, no smell of burning flesh.

Deep, heavy breathing filled his ears, mixing with the sound of his own heartbeat. The warmth of the Devil's breath made his skin crawl, such a drastic contrast to the cold, hard earth beneath his back. The damp smell of soil reached his nose, but the stench of death that went wherever the Devil did overpowered the smell of the dirt.

"Alexander," the Devil ground out in a sing-song tone. "Why won't you look at me?"

Pike took several measured breaths.

"Why don't you explain what has happened to your resolve in the past month?"

Nearby, the drip-drip-drip of melted snow on the trees counted the beats of Pike's heart along with his breaths. The squawking from the murder of crows that had fled moments ago echoed in the distance.

"Alexander," the Devil hissed.

Pike's body lifted high off the ground.

"Look at me!" the Devil screamed in fury.

Pike felt the air rush past him as he slowly opened his eyes, though still squinting to avoid seeing this beast as much as he could. The waxing moon shed light to everything but the Devil.

Terror filled Pike's heart like it had done many times before when met with that face, long and dark and ragged. The hunched yet looming figure stood tall against the almost full moon. His eyes blazed red against the darkness of his skin.

"My patience has run thin," the Devil growled. "You have one more job. If you fail this, you die and your mother is mine. If you succeed, I will release my debt. I am tired of these human games."

The Devil lifted his free hand, long fingers contorted and mangled. "Do not fail me again." He pulled his fingernail across the front of Pike's chest in a diagonal line from his shoulder to the bottom of his ribs.

Pike let out a scream, clenching his teeth shut. His chest burned, silver flames bursting from the wound. It wasn't unlike the dozens of other scars he'd been given for misbehaving. Silvertongue dropped him to the ground with a thud. Pike lay on his back, body refusing to move.

His chest still ached, his skin stinging from the fresh wound sticking to his shirt.

A gust of wind rushed past him and the clearing in front of his house felt lighter and less suppressing. Leaning his head up looking for the Devil, he sighed seeing that he had disappeared. Pike crumpled back down, eyes looking heavenward.

At least Hickory didn't feel much pain before the end.

"God forgive me for what I've done," Pike muttered to himself, struggling as he took deep breaths.

Behind him, a screen door squeaked open. His mother knelt next to his shoulder, head hovering just above his own.

"Welcome home, Pike." She smiled, eyes brimming with tears reflected in the moonlight. "I'm glad to see you breathing."

"Mother," Pike breathed.

She brushed his hair gently out of his eye. "Let's get you inside. We can catch up over dinner."

She helped him up, and together they went inside the relative safety of their cabin in the woods of Morville. She tended his wounds well, cleaning and slathering a salve over the gash. She wrapped a bandage over his torso and shoulder, covering the whole wound.

Unfortunately, it had been quite common between the two. Pike showed up injured all too often with his occupation. And Mrs. Pike had become accustomed to cleaning his wounds with relative ease. Most of the time, Pike would discuss what had caused the wound, but this particular night, he didn't have many words to say.

"Where all have you traveled since I last saw you?" his mother put away her medicine kit and set out the dinner plates.

"Here and there," Pike shifted in his seat. "New England, Oklahoma, Montana. . ."

"Oklahoma is new isn't it?"

Pike shook his head. "I was there in the spring of seventy-five."

"That's right. The left shoulder scar."

Pike glanced down at his left shoulder. Hidden under a fresh shirt, a one inch scar remained of a knife fight he'd been involved in with some soldiers.

"Mother. . ." he thought of how well she knew his scars both visible and unseen. "I messed up. I only have one more assignment. But if I complete it, then–"

"You're free?"

The amount of hope in those two words was so evident.

Pike only nodded.

He was balanced on a very unstable cliff.

One more wrong move and he would die.

One last job and he would be free from this cursed line.

And if Pike didn't complete that job, his life and his mother's were over. Everything they'd ever loved would be gone.

❧

And so Pike sat on the front porch from dawn to dusk watching the rain fall for three agonizing days. Waiting for his next assignment was almost as painful as waiting for his wound to heal. In fear of missing when the Devil returned, he rarely left his post, knowing that the Devil could show up at any moment.

While Pike sat on the porch waiting, his mother kept very busy. She knew what his occupation entailed, but she loved him despite his path. In the lowest moments, she brought their meals outside and tried to take his mind off of things the best she could. She had always said that any mother would've done the same, though he wasn't sure there was another relationship quite as complicated as the Pike family's situation.

To take his mind off of the pain, she updated him on local news. A new doctor had moved into town. Everyone seemed to love him and his family, his little girls. There was talk of some outlaw cowboys that had been seen outside of town though they hadn't really made a stir yet. And of course all the old ladies at church had asked, "how is Pike?" and "When will he be back in town?" always wanting him to stop by and say hello. And like she'd done for the better part of her life, his mother had lied saying he still traveled for business and that he did just fine.

Though he felt like he didn't show it enough, Pike appreciated his mother's support more than anything. She never chastised him for what he did. He assumed she'd had to be accepting of it when her husband inherited "the family curse", as she called it. He also couldn't help but think that even if he chose the job, that she would've been loyal until death. And that nearly hurt worse.

Nevertheless, it pained Pike to be such a burden on her life and spirit. People were often arrested for being accomplices in crime. . . He wondered if God would at least accept his mother into Heaven despite her connections on earth.

Maybe He would understand.

After lunch one afternoon while his mother did his laundry, he'd been washing dishes. She brought out the wild rag he'd gotten from Ethan along with the framed photo of the Moore family.

"What would you like me to do with these?"

Pike's vision blurred, remembering that moment by the fire with Watson after his last meal. Pike cleared his throat of emotion. "You can put the photo back in my coat. I'll. . ." he looked down. "I'll put that with my keepsakes."

She laid the wild rag gently down on the kitchen table and went back to the laundry. After drying his hands, Pike ran the silk fabric through his hands, its cold feel running against his palms.

"Will you ever forgive me?" he asked, knowing the question would never be answered.

With a shaky breath, Pike headed back to his room where an old wooden wardrobe stood against the wall. Above it, he pulled down a decently sized chest made of wood and leather.

The hinges creaked as he opened the lid, revealing trinkets and baubles of all sorts. Amongst letters and photos, a mixture of little things from his assignments shifted as he placed the wild rag with them. A scallop shell from one of his first jobs in California lay against a bobwhite quail feather he'd picked up from Kentucky. He placed his stolen watch and ring from the Stooksbury's garden party in the chest next to a dull knife from Maine and a disused pipe he'd bought in Boston.

So many memories.

His heart ached running his fingers gently along items from his past. Each had a story, some version of heartache attached to each one. And now Watson's story lived among them.

On the third day with no Silvertongue in sight, questions still raced in Pike's mind going over the encounter with Hickory. He wondered if anyone would miss the old man. He wondered if Watson and Hickory were being introduced in Heaven. He wondered if Hickory forgave him for what happened.

His mother had gone into town before the sun was up, leaving behind a list of things he could do to help her around the house if he felt inclined to do so. Instead, Pike had made himself breakfast, instantly regretting it. It made him feel queasy.

His stomach rumbled unhappily while he sat on the porch watching the horizon. The moment he had stepped outside the front door of his childhood home that morning, harsh winds whipped his loose shirt and pants against his skin, slinging his blonde hair in his eyes.

The locals were probably saying that winter had blown in, but Pike knew better.

The waiting had started to make his hands shake again. Silvertongue was unusually quiet. It rarely took him long to bring a new assignment which only meant that the Devil had cooked up something terrible for Pike. Pike had no doubt that it was payment for all of the mistakes he'd made in November.

As he rocked in the creaky chair on the front porch, he thought back on the past seven years. Countless cities and assignments, faces and names. Too many aliases to count. Having so many masks was an easy way to lose oneself.

"After all these years…" he said to himself.

Somewhere around one hundred and fifty years ago, Pike's great-great-great-grandad had done something so crazy or made the worst imaginable deal with the Devil that it caused himself and five other generations, including Pike, to be subservient to the Devil. And some one hundred and fifty years later and five other Alexander Pikes, it was finally coming to an end.

"The end of an era," Pike muttered.

Despite being hopeful for freedom, he wondered if Silvertongue was actually going to let him leave after completing this job. Pike knew way too much, and that made him feel even worse.

The wind picked up as a storm blew in from the coast. Clouds hung low over the earth, hiding its many secrets. Thunder boomed in the distance, an ominous warning.

Pike overlooked the yard as he'd done seven years ago. Except this time, death walked up the path on the winds of November. The Devil, dressed to the nines as usual, strode up the walkway towards Pike with a roguish look on his human face.

"Silvertongue," Pike muttered, a cautious tone in his voice.

The Devil stopped an arm's length from Pike, watching him with observant, soulless eyes. He chuckled before responding. "Well, Alexander Pike, it seems that our paths are diverging." He checked his human nails nonchalantly. "But I'm generous enough to give you one more simple job as a thank you for all your hard work these past seven years."

Pike tensed. "That's very thoughtful of you," he said, afraid to sass the Devil. "Name?"

"Now, now," the Devil tutted. "So quick to rush this bittersweet meeting. This is the last job brief we'll ever have! Are you ready to leave me so soon?"

Pike clenched his jaw, biting back words. Whatever he had couldn't be easy for Pike. Silvertongue toyed with him. A list of names ran through Pike's head of potential people that the Devil could assign to him. He hoped it wasn't his own mother.

God, let it not be my mother.

"Thank you for your patience." Silvertongue grinned, sharp teeth showing. "One more job. There's a new doctor in town."

"My mother has mentioned him."

"How is your dear mother?" the shadowy man asked like a close family friend.

"She's fine," Pike swallowed. "What about the doctor?"

Silvertongue lazily rolled his eyes. "Well, he's *very* classy. Fancy wife, fancy children. The youngest daughter."

"What do I do with her?" Pike regretted the question as soon as the words escaped his lips. She was a person, a human, whose life they bandied about like a game. He wondered how old she was.

The Devil let a menacing chuckle escape him, then responded, "Well, if you must ask, I only want her gone. You can do whatever you please with her, only kill her in the end. And this time," He rolled his neck in an exaggerated circle, "I'd love to watch."

Pike opened his mouth to ask why, but Silvertongue held up a finger.

"Ah, ah, ah. . ." he wagged his finger. "No questions. I take it you remember what happened last time you asked questions.

Pike subconsciously rubbed his mostly healed nose. It sat slightly crooked, but thanks to Dr. Jackson, he hadn't turned out quite so hideous. But the thought of Dr. Jackson brought images of a distraught-looking Cass after the debutante. He briefly wondered where they ended up moving to and where they settled in Washington.

"Okay, no questions." Pike resigned, clenching his fists.

"Good," the Devil purred. "I want you to kill Hallie Jackson."

22

Pike's hearing disappeared.

For what felt like eons, he only heard a faint ringing sound echoing against his eardrums. The sight of the Devil wavered and swam, and a wave of nausea turned his stomach. His knee thudded with sickening force on the wooden porch of his mother's house, and he clutched his chest tightly, acutely aware of the sharp pain radiating there.

"Oh dear." The Devil grinned. "I do hope this isn't too much for you. After all, you have until the last day of November to complete this task, so three more days. If you fail. . ." His beady eyes bore into Pike's soul. "You die. And your mother will be my servant until she dies or someone else takes her place."

"But the last job—"

"If you fail, you die. Understand? Someone will die by the end of November."

"No, please." Pike breathed.

He sneered at Pike. "Don't beg now. You're too far past that point.

A life for a life. Either Hallie Jackson dies within the next three days or you die and your dear old mother is mine for whatever I please."

Pike gasped for air. His vision swam with every beat of his heart. Long crooked hands clung to his throat and that sickly familiar burning sensation accompanied it.

"Do not fail me, Alexander," the gravelly voice growled. "This is your last job, and you'll never have another one from me. Finish this."

He flung Pike to the ground and disappeared in a gust of wind like he was only dust or smoke drifting in the air. Pike shook violently now, heart racing and hands sweating. Everything hurt— bones, joints, and muscles. His brain wouldn't function correctly. His legs didn't want to move. And his throat burned.

He felt dangerous. Something unhinged in his mind.

Hallie.

He pressed his forehead against the dirt and cried until tears wouldn't come anymore. His chest ached so much that he wasn't sure that the pain would ever leave.

He barely knew Hallie. But what had she done that was worth all this? What had her father done? Or Cass?

Cass.

Just the thought of her name or her deep brown eyes that felt like warmth made Pike feel even more nauseated. She would be furious.

No.

It will break her.

Pike leaned against the steps to his mother's house. And he saw nothing but what he imagined Cass would look like when she saw Pike murder her younger sister. She'd cry and scream. She'd be furious.

And she would hate him.

She would never forgive him. It was the worst kind of cruelty. Being kind, then turning around and betraying someone you cared for deeply. It was inhuman. And his hopes of courting Cass after receiving freedom were dashed to the ground beneath his feet.

Pike began to wonder if his soul had been corrupted as much as the Devil's. After all, people who assisted criminals were often arrested for the crime even if they didn't actually commit it. What made this any different?

He had dreamed that he was good, dreamt that he was enough. Hoped that he was.

But Pike would answer for the Devil's sins one day.

And maybe that day would be sooner rather than later.

P ike stumbled into the town in a daze, still shocked from his assignment.

Could he do it?

I am not my father.

I am not my father.

I am not my father.

He repeated it to himself so many times that he started to think he said it for all to hear. He wondered if the people around him noticed, if they could read his anguish like it was written plainly on his face.

A chill crept up his spine.

He knew that the Devil and all the demons in hell were watching to see what decision he would make. They watched to see if he would fail. Perhaps they were eager for him to fail. Maybe that meant something more for them, like something delicious lurked in the depths of Pike's marred soul.

With the growing feeling of being watched, Pike looked over his shoulder, watching every person he could see. He tried to quell his fears, telling himself that the Jackson family couldn't possibly be in Morville, until he met eyes with a woman across the street standing rigid.

Cassidy Jackson.

And Hallie stood with her.

To be precise, Hallie talked to the side of Cass's face. After several moments of irritation with her sister's lack of attention, Hallie followed her sister's stony gaze. Unlike Cass, Hallie Jackson's face lit up in recognition when she met Pike's gaze on the opposite side of the street.

"Mr. James Pike! What a surprise!"

Pike crossed the street with a stoic gait.

Cass hadn't told Hallie.

Why would she? It would no doubt be embarrassing for a girl to admit to her family that she had been gullible and believed lies so easily. And that she had offered to let go of everything in order to chase a man she had just met. A man that had turned out to be a monster.

Pike cleared his throat. "Good afternoon, ladies. It's a pleasure seeing you all in my hometown. You make these streets more beautiful."

Cass scoffed, tearing her eyes away from Pike, yet her derision drew attention to herself.

"Cass, aren't you going to say hello?" Hallie muttered, meaning laced in her voice.

Cass swallowed, eyeing Pike's plain clothes that had replaced the debutante suit from the last time she had seen him. "Good afternoon. You're from Morville?"

Pike nodded once. "How do you like it?"

Cass hesitated then said, "Small."

Hallie rolled her eyes. "Oh, please! You love it here!" She turned to Pike. "She drags me out of the house on a daily basis to explore more things. The shops, the sights, the park. Anywhere she can go, she's gone or has a plan to go eventually."

"Harriet, you are a nuisance," Cass hissed.

Hallie scowled at her older sister for a moment, muttering something about a grumpy mood. She turned to Pike with an excited look.

"Wait until our father hears you live here! You must come to dinner at our house tonight! We're celebrating Thanksgiving as a family."

Pike's heart lurched. "I—I wouldn't want to intrude."

"Precisely," Cass said, pointedly. "It won't be enough time to plan for his arrival with all of the food preparations. Plus what if Father works late today?"

"You know he won't," Hallie retorted. "He's getting settled in the office, and he wasn't planning on working at all really. He could be home already."

Cass finally met Pike's eyes. She looked hopeful, yet a vulnerability had disappeared. She'd boarded up her doors, and he had been abandoned on the outside. But would she want to open up again? Would she let him explain the difficult and impossible situation he'd been put in? Instead, she sat at the window, looking down at him but unwilling to unlock the door, to let him inside the safety of her heart and away from the demons that tormented him.

"I will only join you at dinner if Miss Cassidy Jackson allows it. If not, I will say my goodbyes and step away, leaving you all to enjoy the rest of your afternoon in peace."

Pike simultaneously hoped for both the allowance of dinner and for the chance to say goodbye so he didn't have to feel guilty for an entire evening of dinner and chatting.

Cass bit her tongue. Pike saw through her feeble attempt at a smile, but appreciated it nonetheless. "Of course. I would love it if you joined us for dinner, Mr. Pike."

Pike assented gratefully.

Hallie clapped her gloved hands excitedly. "Father would love to catch up this evening, I'm sure. Why don't you join us on our morning walk?"

And with no shame at all, Hallie wrapped her arm around Pike's and gave her sister a raised-eyebrow look. Pike froze at Hallie's touch. She felt like a lit fuse, sparkling out of existence right on his very arm.

"Mr. Pike, are you feeling all right?" Hallie gazed up into his face.

Pike must've shown his hesitation, or maybe his face still looked pale from his shock earlier that morning.

Was it really only an hour or so previous?

Blinking a few times, Pike forcefully nodded. "I will be perfectly fine soon enough."

"James?" Cass asked, anxiousness evident in her tone, all formalities dropping away. She laid a gentle gloved hand on his opposite shoulder, coming around him on the other side.

Pike smiled weakly, chill running its course through his body. "I haven't felt the best today."

"You do look awfully pale," Cass muttered, gently tilting his head down with her covered fingers to examine his face with quick, observant eyes. "Why don't we take you to see our father?"

Pike nodded.

Cass turned to Hallie. "Will you stop by the office in case he's not at home?" When Hallie protested, Cass put a hand on her sister's arm. "Please?"

Hallie reluctantly agreed and walked the opposite direction, farther into the commercial district of the town.

After a minute or two of tense silence, walking down the street, Pike cleared his throat. "He won't be there, will he?"

"No, Hallie was absolutely right when she said he'd be home already." Cass smirked. "If I'm being honest, I wanted a moment alone with you."

"Is that so?" Pike asked, a grin in his voice despite his quickening heart rate.

"Don't flatter yourself. I need you to be honest with me, and I knew you'd keep face in front of Hallie."

"Right." Pike cleared his throat again. "Very astute of you."

"Pike," Cassidy began. "Why are you here? What job are you on right now?"

Pike shook his head. "I can't. . . I can't talk about it. I'm sorry."

"Don't apologize. I know that you don't mean it."

Pike momentarily held his eyes shut, holding himself back from flinching at her tone. The edge in her voice cut more than the words.

"Cass," He took a deep breath. "You don't *want* to know."

"But I do! I want to know everything! I want to know why you're here. I can't trust what you say about this being your hometown. I'm pretty sure you lied about everything else the first time we met."

"Not everything, Miss Jackson," he whispered.

She bit her lip, and Pike wondered if she held back emotions or tears or a mix of both. He waited, hoping she would say more.

She swallowed before she continued, "I have played our conversations over and over in my head, desperately trying to read between the lines to figure out what went wrong. My father wanted to invite you to come with us to Washington to work for him. That's how much you impressed him. And yet, you still operate with a façade. Even when I hold your words to the light, I still can't figure out the truth."

"Cass—"

She stopped and turned to him. "Are you really Alexander Pike?"

He swallowed, wishing the lump in his throat would go away. "Yes."

"And you really work for *him*?"

"Yes," Pike breathed the word.

"And you're in Morville for a job?"

Pike licked his dry lips. "Yes, but I grew up here. My mother also lives here. She—"

Cass held up a hand, eyes closed. "And your job. . . is to harm someone."

Pike nodded, desperately wanting to control the beating of his heart.

Cass resumed their walk without another word.

A few more minutes passed while Pike tried to think of something to say, anything to convince her that he wasn't as bad as the Devil. But he couldn't even convince himself of that. They arrived at a small townhouse before he could think of something worthy and the moment had long since passed.

The building was modest, but clearly updated with fresh paint and decorative pieces. It had been painted a pale blue color, seeming gray in the cloudy light. The wooden door looked inviting as they stepped to the porch. Cass pulled out a key and unlocked the front, pushing the door inwards. Henderson, their butler, arrived in a moment.

"Henderson, you remember Mr. Pike," Cass motioned to Pike who stood half a step behind her.

"Of course! What a surprise!" He beckoned them both further inside the warm, welcoming house that now belonged to the Jackson family. "Might I say, sir, your nose looks to have healed wonderfully!"

"All thanks to Dr. Jackson!" Pike said with more happiness than he truly felt.

He stepped past Henderson into the foyer. The arched ceiling let in lots of afternoon light to bounce off the pale gray paint. Packaged paintings leaned against the wall, waiting to be hung, and the furniture had still not been positioned, but the smell of something sweet drew Pike's attention.

"Something smells divine," he murmured.

"Let's get you a bit of something to eat," Cass's hand returned to his shoulder as it had in the street. Her instinct to help overpowered despite feeling hurt herself which broke Pike even more. She deserved so much more than he could give. She turned her head to the butler. "Henderson, can you tell Father that Mr. Pike is here and needs to be looked at?"

"Really, I'm fine." Pike waved a hand in the air.

"Nonsense." Cass met his eyes. "You seemed deathly pale in the streets, like you'd seen a ghost."

"Something like that," Pike muttered.

Cass's expression shifted into something resembling suspicion but much more personal. It made Pike's stomach turn.

Acid threatened to make its way out of his stomach. Pike swallowed it back. "I may need to sit down."

Cass snapped out of whatever emotion had previously held her captive. She led Pike to a sitting room mostly furnished, looking similar to what Liam had in Greenwich, a fire roaring and plush furniture. Sunlight drifted through the window and cast long shadows in the room, dust drifting in its wake. The grandfather clock in the corner read four o'clock in the afternoon.

"Can I get you tea?" Cass asked after getting him seated in the over-stuffed chair. "Or maybe coffee?"

"Coffee. Thank you."

After she left, Pike dropped his head into his hands. Despair toppled over him like a crashing wave. His thoughts roared like the wind.

I am not my father.

I am not my father.

I am not my father.

A firm shake of his shoulder pulled him from his thoughts. When he snapped his head up, he met the concerned eyes of Dr. Jackson, his eldest daughter hiding in the doorway holding a steaming cup of coffee, concern pooling in her eyes. Pike noticed his own hands shaking about the time that Dr. Jackson did.

"Why don't you tell me what's been going on. . ." The doctor pulled up a wooden chair to sit in front of Pike.

Pike's chest ached while he tried and failed to stop his hands from shaking. "I can't stop it."

"The tremors?"

Pike nodded.

"How long?"

"Seven years. But they've gotten worse the past several weeks."

"What's changed?"

Pike laughed sourly. *Everything*, he wanted to say. *I've finally grown conscious of the disaster that rides in my wake, and I'm tired of it.* And then he thought, *I'm at a crossroads in my life. And the Devil is waiting for me.* To which he shuddered.

"A lot of things are different," Pike muttered, not trusting his voice to do its only job correctly. "My job. My future. . ."

"Have you lost your contract job?" Dr. Jackson asked carefully.

Pike laughed shortly, clenching his teeth to keep his jaw from shaking. "Not yet. I have an assignment I'm not sure that I can complete. I don't think it's morally correct."

"What's troubling you so much about it?"

Pike gripped the arms of the chair so tight that his knuckles whitened and started to hurt from the pressure. He met Cass's eyes for a moment before she turned away, looking everywhere except at him.

"I can't do the job. I have to quit, but—" Pike snapped his mouth shut and swallowed. The muscles in his neck tightened with the amount of effort it took to keep himself composed.

"What's the worst that happens if you quit?"

Dr. Jackson didn't know the repercussions of what he'd just asked, but Pike wasn't about to tell him. At least not fully.

"My employer is. . . short tempered. At least with me. He could kill me if he wanted. His rage isn't very contained. And I'm worried about taking care of my mother. She lives north of town. She's a widow."

Dr. Jackson shifted in his seat. "But your employer, surely you could report him to the local authorities, have a mature conversation, get the court involved."

Pike shook his head adamantly, clasping and unclasping his hands in his lap again and again. "He's not like that. He wouldn't—*couldn't* do that."

"So," Dr. Jackson began warily. "What you're telling me is that if you refuse to do this job that you believe to be immoral, your employer could have you killed and wouldn't be reprimanded for it?"

"Something like that," Pike muttered, rocking where he sat now. He couldn't help himself.

"Cassidy," the doctor snapped, calling his daughter's attention away from the broken man in their sitting room. "Can you please get Mr. James a glass of whisky instead of the coffee you brought for him?"

Pike's head fell once again to his hands and his breath came in uneven spurts. The worst thoughts invaded his mind— His body broken and unwilling to move, his mother forced to do despicable things, Cassidy rejoicing that he had died.

Unworthiness.

Self hatred.

Fear.

Thoughts that hissed at him so loudly it sounded like the wind had gotten inside of the Jackson's house, inside of his ears. Thoughts that he would rather die with than let them be known to others.

But he would die either way.

He only had a few days to live.

The sick part was that death itself wasn't what scared him, what would happen immediately after his death scared him the most.

Endless suffering.

"Son," Dr. Jackson began. "I think you're experiencing a good amount of job-related stress. It's causing mental anguish in the form of anxiousness and paranoia, which causes you to have brief paroxysmal displays."

"You think I'm neurotic?" Pike hissed.

"It's a common experience, believe it or not," Dr. Jackson said with dignity. "It makes the most sense for a man in your situation. It would be difficult to keep one's composure in that sort of position."

"And what position is that?" He asked the question with more ice in his tone than he'd intended, but Dr. Jackson didn't even seem phased.

"Somewhere between a rock and a hard place."

"Out of the frying pan and into the fire," Pike grumbled, silver flames dancing in his mind.

Dr. Jackson nodded. "Some people feel better after talking it out. Others start feeling better when they think about the difficult thing passing. And yet others will feel better by simply taking a moment to breathe. Worst case scenario, I can prescribe you something to help mediate your issues, but I'd like to have you in at the office to do a full checkup before we start in that direction."

Cassidy returned with the glass of whisky and handed it to Pike. He finally glanced up at her. Her face flushed but not like it had when he made her blush. She looked like she had been crying.

Pike downed the whisky in one drink and stood unsteadily. He was desperate to get out of the house. He couldn't bear to see Cass cry or speak with Hallie when she arrived. He couldn't answer any more questions. "I need to get some fresh air."

"Will you come back for dinner tonight?" Cass called when Pike reached the door.

He stopped, shaky fingers barely touching the cold brass knob that kept him in the same house of the family he'd been sent to destroy.

Maybe he could explain it to Cass during dinner, or after. Maybe they could solve this problem together.

Or maybe it would make things worse.

Emotion bubbled up inside of Pike, one that surprised him. He wanted to see her again. He wanted to get to know her like she deserved. In a rush, the story came back to him of her future, the one that he'd crafted for her in the garden outside of the debutante dinner. . . Except he wanted it to be him instead of some other gentleman.

Memories he had never made flooded his mind. They'd been married in the spring, moved into the abandoned cottage at the edge of Morville, and started a little garden. They had chickens, and Cass liked to embroider the baby's clothes. Oh, and the baby! He had Cass's eyes and Pike's hair, but his name wasn't Alexander.

And then reality caught back up to him, gravity weighing down his heart. And Cass, the girl who should've been his wife, still waited on his reply.

He cleared his throat and studied his shoes. "If that is something you wish of me, yes. I will come to dinner."

She sighed, shoulders dropping as her lips curled upwards ever so slightly at the corners.

"We can talk more about your issue later, James," Dr. Jackson began. "But only if you want to talk. I won't pressure you to do anything."

Pike's lips twitched. "Thank you."

Turning the brass doorknob, he headed out to the streets again, wind whipping furiously at him. It blew cold and restless, and unease settled in the pit of Pike's stomach.

24

Pike had been lost in thought all the way back to his mother's house, unaware of where his feet were taking him. But he was glad to be back to the place he considered home, despite his terrible memories in that house.

Once, he'd asked his mother why she stayed in that house. She told him that she'd had many happy memories with him there—childhood birthdays and Pike finishing primary school, growing things in their garden and bringing Pike to the shops with her when she had to work in town.

She had also told him about the sweet moments she had shared with his father, even though Pike believed those to be somewhat romanticized. But truly, his mother said she couldn't move away to a house that Pike hadn't grown up in. He meant everything to her, and even when he was miles away doing Lord knows what for the Devil, she still had the memories, the ghost of him running down the hall.

Pike sighed as he stepped onto the porch, boots echoing on the old wood much like they had at Hickory's in Lankin. His heart ached, but he suppressed the feeling like he'd trained himself to do so many years ago. Pike opened the screened door, getting that first smell of his childhood home— pine and dried flowers— then froze.

Inside, the house looked very much the same like it always had. Except that it didn't. His mother always doused her candles if she left the room, or she brought it with her. One flickered oddly on the table, barely melted.

"Mother?" he called out warily.

His heart pounded in his ears like horses in Oklahoma, but he heard nothing else. When he didn't get an answer, he called again.

"Mother!"

He stepped into their living space that housed their mismatched chairs and threadbare blankets. Worn out books were on display next to the couch, and a vase of dried flowers stood on a little side table with a neglected, half-drunk water glass.

"Mother, I'm back. Where are you?" Pike called louder this time.

Paranoia.

She should have been home. She would be sleeping, that's all. Or maybe she had been trying to get the stains out of his clothes.

He moved to the beat of his heart, slowly making his way back to his childhood bedroom, the one he'd occupied while he waited for the Devil to return.

He pushed the door open, but the room remained the same as he'd left it—cowboy clothes hung in the wardrobe minus the boots and pistol, and the bed unmade. Moving across the hall, Pike's mother's room stayed equally empty except her bed had been perfectly made and another vase of dried flowers, her Bible, and a tintype of her and Pike sat on her bedside table.

The only difference was a pristine cutting of a white chrysanthemum that had been placed neatly on the pillow.

They should be out of season by now.

Panic rising quickly, he circled back around to the front of the house. He ripped the door open and jumped off the porch.

"Silvertongue!" His voice cracked against the wind, desperation causing his heart to ache. His eyes were wild with desperation, hands shaking and heart pounding nearly out of his chest. "Silvertongue! Bring her back!"

Pike turned in a circle, scanning the edges of the woods around the house, desperately hoping for a sign.

I allowed my mother to be taken as collateral.

"Silvertongue! Please!" Pike fell to his knees, sobs wracking his body. His heart felt ripped open and deflated, contents seeping out into his chest. Pain filled every crevice. "Please," he whispered into the dying wind.

But the Devil had come and gone, no one there to hear Pike's mother scream. Pike clenched his fists. Despite having a few more days, he would make a decision tonight. One way or another his world would end, and he wanted it to end on his terms.

With some effort, he lifted himself from the ground and went back inside to change. He put on nice pants and a button down along with a coat, and brushed back his hair. He looked in the cloudy mirror, a troubled man staring back at him.

"You're a demon," he growled to his reflection.

His mind played tricks on him, and he could have sworn he saw the reflection grin maliciously. But the moment it appeared, empty eyes gazed back instead.

He stepped back into his mother's room, picking up the photo of them and the chrysanthemum. The Devil had allowed Pike seven days between jobs last year. He and his mother celebrated his birthday with a homemade spice cake, Pike's favorite. She'd taken him into town the next day to the only photo studio north of Seattle. They'd posed in front of a curtained backdrop with Pike's mother sitting in a chair, his hand on her shoulder. She always said it was one of her most prized possessions.

Gently, he laid the photo back on the bed and crumpled the flower in his fist. Everything was on the line now. Things were much more personal.

About half an hour later, he walked back and forth in front of the Jackson's house, debating whether or not he should go inside. He had finally decided when the door opened.

"Are you going to stop pacing and come inside?" Hallie beamed at him. "You'll freeze in this weather. Happy Thanksgiving, by the way."

Pike chuckled uncomfortably. "I must confess, I'm rather nervous about tonight."

"Nervous?" Hallie asked, eyes widening with a quick intake of breath. "You're not—"

"No, Hallie! No. At least. . . I don't mean. . . I wish. . ."

Pike's words failed him after the awkward assumption, though he certainly wished circumstances had been different. He shook his head and took the steps up to the door. "Please, don't tell your sister that I was pacing. I feel that she'd never let me live it down."

"You have my word, Mr. Pike." Hallie gave him a sideways grin then led him to the sitting room.

The family, dressed in evening attire and looking joyful, had gathered along with a few other people. He thought he might recognize a few of them from his childhood spent around town, but he couldn't be sure after seven years. But it struck a momentary fear in his heart that his true name might be revealed and ruin all chances of a future with them as friends.

"Mr. Pike!" Cass, eyes wide with surprise, glided across the room in a floor length dress, bright and beaded at the top, cinching at the waist with a light blue satin band that matched her flowing skirt. A dazzling hair piece twisted into her dark hair, making her look even more like royalty.

"Miss Cassidy Jackson," Pike breathed. "You look. . . stunning."

Cass blushed. "Thank you. I must say that I'm surprised you made it out tonight after our visit earlier."

Pike chuckled sadly. "I was not myself then. But I couldn't miss dinner with you and your family."

"I'm. . ." she took a breath, eyes looking back and forth between his own. "*Glad* that you could make it."

"Thank you for your kind words." He raised her gloved hand to his lips. "I'm sure I will never deserve them."

Hallie raised her eyebrows at him as she walked over to join her mother. Dr. Jackson approached Pike.

"Happy Thanksgiving, son. How are you feeling?" He shook Pike's hand vigorously.

"Much better." Pike forced a smile. "Though I'm worried about my mother. I never did get to talk to her before I came to let her know I had accepted a dinner invitation. I wonder if she stayed in town to shop or visit with someone."

"Have I met her yet? I'm afraid I've met many people over the course of the past week and regret that I have forgotten most of their names."

"I know she's aware of *you* at least. Our home is on the northwest side of town, about a fifteen- or twenty-minute walk from here."

"You'll have to introduce us someday!" Dr. Jackson smiled, turning to the group in the sitting room. "Why don't we all convene for dinner?"

Introductions were made, some more like reacquainting from Pike's childhood. If the Jackson family had noticed most of them calling him Pike, they didn't say. He hoped they assumed it a nickname, and in a way it was. They all stood and followed their host to the dining hall.

Polite conversation among the Jackson's guests filled the dinner, easing Pike's heart even if for a moment. His thoughts often drifted to his mother, knowing that if he could at least figure out what he would do about Hallie, he could find his mother. He found himself sitting between Hallie and Cass making him feel all at once safe and terrified. What if they read his thoughts? What if somehow, Cass outed him during the course of dinner?

Pike ate the turkey and green beans despite feeling sick before clearing his throat and dabbing the corners of his lips with his napkin. Cass eyed him curiously.

"You haven't spoken much tonight. Are you still feeling ill from earlier? Or are you that worried about your mother? We can always have Henderson get someone to run a message out to her."

"I fear she'll be rather worried about me, with my position and all."

Cassidy's eyes darkened under a shadow of doubt as she lowered her voice to avoid suspicion. "Does she know?"

Pike nodded.

"Does she worry often?"

Again, he nodded.

Cass smoothed her napkin on her lap, running her hands over it, despite it being perfectly flat already. "Does she know about your next job?"

Pike shook his head. "I haven't seen her since. . . Since I received the assignment." He swallowed. "I fear she may be *held up*."

He met Cass's eyes fully now, taking in the intensity of her gaze. Something like pity mixed with anguish and despair swirled in the midst of her brown tourmaline eyes that searched his own. He wished he could wash all of those bad emotions away, hoping she would always be happy whether her future was with him or not.

"I'm sorry," Cass breathed quietly, like her life waned instead of her sister's.

She turned her head away slightly, and Pike caught Dr. Jackson's observant gaze. The edges of Pike's lips curled slightly in a half-hearted smile.

He wondered what the doctor truly thought of him.

After eating a dessert of pecan pie and sweet potatoes, Dr. Jackson cleared his throat.

"Well," Dr. Jackson placed his napkin on the table, "shall we reconvene for drinks and cigars in the lounge?"

The guests mumbled a grateful consent, and everyone stood.

When Henderson moved from his position by the serving table, one of the guests stumbled into the table and knocked a water pitcher onto the serving knife. As water spilled onto the floor and guests shouted, the knife ricocheted past the clumsy guest, over the table, directly towards Hallie.

In a moment of panic, a woman screamed, and one man uttered curses. Cutlery clattered against plates, glass shattered, and chairs squealed on the floor.

Then everything froze.

Faces of shock, hands over eyes, arms reaching uselessly out. . . And Pike, right hand dripping blood on Hallie's dress, the serving knife held tight in his bare hand.

The silence was deafening, and for a moment, Pike thought time had truly frozen as his instinct had kicked in to catch the knife. But time had resumed as quickly as it had stopped.

"My God," Mrs. Jackson muttered, reaching out to her husband.

Dr. Jackson moved around the table before anyone else stirred, pulling his jacket off while he moved. Pike finally dropped the knife back on the table, hand trembling, whether from the adrenaline or the pain, he wasn't sure. Drops of blood stained the white tablecloth, a picture of what Pike was—the stain on humanity. Pike moved to speak, but no words came. His eyes glazed over, and the room seemed vignetted.

His vision swam, and his body swayed where it stood. He turned his eyes to Dr. Jackson, who checked on Hallie first.

Pike had stopped a perfect accident that could've done the job for him without being implicated. The weight of the realization made his knees weak.

"James." Dr. Jackson shook Pike's shoulder.

Pike's vision faded in and out of focus as he turned to look at the party guests. Some turned away covering their mouths and others fixated on his still dripping hand. He looked down, hating to see his own blood. Nausea bubbled in his stomach.

"Cassidy," Dr. Jackson snapped sternly.

Movement rustled around the chair next to him. Pike was vaguely aware of hands guiding him to the kitchen, but he didn't hear anything else. Only the rush of blood in his ears and the beating of his own heart, faster and faster.

Pike collapsed in a wooden kitchen chair by the sink, hand stinging when alcohol slid over it. Involuntarily, he clenched his hand into a claw, not able to stop the pain or itch his wound.

He groaned, finally snapping out of his stupor. His feeling had returned fully now, and he was keenly aware of his lightheadedness and the pale face of Dr. Jackson as he worked on cleaning Pike's hand.

Without a word, Dr. Jackson placed a glass in Pike's left hand. Pike downed it, wincing when the liquid burned his throat. Dr. Jackson instantly refilled Pike's cup then stopped the bottle and grabbed a kitchen towel to staunch the blood flow.

Pike's head swam again, and the edges of his vision blurred. Sweat coated his clothes, beading around his neck and his brow. His hands still shook, and his knees still felt weak despite being seated.

And his head. How it roared with the wind that beat against the window, banging and battering the house to be let in.

It wanted Hallie's blood so desperately.

He wanted Hallie's blood so desperately.

Pike was the wind now. There wasn't anything different between them anymore. They were one and the same. And they would always be one and the same.

The wind and Pike.

Pike, the witching winds.

The guests left a little at a time until only the Jackson family and Pike were left in the half-decorated house. Pike's hand had now been bandaged and rebandaged until finally it had stopped bleeding profusely.

The table had been cleared, blood stains worked on, and Hallie reclothed in an unsoiled evening dress. Mrs. Jackson had brought Pike coffee while they sat in semi-comfortable silence by the fire in the sitting room.

"I'm sorry to have ruined your dinner, Mrs. Jackson," Pike finally spoke, voice cracking from disuse.

"Young man, don't feel guilty one bit," she smiled as warm as the fire, and her eyes glistened in the firelight with unshed tears. "You saved Hallie from what would have been a terrible accident, and for that, I would ruin one hundred dinners without thought."

Pike swallowed, lump still present in his throat. The horrible guilt of what would happen hung in the silence, though Mrs. Jackson wasn't aware of that. After some time, Cass came down from assisting Hallie.

"Thank you, Pike," Cass said, after her mother left them to speak alone. "Though I'm sorry that saving Hallie meant injuring you yet again. It seems that our house may be bad luck to you."

Pike nodded. He ground his teeth together, still shaky from the evening. There was so much he wanted to tell her, so much he wanted to say. But he wasn't free. And he'd already hurt her so much.

Cass sat beside him, inspecting his bandage once again. "What will your *employer* say?"

"Nothing," Pike grumbled. "He couldn't care less what happens so long as I survive. I bet if I almost died. . . Well, never mind. No rest for the wicked."

"Pike," Cass chastised him. "You can't say things like that. Surely you aren't beyond redemption."

"But it's true. I am practically a demon in human skin. Nothing and no one can save me from what I've become, what I've made myself to be. I am destined to die a monster, not a savior."

Cass didn't answer. She probably detested being in his presence after such an honest confession. Pike could see the firelight reflected in her tears much like her mother. And he thought of *his* mother, what she would have to go through, or maybe *was* going through.

It made him hate himself even more. He hated his eyes, his hair, his name. All of it. And he hated that he had to hurt Cass.

"Cassidy," he started, voice barely above a whisper.

He needed to leave, needed to finish this game.

She looked him in the eyes. "Yes?"

"Can I talk to you. . . outside?" He set down his nearly empty coffee cup.

Cass stood, helping Pike to stand on unsteady feet.

Damn this alcohol, he thought to himself. It clouded his senses. His words felt strange on his tongue, and his thoughts jumbled together. But they donned their coats and stepped into the merciless wind.

Pike stared into the night. A few men smoked their cigars and pipes heading home from gambling. Dogs barked, and somewhere a child cried.

He refocused his gaze on Cass. She watched him, face refusing to tell him any secrets that she held so tightly to her chest.

"What was it you wanted to talk about?" she asked.

Pike cleared his throat, eyes attempting to focus on her. "Well, Cassidy. . . I—"

Someone nearby laughed heartily, slicing through the wind and causing them both to tense. Apparently, Pike wasn't the only one on edge.

"Cass," he began again, this time quietly and fervently. "I first want to apologize for leaving you like I did before, back in Greenwich. While I don't have much control over my life, I shouldn't have left how I did. And for that, I am sorry."

Cass bit her bottom lip, eyebrows furrowed. "Well, thank you. But. . ."

Pike shook his head slowly, feeling a little heavy both physically and emotionally. He lost a decent amount of blood. And he'd had at least a drink or two at dinner, plus two while Dr. Jackson worked on his hand. It showed.

"What is it, Pike?" Cass begged, hand sliding into his good one. "Be frank with me, please. I at least deserve that."

Pike inhaled deeply, lungs expanding until they ached. He released his breath slowly and glanced up at the sky. "Cass, I'm going to die."

"I don't—"

"No, Cass. Let me speak." Pike swallowed. "I am going to die so that Hallie doesn't have to die." He looked her in the eyes now, grasping tighter to her hand in his. "My last job is Hallie. It's a sick joke. He knows I can't do it. He gets my soul either way. If I obey, I betray your family and hurt people I've come to love. If I disobey, I die. Either way, I will not win."

Pike shuddered and closed his eyes, afraid to see Cass's reaction. She didn't speak for what felt like eternity. Seconds stretched into minutes into what felt like ages until she finally spoke.

"I won't let that happen to you."

Pike opened his eyes, shifting back on his feet. "Cass, who do you

201

think you are—a human standing up against the Devil?"

"There must be another way." She pulled her hand away from his. His confidence wavered. "You are capable of making your own choices. So there must be another option."

"Don't you think I've tried?"

Cass straightened. "I will not give in to him. I refuse to lose to a beast whose past is decorated with the lives of those he's ruined."

"There's nothing you can do, Cass. It's over. What more can I say?"

Cassidy's jaw quivered slightly, causing something in Pike's heart to snap. He only wanted to make her smile, to love her like she deserved. And the Devil had done a fantastic job at ruining any chance of hope.

"Cassidy," Pike whispered, breath leaving him. He moved closer, hoping to hold her at least once. He knew there wasn't another option for him. The Devil's plans were unavoidable.

The front door opened, and Hallie's face peeked out. "Is everything all right? It's cold out, and you're both being ridiculous standing outside like this."

A frantic look filled Cass's eyes as if she believed the Devil himself would rush up the stoop and whisk her sister away. "Harriet, get back inside. Now."

"I want in on whatever secrets you two are sharing. Is it about me?" Hallie gave a suspicious look to Pike, who felt like he would be sick in their rose bushes.

Hallie shut the door behind her as Cass pulled her into a tight hug. Cass's eyes watched Pike.

"We *will* find another way," Cass said forcefully.

"No," Pike stated, a little harsher than he'd intended. "I end this tonight."

"Pike, I won't let you. There's always another option."

"Cassidy Jackson," Pike shouted with more anger than he'd ever felt towards a human. She shrank from him and Hallie cowered behind her, confusion swirling in her eyes. He was doing the one thing he didn't want to do and it killed him. "I will not listen to this any longer! I am taking Hallie's place. This was supposed to be a goodbye, not a match of wits!

202

Stop fighting me."

He staggered down the steps, rubbing his chin with his good hand and swearing under his breath. Heels clicked down the stairs after him.

"You don't get to walk away again!" Cass shouted back. "Not again. You come into my life, into my home, and you disrupt everything. You confuse and excite me, and I would like to know you. And when I confess my feelings, you act like you don't care. So you don't get to walk away from me."

Pike wheeled around, eyes blazing with frustration. "Then you don't get to doubt how much I care about you, Cassidy. Or how much I care about your family. I would die for any of them." He gestured to Hallie and the house. "And to hell with your thoughts on the world; none of this makes sense to anyone! Why should it make sense for you?"

Cassidy moved to hit him. He easily stepped to the side, grabbing her arm.

"Do you see yourself, Cassidy?" Pike asked, incredulous.

"Pike," she swallowed. "Surely—"

Proof. Her science focused mind needed proof.

Exhaust all possibilities.

Pike laughed, frustration boiling under his skin. "Do I need to prove it to you for you to believe that there is no other option? Would you like to watch me die so you can see that there is no other way?"

Pike threw her arm back at her with a gentle shove. She breathed heavily, hair blowing in wisps across her face with the furious wind whipping around them. She gave no answer. Pike looked back up at Hallie who seemed like a statue she stood so still, shocked.

"Hallie, tell your parents that I give them my best, and thank your father for all he's done for me. Please look after my mother. She'll be glad to have daughters to fawn over. She always wished for one." Pike turned his gaze back to Cass who held her arms close to her body. "She would've loved you, Cassidy Jackson."

And with that he turned around and headed for the road that crossed Main Street where the Jackson's house stood. His resolve wore thin and he knew that if he turned back now that he'd never go through with this crazy plan.

He moved like a man on a mission, or maybe a man with a death wish. Or somewhere in between. But he was relentless with his pace, heart beating furiously in his chest. He wanted to turn back and apologize to Cass and to Hallie, to hold Cass in his arms until they turned to dust. He wished he could crumple to the ground outside his mother's house and gaze at the stars instead of facing the terror that lay ahead.

So he didn't look back.

Pike shouldered his coat closer to himself as he stepped into the road. Setting his foot down in the path, the winds immediately hushed to a whisper.

"Show off," he muttered.

And a laugh like nails on a chalkboard crackled through the night as a figure dressed in a suit strode up to meet Pike in the middle of the crossroads.

A harsh, near soundless wind rustled past Pike.

It always began with the witching winds.

It was superstition really, though outwardly the people of Morville shrugged it away, reassuring themselves that the Devil didn't care for quiet, little towns.

Except that he did—*does* care for quiet, little towns. Because quiet, little towns are the place to hide one's secrets.

Until those secrets ask to die.

"Well," Silvertongue crooned. "What a nice little surprise! You bring me two Jackson sisters instead of one!"

"I didn't—" Pike snapped his head around catching sight of the two Jackson sisters lingering in the shadows of the trees. "Cass, no. What are you doing?"

"You think this is heroic!" she called. "But I don't believe you. Help me understand."

Chuckling pulled Pike's attention back to his employer.

"How touching," the Devil smiled, turned up too high to be natural. "I'm impressed with your bravery, Alexander. But it's a fool's errand. You brought me exactly what I wanted!" The Devil stepped to the side, calling out to the sisters. "Did he explain that he was manipulating you? To convince you he was heading to die as a sacrifice for you while only bringing you within grasp of the Lord of Hell himself?"

"No, that's not true," Pike rushed to correct the Devil's lies. "I wasn't manipulating you. I was trying to—"

"Oh, Pike. The game is up! Don't you see?" the Devil hummed. "You've done your part. Your debt is—"

"Stop it!" Pike shouted, cutting Silvertongue off before he could finish his sentence. "You said someone has to die. I want it to be me."

The Devil's smile faltered ever so slightly. "I'm sorry. . . *You*?"

Pike straightened, holding his shoulders back. "I want this to end here. There are no more Alexander Pikes to manipulate and control like a puppeteer. No more games. I die, and this hellish reign ends. Morville, Washington has no more servants to pass it on to and your little small town secret dies with me."

The Devil chuckled, wind circling around him, picking up speed. "But what's stopping me from killing the girls myself? Or making your sweet mother carry on the curse?"

Pike stepped forward. "You said—"

"I *said*," the Devil boomed, the nearby trees quivering under his volume, "if you fail, you die. And your mother will be my servant until she dies or someone else takes her place."

Pike swallowed his fear. "How about I make you a deal?" Behind Pike, one of the girls cried, but he didn't dare turn around now.

Silvertongue tilted his head to an unnatural angle. "You think you're in the position to make a deal? With me?" He threw his head back roaring with laughter that crawled under Pike's skin. Pike held his stance despite wanting to cover his ears.

"Pike, you insult me!" the Devil hissed. "This is why the original Alexander Pike sunk into this mess in the first place."

"And what deal did he lose?" Pike asked, desperate to know what caused such a generational curse.

"He offered to sell his soul along with the blood running through his veins if I could bring his wife back to life." The Devil grinned maliciously, licking his human teeth. "He never said for how long."

The Devil laughed again, stepping to Pike quicker than humanly possible. He stood seven feet tall now, human form stretched thin in a nightmarish picture of evil.

"I am capable of far worse than you've seen Alexander Pike VI. I won't hesitate to kill you if you ask me again!"

Silvery flames leapt up in a wide circle in the center of the crossroads, caging Pike in with the Devil. The flames reflected in Silvertongue's solid black eyes as he sneered at his servant. Cass screamed behind him, and he turned to look, though the flames were too high to see. He prayed that the Devil's servants wouldn't be able to touch them.

"What will it be, Pike?" The Devil growled, looking down at him. "Now that we're alone, do you have any *burning* questions for me?"

"Where's my mother?" Pike asked.

"At home enjoying a night off."

"Liar."

"Unfortunately, not this time."

"But–" Pike swallowed. "The chrysanthemum. . . and the candle."

"Tricks, Alexander. Do you really think so highly of me?" The Devil chuckled. "Let's stop these games. Speak man to man."

"You're no man," Pike growled.

"Then you're not much of one either," the Devil snapped back. "You're giving your mother to me by default, and you think you deserve to be called a man? Do you remember the things you've done? Beating women, Terrorizing children, breaking men down with your weapons and your words." Silvertongue hesitated with a malicious grin. "There are ways of dying that don't end in funerals, Pike. There is a type of death that one cannot smell. You and I both know that this *little game* we're playing ends in blood."

A groan escaped Pike's lips and his past overtook his mind. He thought of the cruel things he had done under the name of the Devil, all out of servitude. But he still *chose* to do those things. It had always seemed like a simple choice to make: Survive. Do whatever you can to stay alive. But didn't he have a choice the whole time?

"Alexander," the Devil began again. "It seems we have reached our *quatervois*; a crossroads, if you will. I only want to make sure that you've made some good memories in the past month, seeing as it will be your last." He stepped to Pike, crooked finger lifting Pike's chin to look up at him. "Shall we review then?"

Pike bit his trembling bottom lip.

"Do you recall Watson, Pike? Do you remember his face when you murdered him on top of that mountain?"

Watson looked once more at the painted skies that stretched for forever. When he faced Pike again, something in his demeanor was more set, more resolute.

"I forgive you, Pike."

"What about Mrs. Harper Benson," the Devil purred. "Destined to burn from the inside out for her husband's sins?"

The heat from his hands felt like a fire radiating from Mrs. Benson. He wondered how her body could withstand such a brutal force.

"What about your sweet Hickory who will never be missed?" the beast before him chuckled. "Reunited at last with his dear wife and child and no one left to mourn him."

Hickory slumped to the ground in a daze. With little effort, the shadowmen, stiff and tree-like, grabbed Hickory by the straps of his overalls and dragged him into the silver flames behind the Devil.

"What about young Oliver? Didn't you ask? Don't you want to know what I did to him?"

Pike clenched his left hand tight, not trusting his voice to answer.

"He's like you now, Alexander." the Devil beamed. "He's excellent. A natural, I must say. It would've been a real treat to see you two working together, but you had to come seek me out instead, asking to die." All twisted joy left his eyes. "Pity."

"So you've created another monster against his will?" Pike asked.

"Oh, on the contrary!" Silvertongue chuckled menacingly. "Oliver *asked* to become like you. Seems you inspired him to be something. . .

greater."

"*How did you get this job?*" Oliver ran his hands down his pant legs, tilting his head in curiosity.

"*Why? Are you interested?*" When tense silence from the boy greeted him, he shook his head. "*You want to become* greater *and strike fear in peoples' hearts when they set eyes on you?*"

Pike shook his head, willing himself to hold it together. The Devil roughly grabbed his face and turned him to the side. The silver flames parted and a dark figure emerged, a glower plastered to his young face. The flames merged once again, caging the three figures in together.

"Oliver?" Pike cried.

The past few weeks had aged him. He looked stronger, darker, more dangerous. The joyful smile had been replaced with a menacing grin.

"Your friends are delightful, Pike." Oliver barked out a laugh. "I must say, I enjoy the company of beautiful women."

Pike moved to hurt Oliver, make him feel any amount of pain, but the Devil wrapped an arm around him. Pike screamed as his flesh singed from the contact.

"How does it feel, Alexander?" the Devil taunted, whispering in his ear, rank breath curling around his face. "How does it feel to know that you've single handedly started the next generation of my human servants? How does it feel knowing that you'll have such an incredible *legacy?*"

"No," Pike muttered, closing his eyes. "I don't want it."

Oliver laughed now standing next to them. The Devil released Pike, shoving him roughly forwards.

"What *do* you want, Alexander Pike?" the Devil howled.

Names. Countless names.

"Tell me!"

Faces. So many faces.

"What is it that you so desperately crave?"

In a moment of terror, all of Pike's pent-up rage from the past month exploded in silvery fury. "I want to burn! I want to burn up and disappear."

The Devil laughed as Pike fell to his knees, disoriented in the ring of silver fire, skin hot, head fuzzy from the drinks he had ingested earlier and the amount of blood lost, and mind cloudy from the pain he'd already endured. His heart ached as he prayed.

Please, God. Kill me.

Let me die.

End my suffering.

"Do you seriously think it will be that easy?" the Devil barked. "You think you can disappear? Will that save you?"

"I never wanted to be this," Pike cried, tears evaporating even as they rolled down his cheeks.

"You get no choice in life!" the Devil roared, skin melting in parts to reveal the beast that he actually was. His eyes faded once again to the glowing red, his skin looking shredded and mangled. "You play the cards you're dealt until you run out of time. You never win! *Fold*, Alexander."

Pike sobbed openly now.

This was his torment.

This is what he deserved.

This was his eternal punishment, eternal misery. He had been a fool to believe in fairytales.

He pulled his knife out of his boot and threw it blindly towards the Devil in a feeble attempt to do something, anything to stop whatever hell he lived in. With a careless attitude, the Devil kicked the knife away. Oliver smirked behind his master.

"I see your soul, young Pike," the Devil hissed. "You're breaking as we speak and soon you'll belong wholly to me for eternity."

Something about that half human grin caused Pike's head to throb, heartbeat pounding so loud that it blocked out any more words. But he watched the Devil through his tears.

Then the silvery circle faltered. The Devil turned his attention to the side and stumbled back, shouting and clutching at his chest.

A familiar face stepped into the ring.

"Has no one told you that the Devil wears a suit and tie?" the rough voice called. "You ought to be more careful, son."

27

atson Moore.

"Watson!" Pike cried, tears distorting the image of the man that he thought he had killed. "You're alive?"

Watson smiled. A genuine smile like he was cracking jokes on a gentle horseback ride in Oklahoma instead of a circle from hell.

"Pike, you still have quite a bit to learn." Watson turned to the Devil and Oliver and raised his eyebrows. "And it seems so do you! When are you going to learn that you can't get rid of me so easily?"

The Devil raged and the circle of fire sprang higher. The last of Silvertongue's human costume disappeared as if burned in the fire and the beast stood taller than the flames.

Pain. So much pain.

Pike couldn't stop his hands from shaking.

The Devil roared something in his own language while he stretched his arms out to the sides, letting out a terrible screech. Pike couldn't look at the Devil so he watched Watson. The dark skinned man looked so much lighter compared to the evil that stood before him, yet Watson stared the Devil directly in the eye.

Watson.

"I'll do you a favor, for free," Watson commanded, speaking to the tar-colored beast in front of him like it was absolutely normal. But then again, he'd seen the Devil before. "I'll give my life right now. You can kill me in place of Pike or whatever evil you assigned to him. But you have to swear on the blood of Christ that Pike, his mother, and whomever else you've thought of—they are free."

"Watson, no," Pike sobbed, voice hoarse.

The Devil's body warped, and silver flames exploded from his chest. His skin fused back around the wound, healing it immediately. "You have no power to make such demands, human."

"Not in my own power." Watson tossed a small object to Pike from the inside of his coat pocket.

Pike wiped his tears with the back of his left sleeve and picked up the small book. In the top half, through the black leather and well-read pages, a tear that looked like a bullet hole broke up the otherwise intact cover.

Watson had never died.

"How did you find me?" Pike shouted, mind swirling.

Watson smirked, but didn't take his eyes away from the beast before him. "No matter how much you lie, there's always going to be a little bit of truth. . . Even if it is about where you came from. I figured your hometown would be my best bet."

The knowledge of Watson making it all the way to Washington from Oklahoma for Pike's sake overwhelmed him. The idea that someone cared about him that much made something inside him ache. He clutched his chest as he moved to get over to Watson.

"Watson, you can't do this." Pike's voice cracked . "You can't—"

An ear-piercing screech stopped him in his tracks. The earth shook, and Pike braced himself with a hand to the ground. He snapped his head back up, and the Devil looked even more twisted than before, limbs bent at unnatural angles. His face had the cruelest look Pike had ever seen, and it sent terror shooting through his veins.

Oliver screamed along with the Devil, his body contorted from invisible chains, anguish visible on his face.

"Pike!" Watson shouted over the Devil's hideous roar. His sharp gaze watched Pike. "Let this be your answered prayer!"

And with a grin, Watson shook hands with the Devil, a silver flare springing up as they touched. Wind, heat, and silver flame whooshed, and three figures disappeared into the clearing, leaving nothing to prove that anything had occurred in that spot.

Alone.

There were no words to explain or justify the silence, only a yawning hole where sanity should be along with answers and innocence.

But despair.

Heaping amounts of despair remained instead.

Let this be your answered prayer.

When Pike could finally convince his hands to work like they should, he opened the book of verses that Watson had thrown to him, gingerly holding it with his wounded hand. He opened to a ribbon tucked into a section labeled by a name: Jeremiah.

One line had been boxed. Pike, not knowing what else to do with it, read it aloud.

"Thus says the Lord, 'Stand by the roads, and look, and ask for the ancient paths, where the good way is; and walk in it, and find rest for your souls.'"

The page wrinkled from the tears falling from his chin.

"I'm so lost," he whispered, crying heavily. "I'm so lost."

And in that moment, he thought of his father and wondered if he had ever felt this way. Pike wondered if he had grieved for a stolen destiny. He wondered if all of his ancestors grieved that lost innocence and tragic future. He wondered if they ever felt torn between doing what's good and right or doing what had been required of them. And most of all, he wondered if all of the unspeakable things he did made him a monster as evil as the Devil himself.

Words came out of Pike's mouth without him trying. "I want to

 213

become more than the monster in me."

And a gentle breeze fluttered past him like an embrace rather than a fierce storm. He turned his head to follow its path and saw Cassidy and Hallie sitting in the grass watching him from a ways away, both holding tight to each other, seemingly unharmed.

"Cassidy," he croaked.

With a great amount of effort, he pushed himself to his feet and stumbled, catching himself again. He moved one foot forward again and again until he fell at their feet. Cass let go of her sister and pulled him to her, as close as possible.

And in her arms, Pike cried. Every tear he held in his body rushed out, emotions desperate to escape after so much had happened to him.

It felt like a release.

Like freedom.

After what felt like hours, Pike held Cass close and sat in her embrace content to never move again. And neither of them moved until the nearly full moon began to set over the horizon.

"Pike," Cass whispered.

She pushed his sleeves up.

Where his tattoos had once been unholy flames, they were now faded like the white scars on his torso and back rather than dark black lines marring his pale skin. Pike's hands shook as he took a deep breath.

"Let this be your answered prayer," Pike repeated Watson's last words almost in disbelief. He might not have believed it to be possible had it not been his own skin.

He thought of the day he had earned those marks when his father had died. He stepped in as the next Alexander Pike. His poor mother's heart must have shattered thinking of her young boy working for the Devil.

No longer.

"My mother," Pike's voice cracked, hoarse from crying so hard and for such a long time.

Cass nodded, and Pike pulled both of them to their feet.

"I'll walk you two home first."

As they stumbled back into town, only the gamblers and drunks were out in the street. Cass and Hallie both had hair falling out of its place and down in waves, and dust and ash kicked up by the fire dirtied their faces. Pike had no idea what he looked like, but it couldn't be good. And a man alone with two women he wasn't related to was already scandalous, though he'd never before been too concerned about his social status. Things changed when your future shifted in one evening.

None of them spoke as they walked. Pike wished to talk to Cass alone.

It has to wait.

At the steps by the Jackson household, Pike wrapped them both in brief hugs, holding them tight. "I'll be back later to check on you two. Thank you. . . for everything."

As he backed up, Cass held tight to his hand. "You aren't going to leave me again, right?"

"Only a woman like yourself would love the damned. How could I make that mistake again?" Pike placed a soft kiss on her knuckles. "I promise. I won't leave you."

28

By the time he'd stumbled alone and weary onto his mother's property in view of the front porch, she ran to meet him.

Pike's mind flashed back to his childhood.

Whenever he'd have nightmares about evil things, his mother's hugs were always the antidote to his fears. She would hold him and hum old hymns until he fell back asleep, her soft voice lulling him back to lighter dreams.

This hug felt like one of those times, waking up from a terrible, nearly never-ending nightmare. He sank into his mother's arms, despite being a head taller than her, and cried though it surprised him that he had tears left to shed. She shushed him and stroked his sweaty hair back behind his ear. He knelt to the ground as she held him tight.

Pike pulled back enough to look at her. "I love you, Mother."

With a small smile, she rubbed his cheek with her thumb. "I love you so much more, Pike."

Pike leaned his forehead against her shoulder, wiping away his tears.

"I never meant for this to be our lives, to go to hell and back."

"Of course not," she whispered kindly. "Your father never meant it either."

"But he wasn't a good man, was he?" Pike's voice broke.

"He wasn't always good. But he made sacrifices daily for us." His mother's voice sounded far off despite her proximity. "And he loved you very much. He was so proud of you."

Pike grew silent for a moment, wondering if his father had done all he had for Pike, trying to keep him and his mother from the Devil's reach.

He searched his mother's face. "Am I a good man?"

She shushed him, hugging him once more. "You have always been a good man. Now you can be a great one."

Pike sniffled. "I never meant to hurt you. My intention is always to take care of you. You know that, right?"

"I know, love. I know," she whispered again, still stroking his hair like he was only a child and not a grown man.

They sat like that for a while before Pike leaned back again. "Mother, I'm done running. Our debt has been paid."

His mother furrowed her eyebrows. "Paid? No more jobs?"

"No more jobs."

Pike watched his mother's hazel eyes for signs of her thoughts. The slight wrinkle of her sun-tanned skin between her eyebrows made it difficult to read her emotions. Was she happy? Was she missing his father? Did she regret all these years wasted?

Then she began to chuckle, eyes crinkling at the edges from her joy. Pike sat back even more, eyebrows drawing together. She laughed, one of those laughs that sounded like a babbling river, rushing and wild. A laugh so contagious, a laugh you could get carried away by so quickly without even trying. She wiped away tears then wrapped him in yet another hug as she sang gently. After she had quieted again, Pike took in a shuddered breath.

"I'm sorry, Mother," he whispered.

She cupped his face in her hands, forcing him to look her in the eyes. Eyes that held no judgment. She smiled warmly at him. "I am so proud of the man you have become, Alexander James Pike."

And something like a dam boarding up a river gave way inside of Pike's heart and relief tumbled out like waters finally set free. He pulled his mother close and buried his face in her shoulder, so thankful for someone who stayed with him and supported him. And even now, she loved him more than he deserved.

He leaned his head up, looking past his mother's shoulder. The dark of the night had faded, casting the world in all shades of blue.

His mother held his face in her hands again and kissed his forehead. "How about an early breakfast, hmm?"

⁓◦⑂◦⁓

As his mother cooked, Pike watched the early morning glow of the sun filter through the bright curtains, dust dancing in the spotlight as the light clatter of kitchen items sounded like a symphony of ordinary days. The worn wooden table stood where it always had, one good tablecloth still draped elegantly over the top.

He moved the dried flowers from the living room to the kitchen table and set out napkins and cutlery. Opening the curtains, he brought light to the dark places.

Free.

Despite the lack of sleep, Pike felt so much lighter than he had in his life. For once, there wasn't a looming sense of dread hanging over him like a storm cloud. He felt light on his feet and couldn't stop from smiling to himself.

As he turned away from the window, his stomach rolled from hunger. His mother hummed while she dished out eggs on his toast and her own, and they sat down for a meal together.

He told the events of the previous night and Watson's sacrifice. Pike didn't think he would be ready to share much more than that, but he hoped that eventually he could speak of what miracles had happened in that circle of silver flames. More importantly, he hoped that someday he could sort out the emotions twisting in his heart.

"So," his mother interrupted his thoughts with a mischievous grin, "are you going to tell me more about Miss Cassidy Jackson?"

Pike choked on his toast. Reaching for his water, he took a rather large drink before he regained his composure

"Whatever do you mean?" he asked, feigning innocence.

"What I mean is, why haven't you told me about you and her yet? There's been talk that you've dined with them. From what I've heard, it seems that Miss Jackson is quite fond of you."

Pike grumbled under his breath about small towns. "Mother, as much as I would enjoy a future with such a woman, I doubt she'd want one with me. You heard the kind of hell I put her through this past month. I barely know her, yet she knows the worst about me. Or at least some of it." He scratched the back of his neck, pausing in thought. "I would love to try, but what would her father say when he learns the truth?"

"It takes a lot to follow a man to hell and back. It sounds like she cares for you quite a bit."

"But can she possibly love me? And again, what of propriety? Besides, Miss Jackson has her own life. Even if I wanted. . ." He shook his head.

"You never know." Mrs. Pike shrugged.

Pike raised an eyebrow at his mother. "You cannot be serious. Cassidy Jackson is an elegant young lady, not an accomplice to malice."

"Neither was I," his mother said with a stern look. "And luckily, she never has to be. You've been released. You still have the opportunity to have a normal life if you want it."

"Normal? I have scars that I will have to explain to the woman I end up marrying. And the nightmares. . ."

"And you don't want to see if Miss Jackson would be interested in trying? You won't even give her the chance to try?"

Pike ran his hand over his chin. "It's not that I don't want to try."

"You're afraid of opening up again?" His mother smirked, raising an eyebrow. "You've kept your heart locked up for the past seven years. I think it's time to let it out of its cage."

29

Pike stood at the doorstep of the Jackson family's townhouse, messing with the new bandages his mother had put on after breakfast. So much had passed between him and that family, and yet they were still merely acquaintances in Pike's eyes. He waited, wondering what to say to them.

Yet his mother was right. He'd kept his heart locked up for long enough. He was afraid Dr. Jackson would deny his request, but he still had to try. Cass was worth it.

He inhaled deeply and rapped at the door. Long agonizing seconds passed as his heart seemed to beat louder and louder in his chest.

Henderson answered. "Mr. James! Do come in." He swung the door open. "I must express my gratitude for what happened during the dinner last night. We're all so grateful that you were there. And to think what could have happened had you not come to the rescue!"

Pike bowed his head briefly. "Of course! It was nothing, really. Is Dr. Jackson at home today? I wanted him to take a look at my. . . wound."

He held up his wrapped hand. Henderson nodded quickly.

"Why don't you take a seat in the sitting room, and I'll send him in as soon as he's dressed?" Henderson took Pike's coat and hung it by the front door.

He led him to the sitting room and disappeared up the stairs.

Time slunk by until finally, Dr. Jackson descended the stairs, adjusting his cuff sleeves.

"Mr. James Pike!" he exclaimed, reaching the bottom of the stairs.

"Please, call me Pike." He stood, holding out his wrapped right hand. The doctor shook it lightly before Pike continued. "I have a lot to discuss with you, Dr. Jackson."

The two men sipped on coffee while Pike explained everything from the beginning. He explained about his subterfuge, his aliases, his despicable actions, his growing attachment to Cassidy, his past, his tormented mind, his injuries, and his cursed bloodline that had finally been redeemed.

Dr. Jackson had listened carefully without interrupting, and when Pike had finally come to the end of it, Dr. Jackson cleared his throat. "You certainly have lived a life, haven't you?"

Pike nodded curtly.

"No doubt, that's what caused the tremors and the copious amounts of stress when you showed up here yesterday afternoon."

Pike nodded again.

"What was your *intention* for coming by today?" he asked Pike, choosing his words carefully.

"Well, sir," Pike began. "I would like to ask first for forgiveness for all the mess I've brought to your family. And secondly," he swallowed hard. "I would like to ask permission to court your daughter, Cassidy. Properly, that is. Whatever your wishes, I hope they can be my own as well."

Dr. Jackson's face softened slightly. "You are forgiven, son. As for courting Cassidy, that's mainly her decision, though I do have my doubts. You have proven that you've had a change of heart—or a change of testament— we will see how it plays out. In the end, I only want my daughter to be happy and provided for."

Pike sighed in relief. "Thank you very much, Dr. Jackson."

"Unfortunately, Cass is still asleep from last night's *escapade*." Dr. Jackson motioned with his hand. "But how about you and your mother join us tonight for dinner? Liam is coming into town tonight, and he'll be here for a while. I'm sure he'd be delighted to see you again."

Pike smiled. "It would be my absolute pleasure. Thank you."

Dr. Jackson returned the look. "But let me take a look at that wound before you leave."

They moved to the kitchen before getting to business where they settled at a small table. Dr. Jackson carefully unwrapped the bandages and studied the wound. "It looks like your mother does well in medicine. If you're anything like her, I could use you at the office. It's quite busier than I expected, and I seem to recall that you're in need of a new job." He raised his eyebrows at Pike.

"I'll consider it." Pike grinned, unable to fathom how his luck had turned.

"Good." Dr. Jackson beamed. "I'll be expecting you tonight. Six o'clock?"

"Six o'clock sounds wonderful, sir."

By the time six o'clock rolled around, Pike felt more nervous than he could ever remember being before meeting a woman. But he felt stronger with his mother by his side, knowing they'd avoided a dangerous fate. His mother was finally safe from the Devil's grasp.

She'd dressed up in her nicest dress, looking like a wedding guest. She even brought out her good jewelry and shined Pike's shoes. Pike wore one of his pairs of dress pants, and a white shirt that had belonged to his father along with the matching coat, vest, and tie. He made a mental note to find time to get new business and evening clothes.

Before they left their house, he slid Watson's torn book into his coat pocket along with the photo he promised Watson he'd carry with him. He still hadn't opened up much to his mother about that particular moment. It would come in time.

The pair walked into town arm in arm, his mother humming the whole way instead of speaking, allowing Pike to internally process the last month. Pike tried to remember all the words to the hymn that both his mother and Watson sang as they stepped up to the Jackson's door.

Henderson arrived immediately and took both of their coats, leading them directly to the dining room.

Introductions were made and smiles were passed around. Surprising him with affection, Liam gave Pike a hug and beaming smile.

"My Lord, Pike," Liam chuckled. "You are more of a man than I could ever be. I'd love to hear about all your travels."

And though it was difficult talking about himself after being mostly alone for the past seven years, Pike found himself enjoying the company. Hallie acted a bit awkward around Pike, and he didn't blame her. He apologized to her again and thanked her for her graciousness before they all sat at the dinner table, Pike between Cass and his mother.

They all ate their fill at what Pike would've named a feast. Conversation remained easy and lighthearted. The room felt thick with affection of all levels. Pike had never felt such emotion sitting with people, and he considered them friends, hoping they considered him one as well.

After dinner, he slipped out the front door, taking a moment to contemplate the past month in the gentle, quiet breeze. A chill hung in the air, cold seeping in from his shoes. Leaning against the outer wall, Pike observed life occurring in front of his eyes. Couples walked down the street, families laughed together, and children enjoyed a night in town.

It made him wonder what his future looked like. And he was surprised to find that he'd never really considered much past wanting a family.

The door opened and Cassidy stepped outside, pulling her shawl closer around her shoulders. "You'll freeze if you stay out here much longer."

Pike beamed down at her. "And you wouldn't want me to freeze?"

Cass blushed. "Not at all, Mr. Pike."

Pike looked down at his feet when she said his name. "I have asked so much of you the past few weeks. But I would like to ask one more thing."

He held Cassidy's hands into his own, being careful with his wrapped right hand. "Can I invite you over for dinner, Miss Cassidy Jackson? It wouldn't be anything close to this nice, but my mother. . ." He chuckled to himself. "She's hoping to have another woman around the house."

Cassidy laughed behind a gloved hand. "I'd be delighted to join you all for dinner. Would Saturday be all right?"

"Saturday is wonderful. I look forward to it."

Without hesitation, Pike leaned his head down until their lips met, his heart beating wildly. Every thought in his mind disappeared, leaving him with only the sensation of her, warm and inviting. Hope fluttered in his chest, lit by the fire of passion. For the first time in his life, he felt carefree.

Cass pulled away much quicker than Pike would've preferred, but she was positively beaming. He'd once said that her smile could end a war, and though he knew she couldn't solve all of the world's problems, he did know that he wanted her by his side to brighten even the darkest days ahead.

30

Pike sat at his desk in his childhood room, pen in hand and empty journal in front of him. His mother had bought him a new journal as a gift for the start of a new chapter and a new job working for Dr. Jackson. Which was a bonus in addition to a courtship between him and Cassidy.

There were so many stories he wanted to tell. So many things tumbling in his mind like leaves in the wind. So many faces he wanted to honor. He'd always carry the weight on his shoulders, but maybe this would help ease the pain.

So he wrote:
November 30, 1879

We begin at the end, at an almost happily ever after.
It began with the witching winds. It was superstition really.
A November gale.
Hope has a price, and its name is disappointment.

Joy has a price, and its name is sorrow.

Love has a price, and its name is heartache.

As with all things, there is balance. You hold in one hand something pure and lovely, and in the other you hold something raw and rough. Both can be good, and both can be bad. But we all have the opportunity to balance them, one in each hand.

My past may be full of disappointment, sorrow, and heartache. The future may hold some of that as well. But my future will also be full of hope and joy and love.

I sit here—a man. Very, very broken.

I wonder often if I am merely dreaming. Like I'll wake up tomorrow, bruised and bleeding somewhere with the Devil for company.

But I sit, writing. And there's a woman waiting for me.

I want to tell myself, "Love her like it's the last thing you do."

But is it enough?

There's something purifying about the snow. The snow outside my window fills the cracks in my heart. It washes the mask off my face and reveals the restless man beneath that craves change. It peels back the layers of costumes I've donned for years and unveils my true nature.

Who am I when the Devil is gone?

How can one know grace if he doesn't know sin?

If grace is a wildfire, our hearts are trees. The dead skeletons burn faster, but the ashes of the past will bring nutrients for the young trees' future. If the Creator is water, I am aching soil. That water is providing life, changing the atmosphere, and feeding the trees.

How I long to be watered and fed with the ashes of my past, merely a memory of a life gone by, fading even as we speak.

Pike looked out the window of his bedroom. Snowflakes drifted slowly in the breezy morning. His mind drifted like snow to the hymn his mother had hummed on the way to the Jackson's house, finally remembering the familiar words.

Oh, to grace how great a debtor
Daily I'm constrained to be
Let Thy goodness like a fetter
Bind my wandering heart to Thee
Prone to wander, Lord I feel it
Prone to leave the God I love
Here's my heart, oh take and seal it
Seal it for Thy courts above

Pike set his pen down, wounded hand shaking from the extensive use. Stretching each finger, Pike read back over his words. This moment marked the start of a new life for him. More than a new chapter.

An entirely new book.

He exhaled, aware of the weight of such words that he had written. Closing his eyes, he placed a hand on Watson's old book, leather cover still partially shredded by the bullet that had failed its job.

"Prone to wander. . . Prone to leave." He took in a shuddering breath, muttering to himself.

Here's my heart.

Pike opened his eyes, icy blue almost matching the snow-covered yard. The warmth from his mother's cabin felt safe and comforting. She had cooked something for dinner that smelled like Christmas, and outside, a winter wind whistled quietly against the windows.

But for once, the wind didn't seem so scary.

The End

Acknowledgments

This book came about in a month of unemployment right after moving 800 miles across the country. I was stir crazy and itching to write something. And Alexander Pike VI got his story!

I first want to thank my husband, Cody, for putting up with weeks of crazy while I sat bored and unemployed. Thank you for pushing me to write even when it felt like my words meant nothing. You push me to write for myself. Thank you for loving me.

To my family who were accepting when I told them I wrote a book about a slave to the Devil. Thank you for reading Pike's story during its roughest moments when it was still called *On the Winds of November*, and for helping me make all the decisions.

To Vanessa and Jourdan: I am endlessly grateful for your coaching and knowledge of books and indie publishing. You've made this crazy, hairbrained dream a reality. And you helped me not feel overwhelmed when publishing felt impossible. Thanks for being incredible friends!

To my author group chat buddies: Emily, Maddie, Natalia, and Rachel. Thanks for the endless memes and rants. You all have been so helpful when the weird details of indie publishing have been stressful. And thanks for all the sprints we did where I edited instead of writing!

To my betas: Britt, Chera, Craig, Jordan, Kari, Kyla, Lucas, Madison, and Morgan. I am dead serious when I say that this book would not have been the same without you all. Thank you for supporting me and my book when there wasn't much of a book to support!

To my editor, Megan: Thank you for reaching out to me in 2021 asking if I wanted to claim one of your editing spots for 2022. It pushed me to be serious about my writing. I had no idea that it would be this book, but I am so grateful for your support and passion for this project.

To my cover designer, Maria: Your artistic ability is astounding. With the little I gave you, you crafted a beautiful cover that's equally spooky and intriguing. Thank you for your patience with me when I didn't know what I was doing. The cover is perfect!

To my incredible street team and to you, dear reader: Without you all, I have no job. So thanks for taking a chance on this book. I hope it finds you in the dark places when you need a beacon of hope.

Lastly, a huge thank you to my Creator. This book is our story, and I am humbled and honored to call myself an author. Thank you for being there on nights of doubt when I wondered if I would ever be good enough. Thank you for real life redemption arcs and unimaginable grace. Without you, I am nothing.

About the Author

A story lover at heart, Morgan has always been crafting stories. Growing up in East Tennessee in the Great Smoky Mountains, their mystery and beauty have inspired many of her tales. She's a big fan of rain, stargazing, coffee, and taking the long way home. Currently residing in middle Tennessee, Morgan lives with her husband, writing books and exploring the mountains. When she's not reading or writing, you'll find Morgan outside foraging among the plants or trying new coffee shops.

Keep in touch with Morgan at www.morganhubbbardauthor.com and on facebook or instagram @morganhubbardauthor.

CPSIA information can be obtained
at www.ICGtesting.com
Printed in the USA
BVHW032042010323
659502BV00003B/70